Mile On

DOM NICHOLLS

Lowden Ambrose Publishing

Lowden Ambrose Publishing

First published in Great Britain by Lowden Ambrose Ltd 2023

Book design by Sam Moppett

ISBN: 978-1-7393085-1-3

www.domnicholls.com

For my girls, big and small

1.

The best lies don't care much for travel. To say a lie is halfway around the world before the truth has got its boots on is a gross mischaracterisation. A proper lie has no need to move. It does not seek the limelight. It will suffocate in the oxygen of publicity. Much better to hide in the background and be mistaken for the truth.

Our global traveller meanwhile is mere gossip. Gossip serves a need, that's true, but has no real lasting effect. A brief high, like a shot of caffeine or nicotine, but no more nourishing than that for the human soul. Not like a proper lie. A take-your-country-to-war lie. A rig-an-election lie. A murder-your-opponents lie. Proper lies.

Most lies are born in daylight when their owners are awake. But the truth is just as vulnerable after sunset. Take any slumbering city and there will be lies aplenty down there.

A very old lie, perhaps one of the oldest, was sitting in a car on a dark street in east London.

Betsy Trenmore-Halford stared at her reflection in the rear-view mirror. How many times, she wondered, have I done this? How many nights have I spent alone and cold, silently watching as the world outside did whatever it is that worlds do, when they've got somewhere to go and something to do. Many times, she decided. Too many to remember.

She examined the lines around her eyes, each one a deep valley hiding a decade of secrets. The face was old, but the eyes, heavily-lidded and guarded by the protective shields of oversized spectacle lenses, were still sharp.

She watched the light go out in the hallway of the house she had just left. She forced a smile and waved to the dark doorway, but nobody had lingered long enough to return either. She could still taste the whisky from the nightcaps – no, I mustn't, thankyou Bryan, driving home – oh come on, Bets, he'd said, one won't hurt you. Except that one had turned to two. At least two. The digital clock on the dashboard shimmered and the time 03.00 was displayed in chunky green blocks. Tuesday's bridge night had gone on longer than usual. No-one had noticed, let alone cared. One of the benefits of getting old, she told herself. Time has little meaning to a life without purpose.

Movement. Betsy looked to her right, to see a fox padding between cars packed tight on either side of Wellspring Gardens. She was about to draw on her vape pen when her eyes snapped further up the longest stretch of the 'T' shaped road, perpendicular to where she sat. A figure was approaching from the far end. The parked cars blocked much of her vision. The figure's hooded and seemingly disembodied head skimmed across car roofs. Betsy strained to recognise the…man? Woman? No way of telling at this distance.

The walker moved steadily, staring down. Probably a mobile phone. Betsy tutted.

'Unlikely to meet a mugger at this time of night, but still stupidly reckless,' she muttered.

The figure slowed and stopped by a tree. Looked around. Betsy instinctively checked her mirrors. Empty streets. The figure examined the tree to one side and a garden wall adjoining a house to the other. The person removed something small from a jacket pocket. The item was placed as high as could be reached between wall and house. The visitor then set off back the way it had come. No rush, but faster than it had walked before. The figure turned the corner at the end of the street.

Betsy looked around and checked her mirrors again. It was an old reflex. Automatic. Over before she'd known it had started. Empty streets.

She sat for a minute in the dark silence. Parked far enough from the nearest streetlight, she would have been undetectable to the visitor, she was sure.

The street was still.

The fox had gone.

There were no lights in the doorways.

Betsy tucked the vape pen into an inside pocket of her tweed jacket, opened the car door and tutted again when the interior light came on. She stepped out and closed the door as quietly as she could. It still sounded to her like a thunderclap.

She crossed the road and hurried the short distance to the wall where the person had stopped. A small white cardboard cup had been stuffed into the gap between the wall and the house. With some difficulty, she reached up and pulled it out.

Inside was a USB stick, used for storing computer files. Quicker now, she headed back towards the car. She examined the cup. No markings outside or in. The stick likewise displayed no writing or company logo. A small sticker, about the size of a postage stamp, was attached on one side. In the centre of the sticker was a tiny round metal object. It looked like one of the batteries for the hearing aids her friends wore.

Betsy's heart thumped as she clambered back into the car.

Nothing moved on the street.

She put the cup, still with the USB stick inside, into the door pocket and rummaged in the key tray for a boiled sweet. She blew the dust off, flicked the sweet into her mouth and reached for the keys.

A second person turned the far corner of the street leading away from her. This one was on the other side of the road from where the earlier figure had appeared. Betsy paused, then drew her fingers slowly back from the keys. She knew this was a man. She'd seen countless powerful arms like the ones approaching relax at the sight of a small woman confronting them. They'd always underestimated her; the arms and the men attached to them. They'd soon regretted that.

The parked cars offered only snatched glimpses. The man was looking at a device in his hand, just as the last figure had. Walking slowly, in a tight jacket and a hat snug to his head, the man reached the place where, on the footpath opposite, the earlier figure had hidden the cup with the USB stick. He carried on walking without looking up.

Betsy hunkered down in her seat. She resisted the temptation to twist the sun visor to cover some of the window. If you want to hide, years of stakeouts had taught her, don't make any sudden movements. Sit dead still in a car at night and people will walk right past without noticing you're there. The human eye picks up movement much more easily than the brain reconstructs a stationary shape as a person.

The man approached the junction of the two branches of Wellspring Gardens. He still held the device, although Betsy could see now it was much bigger than a mobile phone. The man stopped walking at the corner. Betsy felt her options, and her throat, narrowing. The man twisted left and right, his eyes fixed on the device. Then he stopped, head down. The object in his hands pointed directly at Betsy's car.

There comes a point when you have to commit. When you have to let go of the old world and embrace the new. Ignore the voice in your head saying '*don't make a fuss, it'll all be fine*', and listen instead to the blood pounding in your ears: '*the cosy scenario is gone, accept it and get over the panic. Prepare to fight.*'

Betsy made a decision.

Her fingers strained on the car keys as she twisted the engine into life. The man across the road looked up at the car reversing fast out of the tight parking space. Betsy spun the wheel hard to avoid the car behind. The seat belt bit into her neck as she craned round to see out the back window. A shout told her she was already being pursued. She accelerated hard. The engine screamed as the car lurched from side to side between the metal walls. Into a dead-end.

'Buggeration!'

She stamped on the brakes. Somehow found first gear. The car leapt forwards like an animal startled from sleep. She looked through the front windscreen, for what felt like the first time in hours. The man was sprinting towards her with a look of determination the woman had seen many times before, on the faces of soldiers or hardened criminals. She had no idea which one was approaching but knew the man wasn't going to stop.

He leapt into the air and his round face appeared just inches from her own. His fingers clung to the rim of the bonnet where it met the windscreen. His eyes were locked onto Betsy's, stretched wide on the inside of the glass. The man still gripped the black object in one hand. Betsy flushed cold as the thought exploded in her head that it could be a gun.

With houses filling up her vision, Betsy's brain registered she must be fast approaching the junction at the end of Wellspring Gardens. She stood on the brake pedal and gasped as the man's fingers were wrenched from the bonnet and he was flung ahead of the car. His face was briefly illuminated as he fell under the level of the headlights, mouth agape in a cry inaudible over the screaming brakes. The car skidded. Betsy felt the front wheels ride up, over the kerb of the adjoining road or the man's body she couldn't tell.

The car stopped. The man was no longer visible, whether under the car or flung to one side Betsy had no way of knowing. She was breathing heavily and became aware of the sweet still clamped between her teeth. She crunched it, grateful for the lemony blast that eclipsed the metallic taste of fear.

What the hell just happened, she asked herself. That was no carjacking. There had been intent, of that she was sure, but intent to do what? To leap onto the bonnet of a moving vehicle required extreme motivation, or possibly narcotics. She didn't want to entertain the consequences of either.

Betsy peeled a hand from the steering wheel and opened the door. Stepped out into the smell of burnt rubber. Looked around. Empty street, all quiet. A pile of clothes on the pavement in front of the car were bundled so loosely against a wooden fence it took her a moment to realise they contained a human body. Tight jacket, woollen hat. A streetlight nearby picked out every detail. She felt badly exposed, wanted to get away as fast as possible from any sleepy eyes woken by the noise. But she'd broken the body against the fence.

'Oh dear,' she said. 'Oh dear, oh dear, oh dear.'

She approached the ragged pile of clothes. Nudged the man's foot with her toe and snatched it back. She noticed a small piece of folded paper between the man's legs. She pocketed it then rushed back to her feet, fearing the man would grab at her. No sign of that though. No sign of anything, pretty much.

Betsy knelt down and pressed her fingers into the man's neck. She thought she felt a weak pulse. Was that a good sign or a bad one? She could see no blood. But just because it wasn't pooling on the street didn't mean it couldn't be slowly filling a lung. Clogging the man's brain. Leaching into a leg from a shattered femur.

She yanked out her phone. Dialled the emergency number. Her breathing sounded ragged as she asked for the ambulance service.

She hung up a moment later, before the call went through. Something deep – self-preservation perhaps, or a lifetime's experience – told her to be wary. This was no ordinary criminal event. The man's actions and the technical device, which was…there, cradled to his chest like a baby, spoke of something bigger. And was she that innocent? Her car was over the kerb and she had whisky on her breath. As far as the police would see it she'd driven into the bloke having had one too many.

Betsy grabbed the black plastic lump. It came away easily from the man's limp hands. She left the body and hurried back to the car. Fired up the engine and reversed off the kerb. She called the ambulance service again. Gave details of where to find the man and nothing more. Betsy then accelerated away, as the rain started falling again, towards darkness.

2.

Shifting the computer had been harder than Betsy had expected. She'd anticipated pain from the hip, but thought her back and arms would mask their slow betrayal for another couple of years.

She wanted to keep the USB stick at least twenty feet from the footpath outside the house. She guessed she'd been about fifteen feet from the stranger when he'd pointed the hand-held tracker, as Betsy now recognised the black device to be, broken though it was, directly at the car. She had examined the stick when she got home. She suspected the small round metal object attached to the side was transmitting a signal. It was stuck fast. Betsy didn't think she'd been followed from Wellspring Gardens but didn't want to take any chances with the bug. Much as she hated bringing the stick into the house, whatever was on it had been worth a man risking his life to protect. Betsy had to look. And that meant getting the transmitter out of range of any other thug walking past the house with a radio-frequency detector in his pocket.

Like the other neat Victorian terraced houses on Hollett Road, Betsy's had a small front garden, no more than ten feet deep. So, drag the desktop computer ten feet from the front window to be on the safe side before plugging in the stick, she figured. Although, she had to admit, it wasn't a foolproof plan.

The computer woke up, blue light bouncing off the circular panes in front of her eyes. She recognised the irony of refusing, for years, to purchase a laptop, preferring the sturdy certainty of a desktop computer with a chair adjusted perfectly for her condition. And yet here she was, aching with the effort of converting the lump into a portable device, however temporarily. The screen flashed then displayed a picture of a black cat curled on a cushion. A car drove slowly past the house. Betsy stared at the window and waited for the sound to die. When she returned her eyes to the screen it had filled up with icons. A new one appeared in a corner. A picture of a USB stick sat atop the words 'External Device'.

Betsy clicked on the new tile.

A window opened. The only folder was named 'pictures'.

She clicked on it.

Three images were listed, all the same memory size. She opened one after another. After a quick examination she concluded the images were identical. Fields, houses, farm buildings, cows on the ground, touch of pink in the sky. Everything where it should be for a generic picture of rural England.

She left the computer and crept downstairs, although an empty house demanded no such stealth. She closed the kitchen door behind her and turned on the light, squinting as she retrieved from a back pocket the piece of folded paper she'd found near the stranger's broken body. She spread it out on the counter next to the sink. Smoothed it over with rippled hands. It was a computer screen shot of a map covering part of London. The map had the word 'Start' near the bottom of the page, indicating a street corner, and 'Finish' at the top, with an arrow pointing to Trafalgar Square. A thick line traced a route from one to the other. It mostly wound along main roads and back streets but also went directly through two parks impassable to traffic.

The number '1.6' was hand-written in thick black pen on the side of the map. It was circled many times. A tighter circle, about halfway along the line between start and finish, had been scrawled over a particular street. The hard, deep spirals had gouged a rut around Wellspring Gardens.

Betsy pushed her glasses higher on her nose and unnecessarily adjusted the frame, deep in thought. She laid the map on the kitchen floor and took a photo of it with her mobile phone. Sent the photo to her email account. Then turned the light off and stepped carefully back upstairs.

She shuffled along the landing to the bathroom. A few minutes later she emerged, without the cacophony of a flushed lavatory. No need for such caution, but old habits born in packed dormitories on training courses with little sleep had left their mark.

Betsy returned to the computer. She selected the image search option from her Internet browser and uploaded the photo of the map she'd just sent herself.

No results. A message told her this could be because the image didn't exist anywhere on the web, or the image quality was too poor to be referenced properly.

'Blast,' she muttered.

The first murky light of dawn struggled through the rain splashing against the front window. Betsy followed the streaks down the panes. Her eyes fell on the scanner sitting on the table in the alcove; her optimistically named home office.

Rubbing her hip, she moved across the landing and turned on the scanner. It protested the early start to the day with more outrage than the computer. It eventually stopped, and a blue flashing light held steady, indicating it had connected to the Wi-Fi.

Betsy placed the map face down on the scanner and set it in motion. Light and sound bounced off the walls as the document was read. She selected the 'Export to email' option from the digital display and decided to leave the scanner switched on, in case the shut down routine involved more ear-splitting screeches. She returned to the computer and waited for the email to arrive.

Betsy opened the image. It was a much clearer picture than she'd managed with her phone. Brighter, no creases, uniform perspective. She uploaded it to the image search tool and pressed enter. The 'no results' message didn't appear. Betsy felt a surge of excitement as the screen instead displayed a swivelling egg timer and the pulsing words: 'searching for image'.

*

Just as Betsy had started looking at the folder named 'pictures', a window had opened automatically on a computer a few miles away in another part of London. A message read: 'User access detected'.

'Oh dear, James. Is there something you should be telling me?'

The message had never been displayed before, for the simple reason that the USB stick had never been accessed by anyone other than its intended recipient.

'So, who are you then, my sneaky little thief?'

A new message appeared: 'Identifying location.'

There had never really been any doubt the malware on the USB stick would not work properly. Still, it was a relief to see it in operation.

A new message: 'Mac address identified.'

'Gotcha.'

Locating the mystery user had only been a matter of time once the stick had connected itself to a Wi-Fi source. Unless, of course, it had been sheep-dipped to clear the malware. But only the most paranoid, or connected, had access to that kind of technology.

A new message: 'Referencing maps.'

A separate window opened showing a map. A large circular red lozenge extended over the entire image. It then shrank rapidly. As it did so the map scale changed. What had at first been an image of west

Europe and north Africa quickly became the south east of England, then London, then south London. After a pause the map came to life again. South London became a jumble of streets between Greenwich and Vauxhall. Then another jerk and the large green triangle of Peckham Rye park came into focus. The red lozenge shrank again to a small blob that rolled across a few streets before resting on Hollett Road, halfway between Windmill Avenue and Ambull Road.

A new message: 'Refining,' then: 'Referencing.'

'Oh boy are you in for a shock.'

Another window opened, next to the map. It contained only one line of text: 'Betsy Trenmore-Halford, 72 Hollett Road, London, SE22 4DF, United Kingdom.'

'You stupid, stupid woman. What the hell are you up to now?' said the person going by the name ChipsWithMayo.

*

Betsy stared at the thumbnail image of the map on the screen, under the heading 'Image results'. It was small, but looked similar to the one in her pocket, bar the '1.6' in thick pen and the hard circles around Wellspring Gardens. The map was linked to the first entry displayed on the page of results. The website was for a company called London War Walks. She clicked on the link.

'London War Walks,' Betsy read. 'Specialists in London wartime guided walks.'

She clicked on a tab marked 'Our walks'.

'The City in the Blitz. Westminster On Fire. Theatreland Under Attack. V-Weapons and Gas Explosions,' she read.

She selected a walk called The Long Night.

'On this walk we look at the terrible fires that swept over London on the night of 10th to 11th May 1941,' Betsy read. 'Starting under the guns of the Imperial War Museum we trace the route of devastation through the old Rotherhithe docks, take in the destruction of London's Oranges and Lemons church and finish at Trafalgar Square.'

Under the description was a map of the walk, with the route marked. Betsy zoomed in and out of the map, watching the line track along streets and through parks. She pulled the map out from her pocket, although she knew she didn't really need to check. The images matched perfectly.

*

Even before Betsy had taken possession of the USB stick, the transmitter shaped like a hearing aid battery stuck on the side had been singing its song. Invisible wiggly-worms of electromagnetic energy had been flying out in all directions, desperate to be noticed. The transmitter's designers knew a busy city like London would be problematic, with towering buildings and a congested radio spectrum. Boosting the power on such a small device was not possible. Instead, they'd built it so the magic worms occupied a very specific frequency. It gave the worms the best chance of being identified through the clutter.

They couldn't crawl far. Down reasonably clear streets with just a smattering of trees and a few hundred cars, the worms might get a dozen miles. Smash their little heads through concrete buildings though and the poor things would collapse after a lot less, dazed and confused. London was slowly becoming littered with invisible photons of energy, cast on the floor like drunks nursing bloody noses after a pub brawl.

For the lucky few however, the effort was one of stamina not strength. The worms that went straight up didn't have to compete with shops and bridges and all the other furniture of a city. Theirs was a marathon, not an obstacle course.

Four hundred miles above London a small cube, measuring only one metre along each side, sat on the edge of space. It was one of six identical boxes in low earth orbit. The number in the constellation meant there was always one box sitting over London, waiting to welcome visitors. They all served the same mission. The satellite's owners had considered using only one space vehicle, but to have it permanently overhead the target would have necessitated a geosynchronous orbit much further away from Earth: technically harder and a lot more expensive. Cubesats, as they were known, were reliable and cheap, even allowing for the greater numbers required. It was towards this box, launched just eight months earlier, that the lucky worms inched.

Those that survived the journey were exhausted by the time they arrived at the cube. The sound of their door-knocking would have been missed had the satellite been busy on any other tasks. Being lucky worms though, this satellite had just one job: to point its receiver at the earth and keep a listening watch for radio energy coming from a very specific part of the electromagnetic spectrum. It did this job very well.

Once inside, the worms caught their electronic breath, told their tale and expired in a microscopic flash of light. Job done. With barely a pause the cube then sent the worms' message a few thousand miles across the black void to another satellite. As there was nothing between the two cubes except empty space, this journey was a lot easier. The second satellite repackaged the message and blasted it back down to earth. A large, round satellite receiver dish caught the message outside a building just a few countries east of London. After a final quick journey down twenty metres of cabling the message eventually popped up on a computer screen. One click later it was printed, and after five more metres the message was placed on a desk in an office. The man behind the desk, who had spent his entire thirty-two year career knitting electronic string, smiled, and gave thanks once more that some worms always decided to go straight up.

3.

Betsy lifted her head from the crook of her outraged elbow. With some difficulty she coaxed her arm from the table. She blinked at the computer screen, nudged the mouse and focussed once more on the London War Walks website. The digital clock told her she'd been searching for three hours, give or take a bit of unsatisfactory kip in her home office, for any hint of what the route of The Long Night had to do with the USB stick.

'You silly woman,' she said, as she eased herself from the chair and shuffled painfully towards to the bathroom.

She went downstairs, most steps visited by both feet, and eventually arrived in the kitchen. A black cat announced its presence and moved to greet her.

'Hello, Thomas. Yes, the silly lady forgot to go to bed again. Never mind, shall we have some breakfast?'

She fiddled with the digital radio, twisting the dial as she searched the station names displayed in the screen on the top.

'News, news, news,' she muttered. 'Bright FM, All The Hits, Calm And Cool. Honestly, Thomas, is it too much to ask to find something called local news? She'll be on the other channel soon, too.'

Betsy selected a station then peeled the foil lid off a carton of cat food and emptied the contents into a porcelain bowl. With one steadying arm attached to the fridge she bent down and placed the bowl on the floor. The cat darted for it. Betsy then poured porridge oats and milk into a plastic jug, stirred the mixture with a spoon and opened the microwave door. The USB stick was in the oven. She took it out, placed the jug of porridge in its place and closed the door. She was about to rotate the timer into life when she paused. She pursed her lips and stared at the USB stick. She then opened the microwave door, replaced the stick inside and retrieved the plastic jug.

'Old fashioned method today, Thomas. We'll use the Aga,' she said.

She poured the porridge mixture into a saucepan and placed it on the cooker.

*

The nerves showed she was taking it seriously. Kathryn Fieldhouse had learned to recognise that and was glad for it. The interview was planned for 7.54am, so she'd been up and ready for about an hour. It was her first time on national radio, with the country's flagship news programme, and it had to go well.

Kathryn paced around her flat. Movement seemed to ease the tension, or was at least an illusion of control, which was good enough. Anything was better than passively waiting.

Preparation was everything. Fail to prepare and you prepare to fail, she'd always been told in the army. Which seemed an age ago. We've come a long way, baby, she said to herself in the hallway mirror. Then paced some more.

How do I want to be remembered after this interview, she asked herself. Professional? Competent? Definitely. Leadership material? Maybe. Likeable? Possibly. Better that than disliked for sure, but best not to aim for it, to come across as needy or trying too hard.

'Just be yourself and people will like you,' she said.

And if they don't? Her majority was beefy enough to take a few hits. Sod 'em.

She sat in the living room in her favourite armchair. Felt her feet on the carpet, her back in the cushion. Placed her hands on her thighs. Inhaled slowly.

The phone started ringing. She exhaled, although it came out more as a sigh.

'There it is,' she said to the room.

Bound to happen, but who would it be? Either the party's communications adviser or the whip's office.

David Passmore, her phone told her. So, whip's office then.

'Hello David.'

'Kathryn, good morning, all ready? Looking forward to it?'

'Absolutely. It's a lovely story, I can't wait.'

'Good girl, excellent. Just remember the World Wide Britain treaty is the key theme right now. It'll only be a few minutes. Be over in a flash, so get the theme in early before the clock runs out, yes?'

'Sure, although it'll be difficult to shoe horn it into this one.'

There was a pause on the line.

Shit, thought Kathryn.

'Look, Kathy – '

It's Kathryn, she said to herself.

' – we're a team, right? All pull in the same direction, yes?'

'Yes, of course, I just - '

'And that means,' he cut her off, voice raised slightly, 'the theme is the important bit, not some old flannel about a wall you've just found, right?' Not a question.

'Right.'

'So,' calm again now, 'of course give them the magic dust about the wall, then push World Wide Britain. The PM's due to sign next Wednesday. That's a week today and we're still struggling with a few foreign leaders.'

'Yes,' she said, hoping the words at the other end of the phone sounded less sheepish.

'And watch out for the gotcha, she'll try her damnedest to trip you up.'

'Oh, I don't think so David, ha, ha. I mean, what could she trip me up on, the artisan quality of the plaster?'

There was another pause on the line.

Shit, thought Kathryn.

'Kathy, you're new to this; Carole Aggerton is a pro. If she wants to she'll pull you all over the place, pin you down for answers, get you to promise the earth. The trick is to speak without saying anything, except the World Wide Britain agenda, obviously. Remember, she's a journalist. She doesn't give a stuff about a bloody wall, she just wants a story, a scalp. Yours. You've got to be on your A game, got that?'

'Yes.'

'Good girl. And don't forget to have fun. Enjoy it Kathy, we'll all be listening!'

'Thanks David, 'bye,' she said, but he'd already hung up.

'Shit,' she yelled into the room, 'shitshitshit.'

David Bloody Passmore. Not Dave, oh no. Not Davey-boy Passmore. She could feel her heart beating fast.

'But I'm bloody *Kathy* and I'm a *good girl*,' she raged.

Calm down, control it. You've handled worse. You've walked into a Taliban village at midnight and planted a British flag. If anyone in the party can handle David Passmore, it's you. Put it in a box and put the box in a corner.

The phone rang again. Not a number she recognised or a name in her phone. Right, game on. Deep breath.

'Hello, Kathryn Fieldhouse speaking.'

'Hi Ms Fieldhouse, it's Tim from the station, we spoke yesterday about the interview?'

‘Of course Tim, how are you? All good to go your end?’

‘Yep, we’re ready, Carole’s just finishing the last one and then she’ll be onto you. Unless you’ve got any questions I’ll leave you to it. You’ll hear her in a moment, then just talk straight away when she comes to you. You’ll be live at that point, ok?’

‘That’s fine Tim, great. Is this level good for you?’

‘Yes, don’t worry, I’ll control the volume from here.’

‘Ok, right, yes.’

Kathryn sat down, then stood up again. She liked to move around when talking to an audience, so standing was probably best. So she stood.

‘The time is now six minutes to eight,’ Kathryn heard Carole Aggerton announce.

‘Now, renovation work in the basement of the Ministry of Defence has revealed part of the original Palace of Whitehall, lost for over five hundred years. Joining me now on the line to talk about this remarkable discovery is Kathryn Fieldhouse, former army officer and now the MP in whose constituency the MoD is located. And it really is a remarkable discovery isn’t it Ms Fieldhouse, good morning?’

‘Good morning Carole. Yes, it really is a remarkable discovery, really remarkable.’

‘Part of a wall thought to have been built in the reign of King Henry the Eighth has been found, I understand,’ said Carole Aggerton. ‘How did that come about?’

'Yes, Carole, well, there's been building work in the basement of the MoD for some time now and they've found part of a wall, thought to have been built in the reign of King Henry the Eighth. It was found because of the building work.'

'I understand. And was this part of a historical excavation?'

'No, it was for a disabled toilet.'

'I see, so not quite what the builders were expecting?'

'No, Carole, but obviously as soon as they found the wall that was thought to have been built in the reign of King Henry the Eighth we knew it was something special and had to be preserved for the nation.'

'It must have come as quite a shock to them, wouldn't you agree?'

'Ha, ha, yes, they said they'd never seen anything like it before.'

'Yes indeed. So they weren't specialist tradespeople, used to handling historic building projects?'

'No, I think they came from Streatham.'

'So has this work been budgeted for?'

'Yes absolutely.'

'But I thought you said they weren't specialist tradespeople. And you weren't expecting to have to preserve a historic wall when the work started, so how has all that been budgeted for?'

'Well I can't go into details, but all this work will be paid for.'

'I would hope so. Out of public funds?'

'Yes, out of public funds. It is important to preserve -'

'How much will the project cost?'

'The toilet or the wall?'

'Well, both, but I'm more interested in the wall.'

'I can't go into details -'

'Why not? It's public money. Do you know the figure?'

'I don't have it to hand, but...'

'And when will the public be able to see it for the first time?'

'Oh it won't be open to the public. It's in the Ministry of Defence.'

'The public won't be able to see it? So what's the point of spending an undisclosed amount of public money?'

'Because it's important to preserve it for the nation -'

'Who will never be allowed to see it. Is that fair?'

'Well, maybe not on its own but it is when you understand that it's actually part of the World Wide Britain agenda too.'

'How so, isn't that treaty just about trade?'

'No! It's much more than that. It's a whole of government effort to showcase Britain on the world stage. Trade agreements, defence treaties, cultural investments. This all-encompassing treaty, that the Prime Minister is due to sign with at least twenty foreign heads of state in the coming days, will be the blueprint for Britain in the twenty-first century.'

'And how does the wall fit into that?'

'It shows what a rich cultural heritage this nation has.'

'Forgive me, but it doesn't show anything of the sort. It won't show anything to anyone if it's not open to the public, will it?'

'Well, the Foreign Office is leading on the World Wide Britain agenda so they will probably want to showcase how Britain is wide open on the global worldwide stage. And that's why this wall is so significant.'

'So what are you saying; that this policy may be reversed, and that the public may be able to see the wall?'

'The government keeps all policies under review.'

'Of course, but that's just parliamentary shorthand for being able to change your mind without admitting you've performed a U-turn. Will it be the Foreign or Defence Secretary who decides whether the public will be able to see this part of the country's rich cultural heritage as you put it, that they have paid for?'

'Probably the Foreign Secretary.'

'The Foreign Secretary, thankyou.'

'Although the Defence Secretary would want to be involved obviously, because of security. We couldn't have people unescorted wandering around the Ministry of Defence.'

'Kathryn Fieldhouse, thankyou very much. It's three minutes to eight, time for the weather.'

Her phone went dead.

Kathryn stared at the handset, which felt hot in her palm. It started ringing again. The screen said 'David Passmore'.

'Shit,' said Kathryn.

4.

‘Oh dear, Thomas, she’s not going to be pleased with that.’

Betsy turned the radio off and returned upstairs with more ease than before, fortified by the porridge, a cup of tea and her vape pen. She carried the radio, retuned to a news station called London Local.

She woke her computer up and stared at the route of The Long Night then clicked back to the home page of the London War Walks website. The new page showed photographs of various buildings and war memorabilia. The central image was of a man wearing a t-shirt with a logo saying ‘Guild of Battlefield Guides’. Betsy rubbed her eyes. She heard a van coming down the road and held the curtains to one side to watch it pass. Must be a lost delivery driver, she figured, but observed the driver closely all the same. She thought again about the man she’d left by the fence in Wellspring Gardens. There had been no report on the radio of a hit and run in east London. The paramedics that attended the scene would have informed the police, for sure. Why had nothing been reported? The man must have wanted to avoid the police very badly indeed if he’d managed to get himself away before the ambulance arrived. It didn’t make sense. Or at least any sense it did make felt worse than having to explain herself to the police.

She looked at the picture of the man on the website. Sean Hambleton seemed about forty years old. He was smiling for the camera and pointing down. Betsy was momentarily puzzled, then realised Sean was pointing to the row of social media icons below the photograph.

She clicked on the Twitter icon. Sean Hambleton's face appeared again. The site had 3,697 followers. Betsy scrolled down through the messages. Sean didn't post that often and only really did it to announce the next date for a guided walk. Betsy flicked through until she stopped on a post dated August 27th the previous year. 'NEW WALK' the message proclaimed, above a black and white picture of Second World War fire fighters tackling a blaze. Sean was promoting The Long Night for the first time. The message had been retweeted by twenty-two followers. Most people had reacted to it at the time, or a day or two after. They must be hard-core fans, Betsy figured. She flicked through the details of all those who had posted the message onto their followers. Her eye was drawn to the last date the message had been retweeted.

'That's yesterday, Thomas,' she said, as she sat back in her chair. 'How very interesting.'

*

The wiggly worms had done as good a job as anyone could have asked of them. They'd made it to the satellite with the message from the surface: trouble.

At least that was how the continuous signal was being interpreted in the drab building in Noginsk-9, the military village twenty miles east of Moscow. One of the many outposts of the Satellite Intelligence Directorate, the small building had tracked the USB stick throughout the dead-drop operation. As usual the transmitter was supposed to be in play during the pick up only and deactivated soon after. That it was still singing, long after the operative on the ground had managed to drag his bruised body away from the street, was a concern.

'I told them this would happen one day, with that stupid one point six game,' the head of the department grunted.

'She insisted on it. And isn't that what we're here for anyway?' his assistant replied. It earned him a stare of reprove.

Obviously the USB stick would have to be dropped off somewhere, safe from inquisitive fingers. Just knowing the hiding place was the usual distance from the start point wasn't good enough; much could be missed if the picker-up just kicked over a few stones after one point six miles. So James had added transmitters to the bag of USB sticks he'd given ChipsWithMayo, the year before. Whoever went to pick the stick up would be guided to it by a handheld receiver. The worms were never expected to travel more than a few hundred yards, worst case. Making it four hundred miles to the satellite had been a Herculean effort. But it had come at a cost. The worms hadn't been strong enough to carry much information. Far from passing on the exact location of the stick the best they could do was to offer a broad area. A very broad area. So broad in fact it described most of London.

'How long has the van been in operation?' the boss asked.

'All morning.'

Sensitive receiver equipment installed in the back of a specially modified grey van was able to narrow down the area. The same vehicle crawling along the same road time after time would be noticed only by the most surveillance aware civilian.

'Well? What have they found?' snapped the man.

'South London, Hollett Road,' the assistant quickly offered.

'Have they gone in with the body-worn kit?'

'Yes sir, an hour ago.'

There was a knock on the office door. A young man was waved in. He handed a piece of paper to the head of the department. Who immediately smiled.

'Right hand side as you head west. Either number 68, 70, 72 or 74. They'll narrow it down as the occupants reveal themselves. The team member on the ground said the tone was unstable. One minute silent, the next so loud she almost had to rip out her earpiece. Whoever has the stick must have shielded the signal somehow.'

'The team will be outside, in the van,' the assistant said. 'They'll grab the phone data and photographs of the occupants.'

‘And grab all the glory after they break in,’ the boss said.

‘They’ll identify the house and go in during the next POD,’ the assistant said.

‘POD?’

‘Period of darkness. Tonight.’

‘Why not just say that then?’ the signals intelligence officer said. ‘You freaks in the GRU like to think you’re so mysterious.’

‘I should report you for that,’ the assistant said.

‘Go ahead. Do you want me to report your online porn habit, Nikolai? You have very niche tastes.’

‘You won’t do that.’

‘You are correct. But only because you won’t report me.’

The assistant’s mouth smiled. His eyes, though, stayed fixed on the head of department, the man who, technically, was his boss for the duration of his secondment from Russian Military Intelligence to Noginsk-9.

His boss smiled back.

‘And they say détente died with the Cold War,’ the boss said.

5.

ClickClickClick.

'Woman. Child. About four years old. From number 70.'

'Understood. I'm picking up one phone.'

'She's closed the front door. On her own by the look of it. Age, thirty to thirty-five, average build, black, medium height, long black hair. Send the data back to headquarters,' the man in the back of the grey van said in a low voice. 'So just 74 left, yes?'

'No,' his female companion murmured. 'We've had an elderly couple from 74. No phones. Young woman from 68, I've got her phone, and this mother from 70. I've got her phone too. We haven't seen anyone from 72 yet.'

'Understood. The battery is good on the camera for another,' the man lifted his eye from the viewfinder, 'thirty minutes, I reckon.'

'I've got four ready in the charging bank right here,' the woman said.

'Understood.' He pressed his face back against the rubber eye socket and continued his watch across Hollett Road.

*

In the upstairs office next to the front window Betsy watched murky clouds blend and swirl. She'd given up listening out for news reports of a broken body lying next to a fence. The apparent disappearance of her assailant was just one more blob of grey to add to the others in her head, colliding, contradicting, for one intoxicating moment explaining, like the ray of sunshine landing on the grey van parked at the end of the street, before it was snuffed out by a shifting cloud.

Why would anyone leave it so long to retweet the message about the war walk?

Maybe the person has only just discovered the post about The Long Night, Betsy thought. Strange though, to push it on almost a year after it was first put up. She hovered the computer cursor over the profile name of the follower that had retweeted the message. The account was called ChipsWithMayo.

A new window popped up to one side with the profile picture of a bag of chips. The biography said 'The best thing since sliced potatoes'. The window showed ChipsWithMayo had eighty-six followers and was following twelve other accounts. Betsy clicked on the account. ChipsWithMayo's Twitter page opened. The few posts consisted mainly of restaurant reviews, but Betsy saw that messages promoting walks from Sean Hambleton's site were also dotted throughout the history.

She scrolled back to the top, to the post retweeted for The Long Night a day before. She could tell only one Twitter user had acknowledged the message as the little red heart icon had a solitary figure next to it. Betsy clicked again and saw that someone called James Easton had liked the post from ChipsWithMayo only an hour after it had appeared. Betsy looked at the profile page for James Easton. A tanned man in his twenties with slick black hair and dark sunglasses grinned at the camera. His biography said: 'Amateur philosopher, failed businessman and news junkie. All views my own blah, blah, blah'.

Betsy sat back in her chair. She looked down at Major Tom, who had appeared silently and unnoticed in her lap. She stroked his head and turned once again to the computer. She went back to the profile of ChipsWithMayo and clicked on the list of followers. Other than James Easton all the other profiles had no actual pictures of real people and only seemed to retweet messages, rather than submit posts themselves.

'They're bots, Thomas,' Betsy said. 'You've only got one actual human follower, haven't you Chips?'

For the next hour she looked through the other tweets from the London War Walks Twitter feed. She noticed a pattern. They all got retweeted by a few people at the time they were first posted, then again by the ChipsWithMayo account months later. Each time, within an hour or so, James Easton had liked the retweet by Chips. All the posts that Chips retweeted were to walks on the company site. Occasionally it went the other way. James Easton sometimes retweeted an old war walk and Chips liked his post. Whichever walk was used for the messages, there was always a map.

'You're chatting, aren't you?' Betsy said. 'Setting up meets on Twitter and handing over USB sticks on the war walks.'

She stretched, causing the cat to jump to the floor.

'I am going to the shops, Thomas,' she said. 'And when I return I expect you to be able to tell me what's so special about these walks and the relevance of mile one point six.'

*

Ckickclickclick.

'Woman. From number 72.'

'Understood. I've got one phone.'

'She's out, alone. Walking slowly. Age seventy to seventy-five, slight frame but sturdy, white, short in height, large glasses, neat shoulder-length hair, smoking a vape pen. Send the data back to headquarters.'

*

A car horn blaring next to her snapped Betsy from her thoughts. The effort to find a link between secret messages, hiding places and broken bones was proving to be an exhausting and annoying activity. She knew the solution was there just out of reach, hidden by memories and regrets. Thirty years ago she'd have found the answer by now, or at least one of her team would have done. No team now, just a cat, which wasn't the same. Her past life stabbed at her. It had been doing that more often in recent years. Loneliness isn't the absence of presence, it's the presence of absence.

'Cheer up, luv, it might never happen.'

Betsy looked at the man smiling at her, leaning against the glass window of a café. He had a half-eaten sandwich in one hand, a mobile phone in the other.

'It already has,' Betsy said, as she bustled past.

'What?' called the man. 'What has?'

The old woman carried on down the street.

'The best years of my life,' she muttered to herself.

She shuffled into a grocery shop to search for cat food. For a moment she stared blankly at the rows of packets and tins on the shelves, seemingly overwhelmed.

'Can I help you madam?' an assistant asked.

'Help – no, I don't need any help. Thankyou,' Betsy said.

You do need help, you silly old fool, a voice in her head told her. Damn your pride, this is serious, and right now it's beyond you. You know what you need to do. And you know you need to take precautions.

She left the grocery and continued along the high street to a charity shop. She bought a handbag, an old book and a pair of woollen gloves. Next door was a newsagents. When she emerged she'd added a packet of tissues and a tube of mints to the bag. She opened the mints, put one in her mouth, scattered three more in the handbag and twisted the foil securing the remainder. It took some searching, but she eventually found a hardware shop that sold her a USB stick in a plastic case. She put it in her bag then darted into a small grocery and bought a multi-pack of cat food. This she tucked under an arm as she headed home. She hated waste so refused the offer of a separate carrier, even though there was no more room in her new handbag.

*

The heavy door closed behind them. David Passmore walked on one side of Patrick Evans. Andrew Heath's long legs flicked in perfect rhythm on the other. As thin as a twig but a clear foot taller than Evans, the Defence Secretary was visible to the chief whip only as a bobbing head and a pair of well polished shoes.

'Remember when we used to call him Sunlight?' Evans said. 'The only shiny member of a front bench full of arseholes.'

'Hang on, Patrick, some of them can probably lip read,' said Passmore.

The men waved for the small group of bored photographers camped out opposite the door to Number 10. They continued their stroll towards the back entrance to Downing Street.

'I feel a pang of nostalgia for that time now,' said Heath. 'Boring, but stable. A complete lack of ideas. Marvellous.'

‘So why, when he only gets one idea, does it have to be the bloody World Wide Britain agenda?’ said Passmore.

‘Because it’s a brilliant bucket, my dear David,’ said Evans. ‘Pour anything you like into it, cover any policy foible, dazzle your friends and allies. All while doing absolutely naff all.’

The trio negotiated the security gate at the end of Downing Street and emerged into Horseguards Parade.

‘What was that guff he was coming out with?’ Passmore said.

‘Which bit?’ said Heath. ‘The “champion the success of free and open societies” bit or the “match our policies to the scale of the challenge”? Take your pick. We’re not going to be able to do either with the deal he’s about to sign.’

‘I was particularly taken with the “guarantee a fairer, greener and more prosperous world,”’ said Evans.

The men crossed the road into St James’s Park in sullen silence.

‘But it can be so much more,’ the chief whip pleaded, once clear of a clutch of tourists photographing a squirrel.

‘We know that,’ Evans said, ‘but he’s lost his bottle. What were once countless strands of British energy, zinging off around the world to make these islands imperious once more, are now coils round his throat.’

The wind snatched at the men and shook leaves onto the path. Another shower threatened from the heavy sky.

'We've still got time,' said Heath.

'Andrew, I do admire your optimism. Even if it is totally misplaced,' said Evans.

'What time is left is ours to use, not his. He's not going to do anything,' said Passmore.

'I agree,' said Evans.

'So do I,' said Heath. 'The ball is in our court.'

'We should remind him he's where he is because of us, and that our goodwill is not inexhaustible,' said Passmore.

'Threaten the PM? Goodness, David, you are an ambitious chief whip,' said Evans.

'And Minister Without Portfolio,' said Passmore.

'Apologies your grace,' said Evans, 'how could we forget?'

'Well have you got a better idea?' said Passmore.

'Actually yes,' said Evans. 'As Foreign Secretary I am able to authorise many actions to keep the secret state gainfully employed. As you both know, for a while now I've tasked the Vauxhall vampires to keep an eye on some of the opposition and let me know their negotiating positions. I've tried to use this to nudge the PM. Regrettably I feel my efforts have been too subtle.'

'Oh God, that bloke in Croatia, the lawyer,' Heath said, 'you didn't lose the subtlety did you?'

'Don't be absurd,' said Evans, 'our people have just been listening. I'm not completely stupid. I'd go down in flames for old Blighty but even I have limits. No, I will make this information much more visible to the public if good old Sunlight doesn't harden his position.'

'And if that doesn't work?' said Passmore. 'And why have we come this way?'

Andrew Heath directed the men to cross the road and head back towards Parliament Square.

'Defence always has a back-up plan,' said Heath. 'I needed to talk to you both away from the crowd.'

'Go on,' said Evans.

'No details gents, not yet. But I need your support. Let's just say I've got something brewing for our recalcitrant leader. Needs must and all that.'

6.

‘We’ve got a problem,’ ChipsWithMayo said.

‘Problem? What sort of a problem?’

ChipsWithMayo had never liked the minister, but always managed to force the feelings to one side. The mission was more important than personal emotions.

‘The last message was intercepted after I dropped it off.’

Parliament Square was packed with tourists as usual, unperturbed by the occasional squally rain shower. A shaft of sunlight landed on the statue of Churchill. ChipsWithMayo was certain he would have approved of Operation Meadowland. The old boy wasn’t against a bit of bloodletting and sacrifice for a noble cause.

‘How is that possible?’ said the MP.

‘No idea, I was long gone.’

The minister was walking briskly. He had an important meeting in five minutes. He always had important meetings. And they were always in five minutes. ChipsWithMayo struggled to keep up.

‘So how are you so sure it was intercepted?’ the Minister said.

Because I’m not a bloody amateur, ChipsWithMayo wanted to shout at him.

Instead: 'I always put malware on the USB stick to tell me where it gets plugged in. James sheep-dips the stick before looking at it so I never get a signal from him. I got a signal this time so I know it was intercepted.'

'So who has the stick?'

'An old woman. A Betsy Trenmore-Halford. Know her?'

'No. How do you know she's old?'

'Her date of birth comes up on the software I have to identify addresses.'

The minister looked at ChipsWithMayo.

'There's no end to your tricks, is there?'

There was no reply.

'How has this woman worked out our business?' the minister said.

'No way she could have. It must have been luck.'

'Would she have seen you?'

'No.'

'What would she find out?'

'Well, I'm ninety-nine per cent sure she wouldn't be able to break the steg.'

'The what?'

They dodged around a snaking line of tourists, queuing at the visitors' entrance to the Palace of Westminster.

'Steganography. The picture code that hid the message. But if she did, it only said the operation name, no change to date and time – that's verbatim - and the trade.'

'No mention of the last request? That deal hasn't gone through yet.'

'I didn't include his name again. I still think it was a mistake including him before we even know if he's a threat.'

'Look,' the man said, 'I've dealt with Bonal before and he's a bloody nuisance. He hates Britain and will do anything he can to make life hard for us. As soon as I heard they were bringing him on the pitch I knew we had to act. We're due to sign next week. He's got to go.'

'How's Sunlight?'

'Out of his depth. His problem is he's never properly negotiated anything. He doesn't realise you're supposed to feel like you're in a corner, that's when you know you're in the right place. He thinks negotiating like this has never happened before. He just wants to sign something and get on to the next bit because he believes whatever comes after can't be as bad as this. He'll sign up to anything and hope he can pick the pieces up later. That's no way to run a negotiation. We're the country's only hope.'

'And we're still going through with Meadowland?'

The MP stopped at the Cromwell Green entrance. He turned to face ChipsWithMayo for the first time since their conversation had started.

'No cold feet now, please. This was your idea if I remember correctly.'

ChipsWithMayo said nothing and just nodded.

He dropped his voice. 'Look, if Sunlight pulls the deal round we'll call off the operation. Easy. Have a nice drink and a canapé. Britain needs us to be strong now.'

'Well there's no way this Betsy woman will be able to connect the dots,' said ChipsWithMayo.

The minister arched his eyebrows.

'A baseless statement if ever I heard one. I'm not at all sure you can be so confident, she intercepted your little game after all. Can't you speak to your friends to get the stick back? Use one of those little phones they have on television dramas. Burner phones, I think they're called.'

The MP drew out his House of Commons pass, ready to show the two policemen at the entrance.

'No,' said ChipsWithMayo. 'We don't use burners. Nothing's untraceable. The phones may not be registered but everything leaves a digital footprint these days. That's why we went back to the dead letter box method, no electronic history.'

'Well, I don't care how you do it, but you need to sort this mess out. We're close to the finish now.'

'I know some people,' ChipsWithMayo said. 'I'll make some arrangements.'

'Good. Are you sure you can't just call the hired help?'

'I'm sure. That's the thing about espionage these days. It's so advanced you've got to be properly old-school to survive.'

*

Kathryn Fieldhouse was annoyed. For the interview, for the glacially slow progress of her career and for being treated like a schoolgirl by the Party.

Boxing helped. Although new to politics she had learned her anger was best directed at a padded head. Better that than swearing at a member of the public. But she still needed a pick-me-up.

She called the agency and gave her password. Asked if Joachim was free at ten that night. He was. The usual hour and a half madam? Kathryn said forty-five minutes would be fine. There's a supplement for any bookings under an hour, she was told. Kathryn said she was happy to pay the extra, she didn't do cuddles and the only afterglow she was interested in would be Joachim's rear lights when he left.

7.

Julianne Fieldhouse had told nobody of her suspicions that there was a traitor at the heart of MI6. She had, hitherto, trusted everyone on the surveillance team, but something had been out of place for months. She'd taken the difficult decision long ago to record and then listen again to their operations for any note in the voices that might betray an ulterior motive. She'd review today's operation on the flight home. Anyone watching would assume she was listening to music.

She watched Sébastien Bonal close the door to his apartment and walk the short distance to his car. Sitting alone in her vehicle two hundred metres away, Jules pressed a tiny switch taped onto the steering wheel.

'Standby, standby,' she said.

'That's a standby, standby from Jules,' a man's voice said in her earpiece.

'That's Bonal out of the apartment and heading for his car,' Jules said.

The three other members of the surveillance team acknowledged the call.

Bonal climbed into his car, started the engine and lowered a window to let some air in. It was already hot, even though it was not yet noon. He pulled out of the parking space.

'He's off, heading towards the main road,' Jules said. 'When he turns at the junction he'll go unsighted to me.'

'Understood Jules,' the man said, from a hotel room a mile away. 'Who can take Bonal at the junction?'

'I'm on it.'

'Thanks, Marcus.'

'He's turning left at the junction now, unsighted to me,' Jules.

'Got him,' said the man called Marcus, in a black Fiat 500.

The other three cars chipped in, one after the other, to make it clear to the whole team who had control of the target.

'Control, understood. Marcus has Bonal heading towards the coast,' said the man in the hotel room.

Although the team had been given just two days to prepare, they had learned all the major junctions and roundabouts in the town. As with every new surveillance job the unusual road layout had been a pain to memorise. Necessary though, for the team to keep the target pinpointed in their collective mind's eye.

Bonal slowed on approach to the small roundabout to give way to a car. It had come from the opposite direction, driven almost two complete circles of the roundabout and taken the back road to St Tropez.

Bonal took the second exit and continued up the hill on the main road, towards the monument to the

Resistance fighters that had operated during the war in this part of France. A small track led from the main road to a parking area in the woods behind the monument. Although some way back, Jules saw another member of the surveillance team move out of the car park and drive down to the main road, timing his run in to the junction as Bonal approached. Don't get there too early, Jules said to herself. Having the target from the front is a nightmare. If he's surveillance-aware the target could get a good look at your car. You'd have to drop him as quickly as possible, which would only heap pressure on the team. And don't get there at the same time as the target, because then he'll get a good look at your car, and at you, gawping through the window. And don't get there too late after he's passed the junction, because, well, 'you'll be too bloody late, you idiot,' Jules said.

Bonal passed the junction to the memorial car park. A silver car arrived from the direction of the trees, passing the black Fiat 500 as it turned from the main road.

'Mike has Bonal,' said the driver of the silver car.

An elderly couple were sitting in the memorial car park, tearing lumps from a baguette. They watched a car drive up the track, pause briefly at the information board, then return to the main road and continue the way it had been travelling originally.

'Touristes,' the man said to his wife.

The road sloped down towards a junction on the main east-west coast road. The islands of Saint-

Marguerite and Saint-Honorat lay surrounded by yachts in the Bay of Cannes. Bonal had always loved this view, even though the hard glitter of the sea hurt his eyes. He slowed to take in the view. The sun inched towards its highest point, as if questioning whether it was worth the sheer effort. Bonal reached the junction. He had to wait for traffic to pass, heading west along the coast to St Tropez. He turned in the other direction, towards Cannes.

'Looks like he's heading for the restaurant as expected. Who can get ahead and cover the front?' the man in charge of the surveillance team said.

'I'll cover that.'

'Thanks, Matt, use the back road to avoid the traffic.'

Jules worried again about the mobile phone on her passenger seat. A wire connected the phone to the communications kit hidden in the rucksack, sitting in the passenger footwell. It was recording the voices on the surveillance operation. She didn't want to think how many regulations she was breaking. It was such an unauthorised action she figured there was a fifty-fifty chance her bosses, if they found out, would just chuck her in the sea rather than bother with any disciplinary action. Probably not she admitted, but her amazing career as a surveillance operator would come to an abrupt end if she was caught. Bye-bye MI6. She figured the risk was worth it, if it lifted the lid on quite why surveillance targets her team had worked in recent months had developed the nasty habit of dying in mysterious circumstances a short time after.

The coast road was typically jammed with traffic. Locals and tourists cruised slowly, enjoying the view or looking for a parking space. The surveillance team flowed through the back streets, ahead, behind and to the side of Bonal's car, unimpeded by traffic as lunch approached.

Bonal inched through the traffic and approached a pedestrian crossing. He smiled for a family and beckoned them to cross the road, heading for the beach. He was looking forward to lunch. It had been a tough week and he was glad to be back on the coast. A bit of swimming tomorrow and a lazy dinner in Théole-sur-Mer at that restaurant on the beach. He might just be able to forget the World Wide Britain treaty negotiations.

The surveillance team took their target, as expected, to the car park of a restaurant overlooking the sea. Once they had confirmed Bonal had parked and entered the *Boucanier*, they regrouped further along the coast road. Another member of the team, already sitting at a table and studying the wine list, would alert them when Bonal was next on the move. Control would call the car team if they were needed. Their part of the operation was over.

In his hotel room Control picked up the handset for the second radio net.

'X-Ray, radio check.'

'Yeah, good to me Control.'

'What's happening, Rob?'

'Nothing. She's still in there. No change from normal routine.'

'Okay. Team in position?'

'Yeah, if she suddenly remembers she forgot to empty the dishwasher at the apartment we'll stop her.'

'Great, cheers, Rob.'

Control was happy. Bonal was tucked up in the restaurant and his housekeeper, the only other person with a set of keys to his apartment, was safely in her own home and showing no signs of going anywhere.

He called the installation team on a mobile phone.

'Green light, Jim, happy drilling,' Control said.

'Cheers, Pete,' said the man dressed as an air conditioning technician.

Control then dialled a London number on a second mobile phone. It was answered quickly.

'It's Pete in France,' he said.

'Everything in order?'

'Yep, no dramas taking him to lunch. Housekeeper's under wraps and installation team are going in now.'

'Let me know when the team are off target.'

'Will do.' He ended the call.

The surveillance team drove to a hypermarket car park and stripped their cars of the flyaway communications kit they used with hire vehicles. They paired up and checked each other's cars for any tell-tale signs of the operation. None were found. They left at ten-minute intervals for Cannes-Mandelieu airport, checking in separately for the two flights that afternoon back to London.

Jules had detected nothing in any of the team's decisions or language that day to suggest Bonal's life was in danger. But the niggling doubt remained. She needed to speak to someone close enough to the spy game to read the warning signs as she had, but far enough away to not pose a threat. Breaking MI6's rules didn't sit easily with her, so it was with a heavy heart that she realised she was going to have to talk to her Godmother.

8.

Betsy took one last pull on the vape pen and tucked it into the pocket of her dressing gown. Her mouth held the cannabis-infused balloon of air for a few seconds. She then blew it out of the back door, which she closed and locked. The steam outside wobbled up the side of the house and escaped her vision, like a fleeting thought.

She carried a plate of biscuits through to the front room. Jules had made space on the crowded table for the tea set and reclaimed her seat on the sofa.

'Shall I be Godmother?' Betsy said, predictably.

Jules smiled. She had expected the line, but right now she was knackered and worried and welcomed the soothing effect of Betsy's simple predictability.

Betsy looked for a place to set down the plate of biscuits. Silver framed photographs of Jules and her sister besieged the tea set on the table. A tide of papers broke against the wall of pictures. On top of one pile of papers was a gun. The old seven-shot revolver, black with a wooden handgrip, sat incongruously like an uninvited guest. Betsy picked it up and moved it to the Welsh dresser against the wall. She laid the plate of biscuits in the space made by the weapon.

'Why do you hang on to that old thing?' Jules said.

'The Nagant? It makes a very good paperweight,' Betsy replied.

'Isn't it a bit, you know, illegal?'

'Oh, stop fussing, dear,' Betsy said. 'It served my grandfather perfectly well on the Eastern Front and now it's serving me.'

Betsy poured two strong teas and handed Jules a china cup and saucer. A slab of homemade shortbread threatened to unbalance the operation.

'This isn't Special Shortbread, is it?' Jules asked.

'No dear, don't worry. Your vetting status is just as important to me.'

Jules sipped her tea.

'When did you get in?' Betsy asked.

'Couple of hours ago. From France, so not too hellish,' Jules said.

'And then straight here. Goodness, we are honoured aren't we, Thomas?' Major Tom dozed next to Jules in the sunshine. Betsy's sharp eyes examined her goddaughter's face.

'Bets, do you ever turn off your Aga? I'm already starting to sweat,' Jules said.

'Horses sweat, dear,' Betsy replied with mock disapproval. 'Men perspire. Ladies glow.'

'Well, I'll be glowing my arse off in a minute then.'

'Julianne, please.'

‘Sorry, Bets, love ya,’ Jules said, blowing Betsy a kiss. ‘And I don’t know how you can wear that, in this heat.’

Jules indicated the navy blue dressing gown Betsy had on over her clothes.

‘My thermostat is just fine, thank you,’ Betsy said. ‘You’re a tad young for the hot flushes, dear.’

They sipped their tea and ate their biscuits.

Jules sank into the sofa. The cushions surrounded her like bodyguards. She exhaled slowly as her tired eyes floated around the room. She had always disliked Betsy’s taste in home furnishings. It wasn’t that the room looked old fashioned. More that it was a bit too Disney; a twee version of the perfect English country cottage. Other than the table, a riot of old newspapers, correspondence and reading material printed from her computer, the whole lot seemingly held in check by the revolver presiding over the chaos, everything was just so. Practical, unchallenging art on the walls and a bookcase that hadn’t been consulted in years, mostly consisting of ghost-authored travel volumes by TV personalities. Every time she visited, Jules half expected to find a picture of the Queen on the wall above the fireplace. As it was there was just a mirror, in which she could see the reflection of the glass chandelier hanging over the centre of the room.

‘I heard Her Highness’s stellar performance on the radio this morning,’ Jules said. ‘The Badger won’t be happy.’

‘What are you two squabbling about this time?’ Betsy said. ‘You and your sister are two of the brightest and most talented women I've ever known. I don't know where this competitive jealousy comes from. And I'm sure The Badger will be happy for her, even if she may not have been in total control of the discussion.'

'Not in total control,' Jules said, leaping upright on the sofa and startling Major Tom. 'I've seen interrogation subjects exert more control over a conversation.'

'I'm sure you have dear, but you know she'll have beaten herself up about it, so no point you adding your two penneth.'

'Bloody politicians,' Jules said.

'How is The Badger anyway?' Betsy said.

'He seemed all right the last time we spoke. Didn't chat long. He never does.'

Her eyes unfocussed and roamed the room before settling on a framed black and white photograph on the mantelpiece over the fire. A pair of brass candleholders stood sentry, one on each end of the stone ledge, guarding the picture in the centre and a carriage clock next to it. The man in the picture, with a happy, fleshy face and full head of hair with long sideburns, was not to be seen anywhere else in the room.

'What's wrong, Jules?' Betsy asked.

'Wrong? Why do you think something's wrong?'

'Because you've hardly said a word since you got here except to tear strips off your sister and your father, you're clearly exhausted and you've never been able to fool me,' Betsy said.

‘It’s nothing, just work stuff. So you know I can’t talk about that.’

‘Indeed. Well, let’s just enjoy our tea then,’ Betsy said. ‘Let me know when you’re ready to tell me the scoundrel’s name.’

‘Oh God, it’s not a man.’

‘If you say so.’

‘Bets, you know I shouldn’t talk about my work. It’s different with you, but still…’ Jules let the sentence fade.

‘If you’re worried about crossing lines, don’t be,’ Betsy said. ‘This barely counts, believe me.’

The women shared a smile. Betsy threw Jules another piece of shortbread.

‘Okay,’ Jules said, fixing Betsy with a stare, ‘you, but no further.’

Betsy glared at the younger woman.

‘Sorry,’ Jules said.

Betsy sipped her tea.

‘You know I’ve been abroad a lot recently,’ Jules began. ‘Well, I mean I’m always abroad, but the last few months have been even more manic.’

Betsy just nodded. She knew better than to break a subject’s train of thought once they were talking.

‘We’ve been taking an interest in a few people overseas. A real interest.’

She fell silent. After a few seconds, Betsy thought a nudge was needed.

‘Well that’s your job,’ she said.

'Yes,' Jules continued. 'But, well, it sounds strange just saying it,' Jules said.

'Not to me it won't, dear,' Betsy said.

Jules smiled.

'Some of them have died,' Jules said.

'People die all the time,' Betsy said. 'Get to my age and you'll realise it's largely a numbers game.'

'Yes, but these have been strange. Not old people, and odd circumstances.'

'Odd how?' said Betsy.

Jules sighed and stared at her feet.

Major Tom raised his head, as if wondering why the room had fallen silent.

'Julianne, have I ever told you about the first time I met your father?'

'No.'

'I was thirty-four years old and thoroughly depressed with life. We were at an official reception about something or other and got talking about skiing. I was mesmerised by the white flash through his beautiful black hair.'

The dipping sun highlighted the creases on her face, casting deep shadows between the ridges of her skin.

'Anyway, I told him how sad I was about the death of the famous American skier Betsy Snite. The next time we met he'd somehow found an old copy of Sports Illustrated from February 1960 with Snite on the cover. She was an Olympian then. It was obvious what The Badger was doing, but I didn't do anything to stop it. I immediately fell in love with that wonderfully imperious stare Snite displayed, as if inviting challenge. I didn't mean to, but was suddenly telling your father how I hated myself for not being as brave.'

For a moment Jules thought Betsy was waiting for an answer to an unasked question. She then realised the old woman was deep in thought, staring at a point on the wall just above her head.

'We kept chatting,' Betsy continued after a few seconds. 'Difficult, of course, but we used to see each other around the circuit. A few months later we were both in Mostar, at a conference exploring the historic depiction of the workers' struggle through art. He made promises to me on the old bridge. And I made my decision.'

'I don't get it,' Jules said.

'The point is, it takes a great effort to break rules one has invested much of one's life living by. But if that effort has been born of sincere thought, perhaps the bigger betrayal is to stay silent.'

'Wait, is that why you took the name Betsy?'

'Jules, please try to stick to the subject.'

'Don't worry, Bets, I'm with you,' Jules said with a smile. She slapped her hands on her thighs and took a deep breath.

'Well, okay then. The guy in Malaysia had an extreme nut allergy but accidentally ate a load of chicken satay, apparently. The allergic reaction closed his throat and he suffocated. Then there's a guy in Croatia who tried to dive a hundred feet into the sea but missed and smashed himself onto the rocks.'

Jules sat on the edge of the sofa, staring at Betsy with her palms open expectantly.

'Exotic, I'll give you, but why odd?' Betsy said.

'Because the Malaysian guy was in his thirties. He'd been managing his condition for over twenty years. And the bloke in Croatia was big into his diving. He used to dive off that point pretty much every day. None of it adds up.'

Betsy poured more tea. Jules sank back into the sofa.

'It is part of your job to be paranoid,' Betsy said.

'I know, but it's also my job to think round corners,' Jules replied.

'All legal? Planned and briefed correctly? No corners cut?'

'Nothing shifty at all. Everything was done by the book in Legoland.'

'Any connection between them?'

'Not that we were told. A lawyer and an academic.'

'Have you spoken to anyone at work?

'No. I wanted to speak to you first.'

'Wise, but I'm not sure exactly what I can do.'

'There is something.'

'What?'

'Tell me I'm not completely nuts.'

'You're not completely nuts, dear.'

*

The photographs were spread over the table in the secure room at the embassy. Good quality, close up, sharp focus. The FSB Resident turned to the man with the bruised face.

'Well, Viktor?'

The stocky man approached the table and looked at the pictures. A young woman, an elderly couple, a woman with a small child, an old woman sucking a vape pen. Viktor looked at the Resident and jabbed a stubby finger onto the photograph of the old woman.

Dmitri Goncharov nodded, and peeled his lips back in an approximation of a smile. He turned to his deputy.

'This one, Misha. Send the team in tonight.'

9.

Betsy stood at the kitchen door blowing smoke into the garden. The roses would need deadheading soon but at least the hollyhocks were flowering. Next-door's pyracantha was invading again. There seemed no way to stop the vicious thorns creeping towards her, like the bad memories of a past life.

Her hip was throbbing and she welcomed what little respite the vape offered. After thirty years of discomfort she had accepted she would never be pain-free again. She took the small mercies where she could.

She was thinking about her goddaughters. With no children of her own her affection for them was as unsurprising as it was powerful. She owed their parents more than could ever be repaid, as if their bond had been forged in blood. Which, in a very real way, it had.

She had always been protective of them, perhaps a little too much at times, but loved them without qualification or favour. She probably had more in common with Jules. Regardless, she recognised the ruthless streak in both and hoped she had contributed to it in some small way.

Contributed. The word lodged in her head as if fired from a gun. When had she last contributed to anything? When had she last been hunted out by anxious colleagues, consulted, considered even? There had been a time – years ago, possibly decades now – when her counsel had been the first to be sought. When operations were running; when events were unfolding. Then retirement. Silence. The silence of the grave she had avoided through all her long years of spying. It was worse than that. At least a grave would have had a headstone. A name. Something to be visited, remembered. She had no such luxuries; at least none worth the effort. Dead, she could have become a legend, but instead she felt painfully, embarrassingly alive. No, she had been denied the honour of a good and timely death. She was now, simply…disappeared.

The thought cut into her soul. She wouldn't accept it. Couldn't, more like. She may be retired, but she wasn't redundant. And anyway, spies never really retire, they just don't get paid for their efforts anymore. She could feel the pull of the secret world tugging at her, taunting, sneering.

Betsy drew hard on the vape pen. The heating element glowed and the cannabis oil performed its brief magic.

Jules's concerns should not be dismissed out of hand, she knew better than that. The deaths did sound bizarre. She was prepared to entertain the idea of murder. But she also knew the consequences of accepting that would mean unleashing a whole heap of questions, with little prospect of good answers. Speculation would be an exhausting and futile activity.

She watched a moth dance around the light above the back door. One moment in the shadows, the next breaking cover to attack the bulb as if it was a mortal enemy. It must hurt, Betsy thought, to keep bashing into the glass like that. Do moths get hurt? Do they even understand the concept of pain? Does it have any idea of what it's up against? Has it spent so long in the darkness the brief illumination is worth the risk to its life?

Betsy needed to think. She closed and locked the back door and collected a small amount of ice in a cocktail shaker retrieved from the draining board. Moving through to the dining room she lifted a whisky glass of cut crystal from a cabinet and placed it on the side. She tipped six splashes of bitters, two of the orange variety, into the shaker, added a dollop of rich, sweet syrup, then swirled the mixture for thirty seconds. She poured in two jiggers of Old Grand-Dad rye bourbon and stirred for another minute before tipping the lot into the whisky glass. She considered adding a slice of orange zest but decided it was late and not worth the effort. Tumbler in hand, Betsy walked through to the front room, tipping the glass to the photograph above the fireplace as she passed. She took a sip, pulled the curtains against the drizzle floating outside the dark window and dialled a number on her phone. One of the towers of books had collapsed onto the floor and Betsy shuffled the pile together with her feet as she waited for the call to be answered.

'Hello stranger,' a voice said.

'Stranger? I don't follow,' Betsy said. 'Can't I just ring an old friend out of a blue for a chat?'

'The blue, dear. And are you ringing just for a chat?' Megan Clover asked.

'No. Yes. Of course,' Betsy said, a note of indignation in her voice. 'I need to come and see you.'

'I like it when people get straight down to business. Not heard from you in, what, six months? Never mind. What's the story this time?'

'I found a USB stick and a man attacked me to try to get it back. He had a radio-frequency detector to locate the stick from a bug on the side. There's nothing on it except three pictures, all identical. I thought you might be able to help.'

'Where's the stick now?' Meg asked.

'In the microwave.'

'Good thinking. I hear owners of fancy cars are doing the same these days with their keys to prevent thieves boosting the signal from outside in order to nick their motors. Not foolproof but you'll be good enough for a short time, at least until the battery dies.'

'Can you help, Meg?'

'When I worked at GCHQ I used to love these picture puzzles. Don't tell me, it's a crowded scene, right? The seaside, snowy mountains, rolling countryside, something like that?'

'Countryside, yes. How did you guess?'

'It makes the translation code harder to crack. Especially if the colours are changing to black and white.'

'Meg, dear, you'll have to back up. What are you talking about?'

'Have you ever heard of steganography, Bets?' said Meg.

'Only in passing. Was never really my department.'

'Right, well it's a technique for hiding information within pictures.'

'What, secret clues, work out the location, that sort of thing?'

'No. It's a technique whereby information is actually hidden within the pixels of the picture. Sounds like that's what's going on here.'

'I'm struggling, dear,' Betsy said.

'Imagine an artist's wheel divided into six equal sections. Now imagine each of those sections is a different colour: red, white, blue, green, black and yellow. Still with me?'

'Yes.'

'Close your eyes and really picture that wheel, Bets. Colour the sections in from the top right, red, all the way round to the top left, yellow.'

Betsy did as she was told and closed her eyes.

'What colour is opposite red?' Meg said.

'Green.'

'What colour is opposite black?'

'White.'

'Good. Now how many steps, clockwise from one section to another, does it take starting on red to get to black?'

Betsy nodded her head slightly as she counted.

'Red to white, blue, green then black. Four.'

'Good. And from yellow to white?'

Nod, nod.

'Yellow to red then white. Two.'

'Good. Now if I gave you the code blue, yellow, red and wanted you to convert that into black, black, white, what sequence would I need?'

'Blue to green then black. That's two. Yellow to red, white, blue, green then black. Five. Red to white. Just one. The sequence is two, five, one,' Betsy said, after much nodding.

'Excellent. That's steganography. Two people share a conversion code, in this case two, five one, then send images to each other. The receiver puts the image through a programme running the conversion code and out pops a totally different picture. Each of those artist's wheels is one tiny pixel on your computer screen. There are about a million on your laptop, sorry, desktop, dear. All the pixels, well, most probably, will be changed in some way by steganography.'

'To make a new picture?'

'You're on the right lines. It could indeed be a new picture that's displayed. But much more information can be passed if you convert every pixel to either black or white, wouldn't you say?'

'Would I?' Betsy said, confused. 'Black or white?'

'Go on, smartypants,' Meg urged.

Betsy thought about the colours on a screen. As she did so she stared at her feet, which had collected a group of books on the carpet. She saw the answer.

'Letters,' she said. 'They're converting the picture into black and white letters and sending text to each other.'

‘There you go, you clever girl,’ Meg said. ‘Get your arse on a train down to Cheltenham and I’ll have a look at that stick.’

Betsy didn’t say anything, but also didn’t end the call.

‘There’s something else, isn’t there?’ Meg said.

Betsy kicked a book across the sitting room. It skittered under the sofa.

‘You know my goddaughter, Julianne?’

‘Is she the MP?’

‘No. That’s Kathryn. Jules works for Legoland.’

‘Got her. What’s up?’

‘She’s concerned about something work-related. Gave me the bare bones and I didn’t like what I heard. Not one little bit. I need a second opinion. A discreet second opinion.’

‘Jules isn’t one to get flustered, I seem to remember,’ Meg said.

‘That’s why I’m worried. At face value it seems straight forward enough. It’s only when you step back and look wider, factor in the USB stick too, that the possibility of something seriously wrong presents itself.’

‘Making two strange occurrences, close together,’ Meg said. ‘I see. Do you remember what you used to say about coincidence?’

‘Of course,’ Betsy said, ‘there’s no such thing. Coincidence is God’s way of saying all the clues are there, you’re just not looking hard enough.’

‘What time shall I put the kettle on?’

'I'll be on the 11.19 from Paddington,' Betsy said. ''Bye, dear.'

Betsy tucked her phone in a pocket and collected the last two novels from underneath an armchair. She left the one she'd kicked under the sofa. She finished her drink, picked up a group of books and walked through to the kitchen. She stacked four paperbacks on top of each other against the back door. The books were arranged so that the first letters of the titles were in alphabetical order from top to bottom: Death Came Slowly To Her; Eye Spy; Old Dog, Old Tricks; The Only Way Is Ethics. She took a picture of the stack with her phone. Betsy then checked the back door was locked, turned the kitchen light off and retraced her steps down the hallway. She built a tower against the front door from another four books. Betsy took another photo, turned off the hallway light and went upstairs to bed.

*

The quadcopter drone emitted a hum rather than a buzz. Not much of a difference, to anyone listening at ground level, but the four sets of small plastic blades were designed to be almost inaudible when the machine was only thirty feet off the ground. The man set the aircraft going in the recreation ground a quarter of a mile from the Trenmore-Halford house and ran back to the woman controlling the device in the back of the grey van.

'Good picture,' the woman said.

'Stable?' said the man.

'Good enough,' she answered. 'As long as the wind doesn't pick up or it starts raining again.'

She manoeuvred the drone across the playing fields and climbed to one hundred feet. The machine flew a racetrack circuit, pointing the camera at Hollett Road on one length and the alleyway at the back of the gardens on the other. The upstairs windows on both sides of the houses were all curtained. No lights. No movement. As expected, at two o'clock on a Thursday morning.

After two laps the woman moved the drone off to one side, hovering above a children's playground. The camera covered the alleyway from the entrance on Windmill Avenue on the near side, to Ambull Road at the far end.

'Air team in position. All clear,' the man said into a radio handset.

'Still all clear at the front of the house,' said a man sitting in a car outside Number 82 on Hollett Road.

'Windmill Avenue, all clear.'

'Ambull Road, all clear.'

'Andrey is deploying,' said the man in the passenger seat of the car on Ambull Road.

Once out of the car the man nodded to his partner in the vehicle and pressed a small switch in the pocket of his jeans.

'Radio check,' he said

'Ambull Road, okay to me,' Andrey heard in his earpiece.

'Windmill Avenue, okay to me.'

'Hollett Road, okay to me.'

'Air team, okay to me.'

Andrey moved quickly off the footpath into the welcoming darkness of the alleyway. He counted the gardens until he estimated he was outside the tall fence panels at the back of the Trenmore-Halford house. He reached into his pocket and pulled out a hand-held infrared strobe. He pressed the rubberised switch on top. He could hear a faint tick every second as the strobe pulsed, although the light was invisible to the naked eye.

'Strobing now,' Andrey said into a microphone in his collar.

'Confirmed visual,' said the man in the grey van. 'Drone can see the strobe. You are outside the house.'

'Acknowledged,' said Andrey. 'Moving from voice to tones.'

The team acknowledged his message.

He turned the strobe off and returned it to a pocket in his jacket. He withdrew a radio frequency detector from the other side. It showed an erratic signal, indicating he was somewhere between five and fifteen metres from the USB stick. He put it away.

He gently turned the latch on the gate. It moved easily but let out a creak. Andrey paused and quickly pressed the switch in his jeans twice, asking for a check by the air team of any signs of movement.

The man in the van checked the back of the houses.

'Air team. All clear,' he said.

Andrey pushed the gate open and stepped into the garden. He pushed the gate almost fully closed behind him, but didn't chance closing the latch. He walked swiftly up the narrow concrete path to the back door. From an inside pocket of his jacket he took out a small wallet. Inside was a set of thin metal rods and keys. He took out four rods and two keys, placing them on the cover of the wallet as he knelt next to the lock on the door. The lock was in almost total darkness, but the earlier drone flight had shown it to be a standard patio door fitting. He inserted one of the rods into the keyhole underneath the handle and gently eased it back and forth. He withdrew it and repeated the procedure with a thinner rod. His breathing was calm. Even so, he had been at the door now for almost sixty seconds.

He gave the double-press signal again on the switch in his pocket, connected to the radio in the small of his back.

A pause.

'Air team. All clear.'

Andrey felt the rod take a more secure purchase. He held it in place with one hand and reached down to select another rod with the other. After a few seconds of searching inside the lock, this rod similarly found a comfortable fit. He carefully transferred the second rod, so that he held both with his left hand, and picked up one of the smooth keys. He inserted it into the lock and eased it against the bolts, increasing the pressure slightly on the door as he did so. The lock twisted. He removed the rods and gently eased down the plastic handle. The door opened.

Double-press of the switch, followed immediately by another double-press; the signal he was about to enter the property and needed a clearance call from the whole team.

The door was open a fraction. As the whole team checked in, confirming no movement, Andrey placed the rods and keys back in the wallet, which he returned to his inside pocket. He took out two thin plastic overshoes. He quickly stretched them over his boots, to cover any muck he might have brought into the house from the alleyway.

He guided the door open, just enough for him to press an ear into the gap and listen for any signs of life. He could hear a high whine. A fridge, or other electrical item. No sound of human activity. He slipped inside the house. He heard a noise from the ground and paused. The noise was not repeated. He guessed it was a hinge registering the movement of the door. He stood still for another minute, listening. With nothing causing alarm he closed the door behind him. Andrey reached into his trouser pocket. He gave two long presses on the switch.

A pause.

'Air team. All clear.'

Andrey allowed his eyes to adjust to the new light level then consulted the radio frequency detector. It still showed an erratic signal. He was annoyed, both at the crazy signal and at the decision to send the team into an occupied house. It was bad enough going into an empty house in the middle of a populated street. The risk went sky high if the occupants were known to be there. He had to use the torch with the red filter - no point breaking in otherwise - but even that could put the whole operation in jeopardy.

He scanned the kitchen with the red torch. Nothing obvious, and he wasn't about to go around opening drawers unless he had no choice. He looked down and saw four paperback books scattered on the floor. He stared at them. Andrey replayed in his mind his entry to the house and remembered the noise. Had he knocked over the books as he opened the door? He bent down and carefully restacked the books, then moved them closer to the edge of the door.

He moved into the hallway, scanned the utility room on the left, and pressed on, to the front room. In a room full of clutter he had to select the most likely places to hide a USB stick instead of searching everywhere. The team would stay off the air unless there was an emergency, like a light appearing in a window. He welcomed the silence.

After five minutes of searching he turned his back on the front room and approached the stairs. He hated stairs. Any one of them could betray the whole job, but the team had identified a possible home office in the front window on the landing. He had to look.

He put a foot on the first step and gently eased his weight forward. Silence. He moved to the next step, his gloved hand stroking the bannister for support. He was conscious of every adjustment to his balance as he placed his feet on the stairs. He didn't dare use the torch, but he sensed around a dozen steps ahead of him, given the size of each and the height of the ground floor. His heart was hammering now, but he concentrated on keeping his breathing level and inaudible.

Four steps up he became aware of more light upstairs. Perhaps from a streetlight outside, shining in through the window over the desk with the computer. His mind raced back to the photographs of the front of the house. Was there a lamppost close by? His stomach lurched when he remembered the nearest streetlight was outside Number 60, which was why the team member on Hollett Road had parked further along. No way that light could be thrown this far, he decided.

Andrey's eyes were level with the upstairs landing carpet when he froze. The light bloomed along the hallway as a door opened. He heard a cord pulled and the light disappeared. He heard a foot clip the metal transition bar between the bathroom and the landing carpet. Andrey's mental map of the house told him the figure had come from the toilet. His mind swam with confusion. If that was the toilet, why hadn't he heard the flush? Faint sounds of cloth slippers being scuffed across thick carpet told him the figure was moving towards his position on the stairs. Abort the mission or attack? Andrey crouched, like a trap-door spider about to leap on its prey, thinking fast.

10.

Betsy woke with a start. Fitful sleep, broken by periods when she had sat up in bed, thinking, second-guessing. It had reminded her of earlier times. She allowed the emerging smile to form. Then, as the morning light streamed through the curtains, she snapped the smile away, found her slippers and got back to work.

The paperback books were still stacked by the front door. Betsy checked the photo on her phone. No change. She walked through to the kitchen, flicking back to the photo she'd taken the night before of the pile by the back door. The neatly stacked books were still there, but Betsy felt a cold wave of shock flow through her when she saw the order: Eye Spy on top, Old Dog, Old Tricks on the bottom of the pile.

She'd had a visitor in the night.

Betsy's mind raced. Someone's been in the house, she thought. Got to be the stick. But what if they've left cameras? Microphones? Have I made it obvious already that I'm suspicious, by standing here staring at the back door? How do I check the microwave? Am I in danger?

She strode to the door and tried the handle. Still locked. Was that worse? Suggested a professional? She moved towards the microwave, calling to Major Tom in as nonchalant a voice as her tight throat could produce, in case her words were being listened to by persons unknown. She blustered around with the box of porridge and opened and closed the microwave door as quickly as the act would allow. The USB stick was still there.

The breakfast routine continued. Without undue haste Betsy moved upstairs to the bathroom. She restricted her ablutions to a splash of water and a quick brush of her teeth, the toothbrush jabbing in and out with increasing fury at the thought of her house being violated. She considered going to the police but knew any story would wind back to a shattered body left unassisted by the side of the road. She couldn't go to the police, not yet anyway. Besides, now she had a score to settle.

She collected her things, ready to leave to catch the train to Cheltenham. She checked the Twitter app on her phone for any activity from ChipsWithMayo or James Easton. Her breath caught when she saw that James Easton had retweeted the post from the London War Walks site promoting The Long Night that morning. It had already received one 'like'. Betsy clicked on the heart icon. The post had been acknowledged by ChipsWithMayo.

Betsy smoothed her crisply ironed shirt and tried to slow her spinning mind. James Easton and ChipsWithMayo were communicating again. They had only just set up the meet, which meant, if they repeated Wednesday's routine, they'd exchange another USB stick at three the following morning. Using as much cover as her small kitchen could offer from any hidden cameras, Betsy retrieved the USB stick from the microwave and tucked it into a jacket pocket, next to her phone and wallet. Her vape pen went into the opposite pocket. She opened the case containing the new USB stick and placed it in the handbag bought the day before. The packet of tissues lay unopened next to the gloves. Betsy broke the seal, pulled out two tissues, blew her nose using both and deposited them into her rubbish bin. She put the packet back in the charity handbag. Next, a pile of loose change on the kitchen counter was scooped in, along with a twenty-pound note. She was ready.

Betsy headed out to catch the train to Meg's house. Chips and James had settled for the route of The Long Night. That was good. Betsy reckoned she knew where they'd be for the handover and when they'd be there. And this time, she'd be waiting for them.

*

Anti-surveillance or counter-surveillance? One meant trying to shake off a tail, the other meant trying to discover who's tailing you. Difficult to do either on your own but Betsy had no choice these days. She was, by nature, guarded, so the routines came easily. Demanding such alertness could be exhausting after a few decades, but at least you'd reached an old age to grumble into.

She left the house and headed down Hollett Road towards the shops. She resisted the urge to look over her shoulder straight away; an amateur move that would let any opposition know she was onto them. There's only one reason you can legitimately look behind you when walking down a street, without looking suspicious. Betsy did so now, to check for traffic before crossing the road to the other side.

She spotted nobody obviously following her.

A blue car with a single occupant was approaching along Hollett Road. Betsy glanced at the number plate: EB60DVY. Elephants Born in 1960 Die Very Young. She matched the phrase with the car and burned it into her memory.

She walked the length of five more houses then stopped. Theatrically patted her wax jacket. Searched the pockets of her tweed skirt. She then broke into an energised shuffle - a movement that would have been a run twenty years ago - back towards her house, eyes ready for any other pedestrian suddenly changing direction. She saw no such activity.

She went into her house and up the stairs. She leant over the desk in the alcove, pretending to search for something but in reality scouring the street for movement. She could see none.

After a short time she emerged back on Hollett Road. She repeated the movement of a few minutes before. There was a silver van parked on Ambull Road with a person talking on a mobile phone. He watched as Betsy crossed the road. NE18LCM. Nearly Everybody under 18 Likes Chocolate Milk.

Betsy joined the main road and turned left. More people here. Good for hiding, bad for spotting a tail. She waited at a set of pedestrian lights. By the time the green man appeared there were about a dozen people waiting to cross. Just as she was about to start walking Betsy pulled out her mobile phone and pretended to read a message, rooted to the spot.

No other pedestrian similarly decided not to cross, and nobody loitered on the far side.

Betsy crossed at the next opportunity, checking left and right for traffic jumping the lights, as any experienced Londoner would. No sign of the elephant car or the chocolate milk van. No obvious followers. That assessment provided little comfort. Whoever had broken in last night had been thoroughly professional, even allowing for the poorly stacked books, so would her skills still be sharp enough to spot them, whoever and wherever they were? The passage of time stabbed at her again.

A young man walked towards her, staring fixedly at his mobile phone. The pavement was too busy to allow Betsy much room to avoid him as he approached. She squeezed her shoulders and tried to fit through the gap between him and a woman pushing a child's buggy on her right. Even so, he brushed roughly past, still staring at the screen.

'Watch out, you silly man!' Betsy said.

The man looked back at her.

'Sorry,' he said. 'I didn't see you.' He turned and continued walking, eyes glued to his phone.

'Nobody ever bloody does,' Betsy said to his retreating form.

She entered the tube station and descended to the platform. She stood by a map of the underground lines. Betsy placed a finger on the glass to mark her position and kept looking up at the destination board above the platform showing the next three arrivals, as if planning her route. She took good long looks down the length of the platform each time.

A train arrived. Passengers swapped positions between car and platform. Betsy waited by the open doors, staring up at the destination board, as any bemused traveller might, unsure if she should take this train or the next. The doors closed with Betsy still on the platform. Apart from her, all the people on the platform had alighted from the train. There had been no similarly indecisive travellers. After a few seconds other passengers arrived to wait for the next train.

She got on it and travelled towards Paddington station. After ten minutes of study she could give reasonable descriptions of the passengers in her immediate vicinity that had got on with her. Approaching Marylebone, two stops from Paddington, she dropped her head to her chest and closed her eyes. She ran through the descriptions of her fellow travellers as she counted the stops: Marylebone, Edgware Road, Paddington. She pretended to wake up just as the doors were closing at Paddington. She clambered awkwardly up from her seat. Too late, she'd missed the doors and was stuck on the train. She looked round, tutting and cursing her tardiness. She produced a sheepish grin that was returned by a couple of other travellers. Nobody had bolted for the doors at the same time.

Betsy alighted at the next stop, Warwick Avenue, with a small number of other people. She and one other traveller crossed directly to the platform heading in the opposite direction. She did not recognise the other person as having joined the tube with her. She got on the first train to arrive and rode one stop back to Paddington, where she left the car. The person riding back down the line from Warwick Avenue stayed in the carriage. Betsy was content she hadn't been followed. She bought a ticket from the automatic machines, picked up a coffee from a kiosk on the station concourse and joined the 11.19 to Cheltenham. She sipped the caffeine. It was strong, but couldn't possibly compete with the adrenaline finally coursing through her system once more, back in action after a long period of retirement.

11.

Betsy clambered stiffly off the bus she had taken from the station. The vehicle accelerated away, blasting fumes into her face. She winced and tried to waft the foul air away. The street, empty but for herself and a man pumping a bicycle tyre, was slick and dangerous, so she proceeded with caution down the gentle slope towards Meg's house. She took the ticket stub for the train journey from London out of her pocket and put it in the handbag, secured in the crook of an arm. The impressive Georgian houses populating the Montpellier district of Cheltenham seemed lifeless, the occupants no doubt elsewhere performing heart surgery, closing billion-dollar deals or winning wars in cyberspace.

A light was visible in Meg's house, fifty yards away in the soft drizzle that had started again. Droplets, unable to gain a firm purchase on Betsy's heavily waxed coat, raced from her shoulders. The few areas of the jacket that had not been adequately protected through years of polishing quickly turned a darker green.

Betsy enjoyed Meg's company and needed her years of experience as a code breaker now more than –

- a hand in her face. The man fixing the bike launched himself at Betsy as she drew level. She was pushed back into a privet hedge. She cried out and tried to fend the man off, but he was bigger, faster and had the initiative. Betsy felt the hedge scrape down her back as she stumbled backwards. She realised she had only been prevented from falling because the man had grabbed her handbag, the strap secured obstinately in her elbow, an action that held her upright. She pulled the strap and shouted, 'off, off,' but the man yanked even harder. The strap snapped, sending Betsy to the floor. Her hip exploded with pain as she hit the pavement. Coins from the handbag landed around her, tinkling as they dashed for the gutter, as if embarrassed by the spectacle of an old woman humiliated on the floor. A sharp stinging in her cheek told her she'd been grazed, possibly even cut.

'That's mine!' she shouted from the floor, but the man was already ten yards away, sprinting down the hill.

Betsy struggled to her feet and shouted again.

'You horrible, horrible man!'

She watched the man run to the next corner and turn out of sight. She looked at the bicycle he'd used as a prop. Betsy knew it was probably stolen but was angry, so pushed it over on the pavement. Her breathing was quick and shallow as she bent to pick up the glove that had been ejected from the handbag. She tucked it into a pocket, checking as she did so that her phone, wallet, vape pen and USB stick were still present and continued her walk to Meg's house, her pace only slightly quicker than before.

*

'You were probably followed from home.'

Betsy winced as Meg padded an antiseptic wipe on the graze across her cheekbone. She slapped her friend's hand away.

'I'm old, but I'm not past it yet. I was not followed.'

They were sitting in Meg's back room, overlooking a large and tidy garden. An open plan kitchen and dining room extended down two steps into a conservatory. Betsy had visited rarely and was surprised at the large amount of art on the walls. Most pictures were of nudes or, with just a few lines, teasingly suggestive of the human form. There was one large black and white photo. It was a close up of a body part. A hip or buttock perhaps, shaded to look like a sand dune. Betsy couldn't tell which but was certain it had belonged to Meg at some point in her life. She quickly looked away.

'There have been muggings around here,' Meg said. 'Expensive area, largely empty during the day. Surprised he went so far as to actually nick a bike first though.'

'It wasn't a chance encounter,' Betsy said. 'He was waiting for me.'

'You don't know that,' Meg said.

Betsy started to disagree, her doughy face suddenly set hard, but was cut short.

'I'll make some tea,' Meg said.

Betsy sat at the small circular metal table in the conservatory, fuming. The shock of the attack was passing, like a wave receding across sharp gravel, exposing a raw and furious surface beneath.

Tea arrived on a tray, accompanied by a Victoria sponge cake. Meg and Betsy sat at the table, which suddenly seemed far too small for the conversation it had to support.

'Well whoever he was you were ready for him. Nice move with the dummy handbag.'

Betsy sniffed and stared at the garden.

'Thankyou.'

'How much did you lose?'

'A twenty pound note. Some change. Other detritus. Mints.'

'A scarf?'

'Gloves,' Betsy said with a faint smile.

'Gloves! Brilliant! You always loved your tradecraft, Bets.'

Betsy turned to her friend. She spoke in a warm and conspiratorial tone, the aggression having subsided.

'I wasn't followed, Meg, and it wasn't an impulsive attack. He was waiting for me. Which means he knew I'd be coming here. They've been watching you, not me.'

Meg picked up a large knife from the tray and started cutting the cake.

'Somebody who knows us both has tipped them off. They know I've got the stick and knew I'd come to you. That confirms my suspicions about how serious this is. There's something very sick happening deep in

British intelligence. It won't take them long to realise I gave them a blank USB stick. They'll be back.'

Meg levered a wedge of cake onto a plate and pushed it across the table. She pulled a face.

'I dare say. All the more reason for us to read that stick and be elsewhere in minutes few, then,' Meg said.

She placed a thin slice of cake on her own plate. She caught Betsy looking at her.

'A moment on the lips, a year on the hips.' She winked at her companion.

Meg loaded a fork with Victoria sponge and crammed it in her mouth. She then threw her hands up in shock, stood up and headed back into the house.

'Back in a tick,' she called.

Betsy finished her cake, got up and shuffled around the room holding her china teacup. She found herself drawn to an alcove in the corner furthest from the conservatory. In the alcove was a low cupboard on top of which were many different bottles of alcohol. She recognised only half the names on the bottles. On the wall above the cupboard was a small collection of framed photographs and formal citations. In one print she could see Meg lying horizontally, held aloft by the arms of six men. She had propped her head up by an arm and was smiling for the camera. The nose of a fighter jet was just visible behind the group. Betsy guessed Meg looked to be in her thirties. The brass plaque on the picture frame said: 'To Meg. Simply The Best! From Signals Detachment, USS America, Northern Gulf May 1991'.

Another photograph sat in a thin black frame. The colour had faded over the years. Even so, a much younger Meg was clearly identifiable. She was straddling a mule and laughing at her companion, a young man, who was struggling to mount another animal. The man was laughing too. A homemade label stuck behind the glass said: 'Chile 1982'.

'Ah, Vicente,' Meg said, appearing behind Betsy with a small black case the size of a paperback book. 'A stallion of a man.'

'Holiday?' Betsy asked.

'Work. Falklands.'

Meg led Betsy into a room on the side of the house that she used as an office. She sat behind the desk and placed the device next to her.

'Nearly forgot to put that on rapid charge,' she said.

Betsy handed over the USB stick. Meg ran a finger over the small circular attachment on the side. She and Betsy shared a look. Meg opened a drawer in a desk. She couldn't find what she was looking for. She opened a second drawer and pulled out a radio frequency detector, similar to the one Betsy had taken from the man in Wellspring Gardens. Meg turned it on and aimed it at the USB stick.

'As expected. Dead,' she said.

She reached for the small black case that she'd retrieved from elsewhere in the house. On the side of the case were printed the words: 'Portable POWER'. She plugged the USB stick into the case. She then pointed the detector back at the stick. The screen promptly displayed a number of pulsing lines.

'Sing, sing, my little beauty,' Meg said.

'Thought so,' said Betsy.

'You've picked up a little bug,' Meg said. 'You were right. This is a tracking device. So if I've got it right, this was the property of James Ernest.'

'Easton,' Betsy said.

'Sorry, Easton. So Mister Easton would use all his, or we should assume possibly her, toys to find this stick,' Meg said.

'Won't they be able to see it now? Betsy said.

'Yes, but it would take a few days to narrow down such a small transmitter after the battery conked out,' Meg said. 'They'd go from a satellite to a ship or an aircraft. Maybe straight to cars if they knew the rough area, and eventually to hand-held. Have you seen anything odd around your house since yesterday? The same cars driving slowly up and down your street, people loitering, that kind of thing?'

'Not that I've noticed,' Betsy said

'This is worst case scenario,' Meg quickly offered. 'Access to commercial satellite products is easy these days, and cheap. This could just be some rich bank doing a training exercise.'

She and Betsy glanced at each other again.

'You are right to consider every possibility, Meg, but we've got to get ahead of this,' Betsy said. 'It's no training exercise for a bank.'

'Fair enough. Anyway, like all good doctors, I'll give you something for your ailment,' Meg said.

She reached back into the desk drawer and brought out a small, stiff bag. She handed it to Betsy.

'Good move with the microwave, but when we finish we'll pop the canary in here and it will sing only for us,' Meg said.

She took the USB stick out of the power pack and inserted it into the edge of a laptop she had on the side of her desk.

'Now, before we go sticking our little whatsits where they're not wanted, let's do a sheep-dip,' Meg said.

She lifted the lid of the laptop and typed in a password. The screen sprang to life. Betsy watched as computer code scrolled down. A window on the right of the computer flashed various messages, none of which looked good.

'Oh, Bets, I hope your personal hygiene is better than your cyber hygiene,' Meg said.

Betsy stiffened. The eyes behind the large circular windows briefly flashed anger at her friend.

The left of the screen was still filled with code. The window on the right was less full. One message was obvious, even to Betsy. Bold letters said: 'ROUTEING SOFTWARE DETECTED'.

'Oh dear,' Meg said.

'What?'

'What you've got here is a bad case of breadcrumbs,' Meg said.

'Breadcrumbs?'

'They leave a trail from the USB stick back to a home location. Whoever put the malware on the stick wanted to know where it was plugged in. As soon as you popped it in your laptop it would have connected to your Wi-Fi and started signalling where it was. All the other party needed to do was convert your Wi-Fi address to a real one, search a few databases, the electoral roll and so on, and find out who you are and where you live.'

'How long have I been in danger?' Betsy said.

Meg pulled a face.

'Unlike the tracker, which would take days to narrow down, the breadcrumbs would have been seen the instant you plugged in the USB stick,' Meg said. 'The malware wasn't put on there just for fun. I think we can assume that whoever planted it has malign intent.'

Meg unplugged the USB stick from the laptop.

'All clean. No more nasties on there,' she said.

'So I guess ChipsWithMayo laid the breadcrumbs,' Betsy said.

'Seems the most likely scenario,' Meg said.

'And James Easton had the tracker put on to find it.'

'Again, seems likely, given the sequence of events and the fact he, or an associate, ended up on your bonnet,' Meg said.

'And left a bloody great dent,' Betsy said.

'Don't hold that against him,' Meg said. 'I've dented a few bonnets in my time.' Another wink for her friend. 'We need to take a few precautions, Bets.'

'We?'

'My dear old frumpy Betsy,' Meg said, gripping her friend's shoulders, 'we're in this together now. Call it old age, call it renewed professional curiosity after aeons on the subs' bench, or blame yourself for endangering me,' – this said with a disarming smile – 'but we're a team now, roomies, besties.'

'I really hope I haven't got us killed, dear,' Betsy said.

'Well if you have,' Meg said, returning to the computer, 'that would be the most exciting thing that's happened to me for years.'

12.

‘Do you know what the Foreign Secretary calls us?’ the woman said. ‘The Vauxhall vampires. Isn’t that funny?’

ChipsWithMayo said nothing.

As usual for a Thursday, the restaurant was full of suits. For a room this size the volume coming from the accumulated babble of voices was one notch above normal. The added decibels were accounted for by the proximity to power. The tables were located within braying distance of the government’s front bench. In the centre of the room, at a table for two, sat a nasty oasis of desultory conversation.

The woman tried a different tack. ‘You smell nice,’ she said.

‘I smell nice?’ said ChipsWithMayo.

‘Yes.’

‘What are you, some sort of bloodhound?’

‘No, I just meant - ’ she tried.

‘What? What did you mean? That yesterday I stank but today I must have washed?’

‘Don’t be like that, babe.’

‘Don’t call me babe.’

‘Sorry. I didn’t mean anything by it. Just trying to be nice.’

She reached across the table for her partner's hand. It retreated from the approach.

'Have you chosen?' ChipsWithMayo said.

'Ooh, well I've narrowed it down to three,' the woman said.

'Yes please,' ChipsWithMayo said to a passing waitress. 'Coconut chicken, no onions, sparkling water. Sarah?'

'Oh, I don't know. Um, um, umm.'

'I've got to be back at one.'

'Cheese burger and fries please,' Sarah said. 'And a coke. A diet coke please.'

The waitress took the menus and disappeared.

'Diet coke?' said ChipsWithMayo. 'Never thought I'd see the day.'

'Well, you were right. I probably need to do a bit more in that department.'

ChipsWithMayo jabbed at the mobile phone on the table. Scanned the latest emails. Snorted a laugh.

'What's that?' Sarah asked brightly.

'Nothing,' ChipsWithMayo said, 'work.'

'How's it going?'

'What?'

'Your work. Still enjoying it?'

'God, now you sound like my mother. One minute you're smelling me, the next asking about my busy day.'

'I, just, I'm just asking.'

'Okay, well, one person thinks he can treat me like a child, and another thinks it's fine to lie to me. Happy now?'

'No, no I'm not happy. Not if you're not.'

'Oh please spare me.'

Sarah fiddled with her fingers. The waitress reappeared. From a tray she placed drinks on the table, said 'enjoy' and left.

'Lunch is going well so far,' ChipsWithMayo said.

Sarah poked the ice round her glass with a straw. The men on the next table suddenly erupted in laughter.

'I've got something that will cheer you up,' the woman said.

ChipsWithMayo said nothing.

'You know those names I told you about, from work?'

'Names?'

Sarah grinned, leant over the table and continued in a low voice. 'The naughty ones. The ones I wasn't supposed to tell anyone about.'

'The chef? And the dog trainer?'

'No, silly, not those ones.'

'Well I don't know do I?' ChipsWithMayo said in a raised voice.

One of the men on the next table briefly looked over at the couple.

'Keep your voice down, I shouldn't even be saying this.'

'Well don't bother then. Tell me about the weather.'

'Oh don't please,' Sarah said, still leaning across the table. 'Look, I'll tell you.'

'Don't bother.'

'I will. Please. You know I love hearing your opinion.'

'Go on then, what's the big news?'

'Well, you know the guy I told you about in Croatia that we were, sort of, keeping an eye on?'

'Yeah.'

The woman sucked her straw.

'Oh save the amateur dramatics,' ChipsWithMayo said, 'either tell me or let me get back to my emails.'

Sarah described Marko Babić's death in Croatia.

ChipsWithMayo drained the rest of the sparkling water.

'What do you think?' the woman said.

'I think you should stop talking about government secrets in a public place.'

The woman sat back with a pained look on her face. ChipsWithMayo smiled at her and leant forward.

'Come round to the flat tonight. I'll make that special pasta dish you like,' ChipsWithMayo said, reaching for the woman's hand, which was quickly offered. 'You can tell me everything then. And maybe afterwards, for being a naughty little girl, we could play mummies and daddies.'

*

'Steg has always been my favourite,' Meg said.

She attached the USB stick to her large desktop computer and tapped at the keyboard. A slight breeze blew in through the doors open to the garden. Still looking at the computer screen, Meg spoke to Betsy over her shoulder.

'It's the dark cousin of cryptography,' she whispered.

'If you say so,' said Betsy.

'Cryptography may be unbreakable, although, newsflash people, it's not,' Meg continued, 'but the mere fact you're sending a message that looks like gibberish makes it interesting to people like me. Much more subtle and clever to send what looks like a real message, in this case a picture, but have all the goodies embedded in it.'

Meg looked at Betsy, who raised her eyebrows.

'Cryptography is like a surfer bum from Bondi beach trying to chat you up after four tinnies. Steg is the silent brooding roustabout with the dusty Blundstones drinking whisky at the bar, in town for twenty-four hours only until his next shift in the deep mines of Broken Hill.'

Meg had stopped typing and was staring at the garden through the open doors.

'This is a good image,' Betsy said, breaking the silence that had descended. 'It's always better when the colours are all mixed up. Country scenes, city blocks, beaches, weather, they're always best.'

'I told you that,' Meg said.

She focussed again on her computer.

'As with men, the part causing all the trouble is the least significant bit,' she said.

'No need to get too technical, dear,' Betsy said.

'Sure, sure, sure, but this is the interesting part. Bets, the Least Significant Bits, or LSBs as we call them in the trade, are the tiny parts of the image that are changed to hide the message. They're the least important packets of data that make up the image. Means they can be spared for the secret message. The colour of the new image will be slightly different from what it was before. Too subtle to find with the naked eye in a busy picture, but visible to those who know how to look.'

She typed a few commands into her computer and pressed the enter key.

'There,' she said. "We're hunting.'

'What do we do now?' Betsy said.

'I'll stay here for a bit. You go and get some lunch,' Meg said.

'Are you not joining me, dear?'

'I'll just grab a cigarette and double espresso.'

'Old faithful,' Betsy said.

Meg turned to Betsy and looked up at her with doe eyes.

'In Paris they call it a prostitute's breakfast.'

Betsy bustled around the kitchen making sandwiches. Her eye was drawn to a framed letter on the wall. Under the image of the Royal Arms, the address 10 Downing Street was in bold type. Below that, to the left, it said ‘THE PRIME MINISTER’ and to the right the date: ‘16 May 2005’. In blue handwritten ink was scrawled ‘Dear Meg’ at the top and ‘Yours ever, Tony Blair’ at the bottom. In between, in black type, were the words: ‘I am writing to thank you for your magnificent contribution to the successful rescue of the British hostages in Afghanistan. Without your dedication and skill they would not be alive today. They, and I, will be eternally grateful.’ At the bottom of the letter was printed ‘Megan Clover MBE’.

‘Ta-daa!’ Meg called from the office.

Betsy hurried back in.

‘Success?’ Betsy asked.

‘Success,’ Meg said. ‘Of a sort. I can read it. Don’t have a clue what it means though.’

The two women stared at the screen. On the left hand side was the original countryside image from the USB stick. In a separate window opposite were printed the words: ‘Operation Meadowland. Date/time: no change. Sell: Gabriel Dubois. Tatiana Petrova’.

‘What does that mean?’ Betsy said.

‘Bets darling, that’s the whole point of espionage,’ Meg said. ‘I have absolutely no idea.’

‘Meadowland,’ Betsy said. ‘Doesn’t spring to mind. Gabriel Dubois, Tatiana Petrova. Never heard of them either.’

‘Okay, let’s thin-slice it,’ Meg said. Her voice had turned hard.

‘Is this suspicious?’ Betsy said.

‘Yes,’ Meg said.

‘Is it a prank?’

'The malware, bug and mugging suggest not.'

'Is it private sector?'

'Probably not, given the scale of the technology involved.'

'Is it government?'

'Probably yes.'

'UK, friendly or hostile?'

'No way of knowing.'

'A training exercise or a live operation?'

'Probably live operation, given resources expended and determination to retrieve the stick.'

'The names will provide a lot of answers,' Betsy said.

'I'll dig around for Dubois and Petrova,' Meg said.

Betsy called for a taxi. She explained why she thought another drop off was planned for the small hours of the next morning.

'Great,' Meg said. 'I'll bring a hard drive with my software to break steg.'

She reached into a desk drawer and pulled out a hard drive, which she placed in another stiff bag with a rubberised waterproof seal.

'What was the business with Jules?' Meg said.

Betsy quickly described her concerns related to the deaths of MI6 surveillance targets.

'What names did Jules give you?' Meg asked.

Betsy passed her a note, on which she had scribbled 'Marko Babić (Croatia). Ravi Marimuthu (Malaysia)'.

'Who are they? Meg said.

‘That she doesn’t know. I’ve found nothing, but then you’re better with computers than I am.’

‘I’ll have a look Bets, but you probably need to go and see for yourself.’

‘I’m not up to that kind of travel. Not any more.’

‘You’ll have to be. You’re already on the pitch.’

13.

Betsy and Meg entered Cheltenham station and walked down to the London-bound platform, in shadow under a heavy sky. They took a seat on the bench closest to the steps. The waiting room was closed. It looked warm and comfortable inside, but a sign on the door said 'Shut for essential maintenance'.

'You shouldn't be coming with me,' Betsy said.

'Tough. I'm involved now, skin in the game, as our American friends say. Besides, we both stand more of a chance if we're together,' Meg said.

A woman walked past, pushing a drinks trolley for the on-board service. She was straining against a freshening breeze. Betsy waited until she had passed before speaking.

'It may not involve the British state at all. Or there may be British operators at one end, probably the ChipsWithMayo end. Either way it's probably illegal, probably high stakes and therefore probably risky.'

'Not the first time we've taken on those odds,' Meg said.

'Indeed.'

'Are we alone?' asked Meg.

Betsy pulled her jacket more tightly around her. She rubbed a deep scratch in the wax coating on a sleeve, gouged out by the privet hedge as she'd fallen back under the mugger's assault.

'There are strings I can pull. But until I know exactly what they are connected to these days I'd rather we just keep it between the two of us.'

'Seems reasonable,' Meg said. She shivered as another blast of frigid air swept down the platform.

The train pulled into Cheltenham Spa station. The women boarded and faced each other across a table located near the doors. A small number of travellers dotted themselves throughout the carriage. The train departed. Betsy stared out of the window. The few flecks of rain that were brushing against the glass changed their direction of travel as the train gathered speed. Instead of heading straight down the pane they raced away from her, increasing their pace until they crashed against the frame on the far side.

They settled into silence. Betsy stared out of the darkening window and realised she was staring at Meg's reflection. Betsy took a small pot from her handbag. The tub was blank but for a handmade label on the side that said 'cream'. She scooped out a large blob, replaced the pot in her bag and rubbed the moisturiser into her hands.

'Of course, apart from being one of the world's preeminent cryptanalysts are you sure there isn't another way I can be useful in this situation?' Meg said.

'Is that a question?' Betsy said.

'Let's pretend it is.'

Betsy stared out of the window into the gathering night.

'I don't think that would be helpful.'

Meg leant across the table, her grey hair, pulled tight in a bun, gleaming under a light in the roof of the carriage.

'Bets, we're in the shit you get that, right? We both know what we're up against - '

She held up a hand to quell the objection starting from the other side of the table.

' – or at least we've both been in this game long enough to suspect where this is going. I'm just suggesting we consider all options for help.'

'I have found,' Betsy started, then corrected herself, 'we both have found the media to be more unhelpful than helpful when conducting our business in the past.'

'But, Bets, we're not in the past any more. It's now the future and we've been dragged back onto the board. We need help. We're old.'

'Speak for yourself.'

'I know these people, I know who to trust.'

Betsy's eyes blazed and the skin across her jaw tightened.

'Who to trust! Listen to yourself, Meg. You write the occasional obituary for the local rag but that is entirely different to inviting a proper journalist into our business.'

Meg pressed on, a note of sobriety in her voice Betsy had not heard before. Tension, perhaps. Or fear.

'They're not so different from us; journalists and spies. We both want the truth and are prepared to bend a few rules to get there.' Meg tried a smile. It was not returned.

'We are very different,' Betsy murmured. 'We may lie, cheat and steal but we do so to get to the truth. They do it to advance their owner's agenda.'

'That's not fair,' Meg said.

'The difference between spies and journalists, Meg, is that spies believe there is only one version of the truth, all they've got to do is find it. Journalists believe there are many versions of the truth depending on their wider needs. Which is usually a manufactured row.'

'That's rubbish,' Meg said. 'What about shining a light in dark places?'

'Oh I'm sure they all believed that once and maybe there are some journalists who still do. But most of them, most of the time use facts as weapons, carefully selecting them to win any argument they like and ignoring the rest.'

'Well doesn't everyone do that? Isn't that just life?'

'Not my life. Facts are immutable, not relative. It may seem strange to some, but spies actually care a great deal for the truth. Many have given their lives for it.'

'That's poetic, but a massive cop out,' Meg said.

'It's no such thing. A fact is either a fact or it's not. Journalists qualify assertions to remain legally compliant, then pass them off as if they're real. They're nothing of the sort. To a newspaper, the truth has to burn. It has to be charged with emotion. By the time their so-called facts have finished getting us there, the truth presented is so demonically powerful, so red hot, we haven't the strength to resist it.'

'And spies? We're all saints I presume?'

'Spies know the truth is an unexploded bomb, sitting in a minefield of other unexploded bombs. Spies have to tiptoe their way to it so they don't set it off, or any of the others lying around. To a spy a fact is a cold, hard, safe slab to stand on, as they inch towards the truth. It doesn't crumble. It doesn't change shape depending who is standing on it. It is clear for all to see, from any direction. Only by approaching slowly over a carpet of immovable facts can we tackle the hardest bit of all. The truth.'

'That's bollocks, Bets and I'll tell you why. First, don't tell me spies haven't got their own agenda,' Meg said. 'We both know enough people who have twisted our analysis to suit a particular policy line they're peddling. Or war they're selling. We have both seen our laughably-named superiors lay those special fact stones like a meandering path, flirting with one truth then veering off to another. All the while, they demand trust without allowing anyone to see what they get up to. Well, everyone can see and understand the media's prejudices. You're washing your hands of all responsibility for the policies that are scattered all over the place when that truth bomb explodes. You're pinning all the blame on the politicians.'

'Politicians? Oh, don't get me started,' Betsy said. 'Journalists are more like them than they'd ever be prepared to admit. They lie, cheat and steal not to hide the truth but to kill it. To reincarnate it in any zombie form that suits them at the time. Compared to politicians and journalists, spies are the most honest of the lot.'

'Honest? We kill people.'

'So do newspapers. And Politicians. At least we admit it.'

*

The month so far had seen greater than average daily rainfall. Major landslips in the road infrastructure around the country had already occurred and a breach of the Union Canal at Falkirk had closed the rail line from Edinburgh to Glasgow for five days.

The line from Cheltenham to London ran directly next to the River Thames just after Tilehurst station, on the approach to Reading. The earthworks in the area had been built over a century before and, although updated, had been weakened by the unprecedented weather.

Train drivers throughout the morning had reported water between the rails. Some had said they could also see stone and gravel building up against the edge of the line, having been washed down the embankment. So close to the river, the area had long been known to be vulnerable to subsidence. Consequently, at two in the afternoon a mobile operations manager had visited the area to assess the danger. He'd reported gravel on the line and a level of water between the tracks that might pose a risk to continued services. He recommended the line be checked again at eight o'clock that evening, which was exactly thirty minutes after the train carrying Betsy and Meg was due to pass through the area. He then returned to the Reading control room and made a cup of tea. The rain continued to fall.

*

Betsy broke the silence.

'I'm a lot older than you, Meg,' she said.

'Not that much,' Meg said tentatively, worried this conversation might also descend into acrimony like the one an hour before.

'I was brought up in a very different world to you. Things were different then. The bullies at school always got away with it because their fathers were important. Queues and shortages at the shops. And all the time the truth we were expected to believe was not matched by the facts we saw every day.'

Meg detected the hint of a rapprochement and felt she should meet Betsy half way.

'Rationing must have been tough after the war,' she said.

Betsy looked at her hard before continuing.

'I used to go to sleep hearing my mother crying and my father raging at his inability – not unwillingness – to provide for his family. I grew up wondering if the old men in charge really knew what they were doing.'

Betsy stared into the wet evening.

'That's why the truth is so important to me, Meg. My mother taught me to question everything. I can hear her now,' she said, wagging a finger into the memory. '"Question everything, Katya. But only if you are prepared to hear the answer".'

'Katya?' Meg said.

Betsy snapped back to the present.

'Oh, it was just a silly nickname,' she said. She moved her handbag from the seat next to her onto the table. Then put it back again. 'There was a cartoon character called Katya I fell in love with.'

'I don't remember that one,' Meg said.

'Before your time, dear.'

'Guess so,' Meg said, her eyes studying Betsy's face.

Betsy placed her hands on the table in front of her and intertwined her fingers.

'Anyway, the point is if we're going to work together we've got to do it properly. The old way. No journalists sniffing around,' she said.

The train wobbled as it went over a set of points.

'All right. Old school, then. You, me, your mother's advice and our collective grey matter,' Meg said.

'Grey does seem to be our colour of choice these days.'

Betsy let her smile fade. Her sharp eyes relaxed and unfocussed as she looked across the wet fields of dun and green, over trees and hills, into the past of another country, another life known only to a handful of people - which didn't include Meg - wondering what advice her mother would have given, in the small cramped Moscow flat, to young Katerina Tereshkova, better known by the diminutive: Katya.

14.

Jules had parked well away from the apartment. She'd made one bold attempt to convince herself this was just good tradecraft. The real reason, as she knew very well, was that she still hadn't decided exactly what was going to happen when she got there. She needed the quarter of a mile walk between her car and his building for thinking. She half-chuckled at the realisation that, unlike most operations she was sent on when she knew what she was going to do but not why, this self-imposed mission was completely the other way round. She'd decided to warn him, and was even confident enough she could carry off a decent Parisian accent to hide the fact she was a Brit. No, the why wasn't the issue.

'It's more a question of what the hell we're going to actually do when we get there, isn't it, Jules m'girl,' she said to herself.

She'd never considered herself to be an impulsive person. Reactive, certainly. Her ability to flick from one mode to another was legendary. At one moment a calm, daydreaming pedestrian. The next a blur of fists and elbows, with a snarl that barely registered as human. The unarmed combat instructor in the gym at the Fort would testify to that, if his fragile ego had allowed. His fragile nose certainly had.

So reactive, yes, but not impulsive.

If you'd told her yesterday that she would wake up and decide to fly to France and warn a surveillance target of a possible threat to his life, she'd have called you mad. And bad. And dangerous to know. She was breaking about a gazillion rules: failure to request international travel in a leave period; unauthorised disclosure of a covert operation; compromising the identity of a surveillance operator. Probably something about bringing the Service into disrepute too. Not that losing surveillance targets to possible murder didn't count as disreputable, but she doubted the powers that be in Legoland, with their special lift to the top floor, would sing her praises for flagging that one up.

She was nearly there. Light and noise on either side of the road reached her from the many occupied apartments. Windows thrown open on another warm night. Cutlery clattering onto plates. Glasses chinking. Normal people doing normal Thursday evening things.

This is not normal, she told herself. Betsy was right; she was exhausted. That and the petty rivalries with her sister had clearly affected her judgement. What the hell was she doing here, risking her career to chase ghosts? Turn round now, she told herself, take your chances at the next vetting review that they hadn't spotted the quick flight to Nice.

She reached the low hedge outside Bonal's apartment. Ground floor, end of the block, thin strip of lawn outside. There were no lights in the adjoining apartment and no movement on the road. Through a large single pane window she could see him relaxing on a white leather sofa. All a bit 1980s for her taste but she figured fashion worked differently on the Riviera. Music coming from a speaker somewhere. Bonal looked happy. Blissfully unaware that in the top corner of his room, awake at the first sound, was a tiny microphone. He was reading a file. Sipping a glass of…red wine. That looks good. Normal life. She resolved to try it some time.

Her eye was drawn to movement near the front door, set in an alcove to her right. She saw two figures. Men. One was reaching up to cover the light with a jacket. The other soundlessly smashed the glass with something held in his hand. Just before the light went out Jules saw that the object was a knife, reversed to butt the glass with the stubby handle. The first man put the jacket containing the broken glass on the ground and pressed the buzzer for the apartment. The man with the knife braced himself. Jules watched as Bonal levered himself off the sofa and headed towards the door.

Jules reacted. She was over the hedge and halfway across the lawn before she realised the gun she was instinctively reaching for under her shirt was locked, warm and snug, in the armoury in London.

*

Betsy wobbled unsteadily through the coach. Meg followed behind. They passed the luggage rack and left the carriage as they headed towards the buffet car. It was noisy by the doors so they hurried through into the next coach. The train raced towards Reading. Betsy had to clutch a handrail as she briefly lost her balance. They reached the door to the buffet car as they went through Tilehurst station.

The door opened automatically in front of them. A woman was serving behind the counter. A man was in front of them, balancing two large cups in a cardboard tray. He shuffled towards the rear of the train. The view from the windows opposite the counter showed the train was running next to the River Thames. The rain had stopped but the view was still drab grey. What few pleasure craft Betsy could see were all battened down.

The woman behind the counter had long brown hair pulled back in a bun. Around her throat was a thin gold necklace. Although late in the day the buffet was still well stocked with food and drink. There was even a small plate with a lemon cut in two, next to an icebox and a packet of straws.

The woman retrieved an empty drink bottle from the end of the counter. She screwed the lid on and tossed it casually into a large plastic bin at the far end.

'Good afternoon madam, what can I - '

The wall smashed into Betsy's face as the train lurched off the rails. The lights failed. She fell back, tasting blood. Noise. Noise everywhere. Something heavy hit her and she was thrown back against the window. She fell to the carriage floor. The heavy thing landed on top of her and let out a cry. There was pain in her eyes. She was hit with another violent sound. Louder. Engine blast as the skin of the train split apart. Wind in her face. She was peppered with shards of glass and metal fragments. She knew she'd been cut. She felt the train collapse to the outside, into the cess, the drainage channel next to the tracks. The coach was still moving forwards. It hit a signal cabinet next to the track and tipped violently. Betsy heard bottles falling from shelves. Debris was landing all around her. The heavy thing – Meg, she now realised – was trying to stand. She was hit in the ribs, hard, by a fire extinguisher. She fell on her knees to the floor, which a minute before had been the window side of the train. The woman behind the counter was thrown out. She landed next to Betsy and didn't move. Her hair was thick with her own blood. The coupling severed between the buffet car and the coach Betsy and Meg had been sitting in. The brake pipe split, causing the air pressure to drop and the brakes to be applied automatically. It had no effect on the buffet car or the two coaches behind as they were no longer on the track. They had all derailed to the outside. The buffet car was moving only by the force of the coaches behind. They pushed it through a thin line of bushes and into the River Thames. Betsy felt another shunt as the coach hit the water and slowed rapidly. The train was unrecognisable. There was no straight line anymore, no order, no human hand. Twisted metal was everywhere she looked. She couldn't tell which way was forwards, which back, what was the roof and what had been the walls. She didn't know what had happened to the train

– derailed somehow – yet miraculously she was alive. But now she could hear water rushing in. The temporary relief at surviving gave way to a surge of panic, flooding over her like a thick black sea.

15.

Jules flung all her weight at the nearest man. He was facing away from her, knife in hand, anticipating the moment the front door to Bonal's apartment opened. Having remembered the absence of a covert holster tucked down the front of her jeans, Jules reckoned her best weapon right now was momentum. Plus, she had to neutralise the immediate threat, which was the knife. She threw herself at the broad flat patch between the man's shoulders. He was light on his toes, preparing to leap forward onto Bonal, so his centre of gravity lent itself to the sudden shove from behind. He was thrown forward violently. With no time to react, his face split against the wall on the other side of the alcove. He collapsed to the ground, a splatter of blood charting his descent.

The collision with the man had thrown Jules to the floor, never a good place to be in a fight. The second man had recovered from his initial shock at the attack and kicked out at her. Jules grabbed the jacket full of broken glass and threw it at his face. He flinched away and threw his hands up. The glass had no effect but did allow time for Jules to get to her feet.

Bonal opened his door. Jules screamed 'Back!' and he jumped away from the entrance, the door still open. He disappeared into the apartment.

She'd momentarily looked at Bonal, taken her eyes off the second man. Mistake. He hit her on the side of the head, a sudden blinding explosion behind her eyes. She was thrown into the wall and tripped over the prone form of the figure by the door. Another punch caught her, but she was already falling backwards so it had lost most of its force by the time it connected with her face. She tasted blood and gasped for air. The man closed on her. His lips were peeled back showing clenched teeth. She raised a knee and drove her heel into his groin. He cried out and fell on top of her. Her fingers were in his eyes. He smashed her head on the concrete with hands clamped tight round her throat, ripping the delicate skin and soft tissue with nails that felt like sharp metal knives.

It's not like the movies, she heard her combat instructor suddenly say in her ear. It's not controlled, it's not aimed, it's not graceful. It's feral, it's wild, it's torn fingernails and broken fingers, it's grab anything you can and yank it until it rips, it's hit and gouge and butt and spit and it's keep on going as hard and as fast as you can because you've got about thirty seconds in you and if you're not on top at the end of that, you're gone.

*

'Up! Up! Move!'

Betsy was in Meg's face, yelling at her.

The older woman was standing in a crouch, one foot on the bottom of the train, one on the remains of a cabinet that had come apart and fallen on them. Meg's arms flailed as she was lifted from the floor. She grabbed part of the side of the counter - now part of the ceiling - that was hanging loose. It came off in her hand. Betsy stumbled and they fell to the floor. Betsy regained her feet. She shoved Meg into a corner.

'Under here!'

Betsy pushed a large black object at Meg. It was the plastic bin. Bottles and empty cartons spilled out as Betsy aimed it at her head. Water exploded into the coach. From what had been the corridor and from behind the units in the buffet, now collapsing off the sides of the train.

'Hold it flat! Air in there!'

Betsy shoved Meg's head down and pushed the bin over her. Water was up to her waist.

'Stay here! They will come! They will come!'

Meg was pushed backwards. By the power of the water or by Betsy she had no idea. She understood that she had to keep the bin level to hold the air in. Pitch black inside.

'What about you?' she screamed, the panic bouncing back at her from the hard plastic.

The water rushed up to her chest, then held. It snatched at the bin, trying to rip it from her grasp. She lost her footing and fell sideways. Meg kicked out, trying to steady herself. Gasped in pain as her shin hit something. Managed to stay upright. All she could hear was her laboured breathing.

'Betsy!' she yelled. Still the panic in her voice.

The water stopped moving. Meg's breathing calmed. The bin was holding and she couldn't hear any leaks or bubbles.

Questions crowded her mind: Where was Betsy? Was she alive? How much air did she have?

16.

The two divers pushed through the murk. Visibility was almost zero. It was evening and the weather up top was still poor. Underwater the current was negligible. That was the only positive element of the dive.

The search had been going on for ten minutes. Two coaches were in the water. The buffet car was completely submerged, the one that had been behind it was half full of water. The dive team had put a safety line into the river. It was weighted down next to the partially submerged coach and allowed the team to orientate themselves for access to and from the dive site. Five people were missing. The divers expected the best they could manage would be to retrieve bodies.

The forward part of the train had travelled a further eighty-two metres after the derailment. The driver of train 7Z25 had made an emergency call on the radio in his cab. He'd reported that an unsolicited brake application had occurred and he thought the rear three coaches had derailed to the cess. He hadn't known the buffet car and carriage immediately behind were in the Thames.

The Up and Down Reading lines had been immediately blocked by the signaller in the operations room five miles away. The driver had hit the REC on his radio; the rail emergency group call button. This had sent an emergency message to all trains in the area telling them to stop immediately. The driver had then asked permission to inspect the train. The signaller had already known something catastrophic had happened because of the number of alarm indications that had come in from damaged signalling equipment. The signaller had also sent a message stopping all train movements in both directions. He'd dialled a number and had been connected to the emergency services. He'd declared a major incident and requested immediate assistance. Twenty minutes later two police divers had entered the water.

Those divers both held powerful torches, or so they thought. The beams managed to cut only a few feet through the brown water. Two bodies had been retrieved from the first carriage. Both men: one elderly, one young. They had been passed back to the police underwater rescue team on the bank. The divers had then returned down the line to the water.

They approached the buffet car. It was unrecognisable as a train carriage. The trees had ripped it apart like a tin can. That, and hitting the signal box, had seriously weakened the frame of the coach. By the time it had plunged into the water it had lost all structural integrity. Sharp metal lay all around the bed of the river.

Taptaptap. Tap. Tap. Tap. Taptaptap.

The divers reached the rear of the buffet car. It was still connected to the coach behind. Forward of that point it was a mess of ripped metal and crushed fittings. The roof of the coach had largely been torn off. It lay on the riverbed. Deep gashes were visible in a number of places.

The remnants of the coach had bunched into two clumps of metal and glass. What had been the right hand side of the train was uppermost. Some windows were still intact. No lights were visible. They approached the nearest mound of metal. An intact window faced them.

The lead diver heard tiny metallic taps. He thought they were the final death throes of the train. Probably metal straining and collapsing. But by the third iteration he realised the sound repeated itself exactly.

Taptaptap. Tap. Tap. Tap. Taptaptap.

The lead diver instinctively knew the sound could not be that of metal sagging under its own weight, or twisting in ways it was not designed for. It had a rhythm. It was controlled, disciplined. It wasn't random. It had to be manmade.

The divers had communication with their team on the bank. The lead diver reported that he could hear a strange sound that he assessed as manmade. The dive supervisor on the bank asked him to repeat his message. Had he said manmade? Yes, he repeated, manmade. Mechanical? Not known. Survivor? Not known.

The divers quickly established themselves above the first shape. They picked up the pace of the search. They aimed their torches through the window. Saw nothing. They searched the twisted metal lying nearby. Nothing. No air pockets. No sound.

Taptaptap. Tap. Tap. Tap. Taptaptap.

They both heard it now. The lead diver recognised the sound as morse code. Three quick taps for S. Three slow taps for O. Three more quick taps for S again. S.O.S.

There must be a survivor.

The divers pushed hard over the three metres to the next mound of debris. A new urgency drove their actions. As with the other pile of metal the window was intact, facing up. The lead diver reached the frame of the coach and aimed his torch through the window. He lurched back and the team heard him gasp in shock.

'Eddie? You all right?' said the dive supervisor on the bank.

'Yeah, yeah, we've got one. Alive.'

'Say again Eddie.'

'Alive! There's one alive in here.'

Eddie pulled himself back to the window. The second diver joined him. Both torches were pointed through the glass.

A woman's face peered back at them through the murky water. Her eyes were tight shut and her short hair floated around her face. The woman had wedged herself against wreckage in the coach so as to sit upright. Her left arm was propped against the window and she was using a ring on her little finger to tap against the glass.

Taptaptap. Tap. Tap. Tap. Taptaptap.

She was holding something next to her head. Her right hand was clutching a plastic soft drink bottle. She held it upside down. A straw ran from her mouth into the bottle. Two more similar bottles were tucked under her right arm. These bottles had their lids on. Eddie shone his light on the woman's face. She squirmed away from the beam. As she shifted her weight one of the bottles under her arm broke free. It bobbed upwards. It was full of air.

The divers watched as the woman sucked the straw and took a breath from the bottle she was holding. She exhaled the air bubbles into the water through her nose.

'What's going on Eddie?'

'Standby!'

The divers searched for a way into the coach. The second diver frantically pulled at parts of the structure. Nothing shifted. The lead diver returned to the window. The woman hadn't moved.

'Get over here, Dan, I need your light.'

The diver watched a large object float past him on the other side of the glass. A collection of black and white material, the heavy thing pushed insistently at the woman's legs. The trapped woman tried to force the thing back but the dead weight didn't yield. She took her left hand off the window and tried to push it away. Her hand became tangled in long hair. It must be a member of the train staff, the diver realised, possibly someone working in the buffet car. The woman snatched her hand back. As she did so, her fingers caught on something that then snapped. The torchlight briefly flashed back at the diver from a gold chain. The woman in the carriage clasped the necklace tight then reached out again for the body. With eyes tight shut she felt the woman for any sign of movement. There was none. She quickly let her go and tucked the necklace inside her jacket pocket.

The second diver raced to the window. Eddie let go of his torch. It floated by his side on a tether line. He pulled a small tool from a belt strapped round his waist. He aimed the safety hammer at the corner of the window furthest from the woman. He hit the glass. On the third blow the window seemed to crack in slow motion. Hundreds of tiny glass particles flowed around the divers. The slack current carried them away, over the top of the wreckage and out of sight. Some sank into the coach to hover around the survivor.

The lead diver unhooked his spare mouthpiece. He reached out and took hold of the woman's left arm. She flinched. He pressed the mouthpiece into her hand. She nodded her understanding. He guided her hand towards her mouth. With her right hand she removed the straw from her lips. She held the straw and the bottle away from her head, but didn't let them go. Before Eddie could do anything more the woman clamped her teeth on the mouthpiece and purged it of the water inside. Eddie had expected her to be shocked by the sudden blast of water from the device. He had anticipated having to purge it fully himself and wrestle her head onto it. The woman took two big breaths, still with eyes tight shut, then nodded.

She allowed herself to be lifted through the window. Eddie gripped her and kicked hard against the frame of the coach. The woman's head broke the surface of the river. She blinked water out of her eyes. Hard white beams splashed across the river from emergency lighting rigged up on the bank. The divers were next to her.

'All right, love? Keep calm, you're safe now!' Eddie had to shout to be heard above the sound of the generator on the bank.

Betsy ripped the mouthpiece out.

'There's one more!' she shouted.

'Don't worry. You're safe now. Try and relax.'

'There's one more!'

She forced her body round to face the lead diver. She shouted into his face.

'There's one more. A woman. Same area as me. You need to go back.'

Eddie looked at his partner. They needed to get the woman to the ambulance on the bank. But she was alive, so the other passenger may be too. The men were torn. Standard procedure said divers never went anywhere in the water on their own.

'There's one more!' Eddie yelled into his microphone. 'Rick, come down the line, take this one, we need to go back.'

A third diver, in full gear, entered the water and yanked himself along the line to join his colleagues. He took hold of Betsy and started back for the bank.

'She's under a bin!' Betsy yelled.

The first two divers disappeared into the water.

*

Does a person's soul recognise when death is approaching?

Meg had no idea about oxygen levels in the blood or how dangerous it was to inhale carbon dioxide from panicky rasping breaths exhaled in the dark. But would her body know? Was that why she had been shaking violently, only to pass into calm numbness? Was it the cold, or her body's way of preparing to shut down?

She couldn't feel her fingers. She guessed they were still in place, gripping the plastic rim, because the bin seemed to be mostly in an upright position. Not that she could see it. But she felt it, every time her head fell, which it had started doing more regularly.

She didn't mind the tears. They were warm, and an indication that life clung on somewhere inside the pathetic body floating in the submerged carriage. And she hadn't minded the leg twitching; a release for the fear and panic, or at least something else to focus on. She didn't mind the warmth blossoming around her groin either, as she let her bladder go. Whether the accompanying tears were of shame or pathetic humour, she couldn't tell.

A noise. Metal on metal. The train collapsing? She felt the bin buffeted by a new current in the water. Light. In the water by her feet. More noise. Tapping on the bin echoing in her dull ears. Bright light by her feet.

They will come, Betsy had said, they will come.

They had come.

*

Lights. Voices. Jules felt herself lifted off the floor. Pain. Blood in her mouth. Eyes that wouldn't open. Dull ears. Mask on her face. Crushed throat that hurt with each breath. Siren. More voices. Blue light. Then darkness.

17.

The two divers carried Meg to the bank, each man under one limp arm. Although her head lolled on her chest Betsy could tell she was alive. Every few seconds she'd lift her face in a grimace and cough violently into the water. Her bun had come loose, sending long streaks of grey hair cascading over her face and shoulders. The third diver joined them when they were at knee depth and wrapped Meg in a foil blanket. Once free of the water the paramedics guided her to the ambulance and helped the divers ease her weight onto a trolley.

'Can you hear me, Megan?' somebody said.

She sucked air in great gasps. Hard white light punctuated by blue flashes assaulted her eyes.

'Megan? You're safe now. Can you hear me?'

She nodded and managed a weak, 'yeah'. She freed an arm from the blanket and held it out.

'Betsy,' she said.

She bustled forward, her own foil blanket crinkling as she pushed past the paramedic next to the stretcher. She grasped Meg's hand in both of hers.

'Betsy,' Meg said again, then allowed the tears to flow freely once more.

'Meg,' Betsy heard the catch in her own throat. 'My dear girl.'

The two women travelled in the same ambulance to the Royal Berkshire hospital in Reading. Their wet clothes were washed and dried, temporarily replaced by blue hospital gowns as they were checked over. Once given the all-clear they insisted on going home rather than stay in overnight for observations.

'What are you going to observe?' Betsy had said, 'a cantankerous old woman complaining about the boring sod in the next bed?'

'I'm coming too,' Meg had said.

'No, no, no,' Betsy had replied. 'I'm no fan of these places, Meg, but the doctors are right. You need to stay in.'

'It's just gone ten o'clock. The drop off is in less than five hours time. I need to be there with you, Bets, you know it.'

She knew it. She called Jules to come and pick her up, but got no answer. She tried Kathryn instead.

'Room for one more?' Meg had asked.

Betsy had stared at Meg, then nodded. And smiled.

'What?' Meg had asked.

'Nothing.' Betsy had patted her arm. 'I'll call Kathryn back, and I'll ask her to pick up some food on the way.'

Betsy had examined the USB stick and hard drive, still in the protective bags Meg had supplied.

'Do you think they're damaged?' she'd said.

'No idea, but let's get hold of the next one together,' Meg had replied. 'Look after it though, it might come in handy as a dog whistle should you ever want to meet the opposition.'

An hour later Betsy watched from the front seat of Kathryn's sports car as Meg, crushed in the back, attacked a Big Mac. For thirty years Betsy had disliked the smell of the burgers. Mainly for the memories they rekindled.

The first, and only, time Betsy had been in a McDonald's had been in 1990 in Russia. Soviet Union, she reminded herself. When the first restaurant in the country had opened Betsy had queued for two hours around Pushkin Square for a burger. Forbidden fruit turned exotic western treat. Given her situation at the time, how could she have resisted?

The burger had been wonderful, the milkshake and fries just as good. Not quite the taste of freedom, as some were claiming, but possibly a sweet hint of future possibilities. She'd played along with that, although never truly believed it.

She had, however, marvelled at the cardboard box the burger had come in. As a mere container its function was plain to see. But to Betsy and her fellow Muscovites, the sheer otherworldliness of the box, and what it represented, rendered it a surreal and hypnotic quality. She'd kept the box and used it to carry her sandwiches to the office for the next few days. Each night she would wash it out and dry it on the heater in her small apartment.

No, the Big Mac meal, in and of itself, had been a delight. It was what had happened a week later that had left a sour taste in her mouth. Getting shot hadn't helped.

'What the hell did you think you were doing?' Kathryn raged into her rear view mirror. 'You're seventy and she's not far behind.'

Betsy snapped her thoughts back from a painful journey in the boot of a car three decades before.

'Who's she, the ship's rat?' Betsy said.

'Cat,' Meg said.

'It's just so irresponsible. What were you doing on that train anyway?'

'Oh, I'm sorry, dear, I didn't realise that after a certain age we were all supposed to hide ourselves away and not go out in public. Retirees are allowed to travel on trains, you know, to pass the time until we keel over.'

'You were nearly killed.'

'Well it didn't say on the ticket that the train was going to derail,' Betsy said. She turned to the back seat. 'This is her soft side, Meg, she saves the rough stuff for the Commons.'

The car blasted along a generally empty motorway, usually in the outside lane – regardless of other traffic – and rarely below 80 miles an hour.

'Any particular reason for our energetic rate of progress?' Betsy asked.

'I've still got work to do,' Kathryn said.

'At this time of night?' Betsy said.

'At all times of the bloody night. The joys of being an MP.'

'Well you don't get your work ethic from your father.'

Betsy's attempt to lighten the mood fell flat.

'Why were you in Cheltenham?' Kathryn said, in the same hard, flat tone.

'Meg was helping me with a problem.'

'Helping you…?' The words died in her throat.

'You seem uncharacteristically concerned, dear. Everything alright?'

'Of course I'm bloody concerned,' Kathryn said, 'you nearly got yourselves killed. Who made you go?'

'The irony of my goddaughter, the MP for Westminster no less, denying me any agency whatsoever, as if the whole movement of female empowerment had been a dream, is not lost on me. Nobody *made* me go. Something your sister said convinced me I needed to make some enquiries.'

'What? Jules? Miss bloody Marple should know to keep her mouth shut. If she's said anything she shouldn't have I won't be able to protect her you know.'

'They were close as children, Meg, not that you'd notice now.'

'What's she said to you?' Kathryn spat. 'If I'd known when you called that you were off on one of her wild goose chases I would have left you in the hospital.'

Over her shoulder Betsy said, 'Would you believe I held her hair back when she was vomiting tequila into the lavatory having split up with Teddy?'

'Bloody idiots,' Kathryn said.

Betsy tried to relax in the ensuing silence. She'd not yet allowed herself to replay her time in the water. A voice in her head she'd not heard before whispered that turning over that particular stone would be a bad idea until she was in a warm and welcoming place. From the moment the train had hit the gravel on the track and tipped over she had been utterly terrified. Still was, she admitted to himself. Even now she could feel her body buzzing, hyper. Energised, but not in a good way. Twitchy. As if she wanted to press pause on the world and gather her breath. Maybe Meg was right, she was too old for this. For the first time in her life she had realistically faced the prospect of her death. She'd survived, yes, but she didn't feel brave. She didn't feel strong. She just felt old and weak and scared.

She pushed the feelings to one side. She and Meg had a long night ahead of them.

18.

Wellspring Gardens felt like a co-conspirator. From the moment Betsy nosed the car off the main road she had been comforted by the tight streets and murmuring trees. Part of her was nervous a return to the scene only forty-eight hours after she'd broken a man's body on the tarmac would be noticed. A bigger part though, and one she thought she had said goodbye to a long time ago, hoped for another meeting with a representative of James Easton.

Betsy was not naturally a violent woman. Assertive, yes, at times obstreperous even, but not one to actively seek out confrontation. Not the old Betsy, anyway. A lot had changed in two days though. Like visitors in the night, a walking tour used to hide secret messages and mugger's fist in her face.

Still, she hated the turmoil she'd introduced to her life. Or reintroduced. Since her retirement she'd become accustomed to a quiet house with a sleepy cat and a safe game of bridge on Tuesday nights. It had surprised her how quickly she had warmed to these new certainties, the constants in her world as she aged. The immovable centre around which all else orbited had comforted her as she'd drifted into irrelevance, increasingly ignored by society and the wider world. Yet now she was upsetting that equilibrium in the name of preserving it. Introducing chaos to maintain the status quo. It didn't make sense. She felt the peaceful world, only fleetingly visible to her now, was slipping away. As if the pools of light under the lampposts were diminishing ink spots of the new life she had created. A cosy existence slowly being swallowed up by the expanding darkness of a past she thought she'd left behind.

She drove past the fence against which she had propelled her unknown assailant, convinced an insomniac neighbour would remember the howling brakes. Her ears and neck burned.

She moved up the long branch of Wellspring Gardens, turned the car round and eased into a space on the opposite side of the road, fifty metres short of the gap between the wall and the house. If that was to be used as the drop off point again she would have a good view of the exchange.

She scraped silt out of an ear and pointed out the gap to Meg.

'You look exhausted,' Meg said.

'You shouldn't have come,' Betsy replied. 'I'm not a helpless old woman,' she added.

'Good,' Meg said. 'We'll be counting on that, I'm sure.'

Betsy hadn't yet decided what she was going to do if anyone turned up. With a bit more evidence she might be able to go to the police. A darker question had started to emerge in the back of her calculating mind though: would involving the police be a good idea?

'Why didn't you tell Kathryn about the USB stick?' Meg asked.

Betsy ignored the question and continued staring at the passenger-side wing mirror.

'Movement,' she said.

Meg inched her head round. Betsy pointed out a figure on the opposite pavement. The individual was tall and rangy and moved with an easy fluidity. Just like the person that had dropped off the USB stick two nights previously. Betsy had parked opposite a streetlight. That might be bad, she thought, but it might also give her a view of the person's face as they passed.

The individual walked under the streetlight. Dark clothes, as before. Betsy could see the figure was wearing a suit under a black overcoat. She wasn't sure if they were different clothes from the last time. It didn't matter anyway as Betsy noticed, by the light thrown onto the figure's face, she knew something much more valuable. She knew the stranger's identity.

'Andrew Heath, you dark horse,' Betsy murmured. 'What are you up to?'

'The Defence Secretary?' Meg said.

The MP strode past the light, hands deep in pockets, back into the semi-darkness.

'That's the one,' Betsy said in a low voice. 'The question now though, is whether he's dropping off or picking up.'

'We'll soon know,' Meg said.

Andrew Heath was ten metres from the drop off point.

'Now, what are you up to, Mr He -'

Fat knuckles thumped the drivers-side window. A gold ring flashed back and forth at the glass like a demented woodpecker. Betsy ducked and Meg flinched from the fist.

'Wotchoo up to then?' A man's voice demanded.

'Hold on! Hold on!' Meg pleaded.

The thumping stopped. Betsy's window was filled with the deep blue of a football shirt. Then a chubby face: white, bald and angry. The face, framed by the window, was squashed on top of a thick neck.

'Who are you?' the face continued.

'Go away, you silly man, you scared the life out of me!' Betsy spat.

'I don't care. What are you doing here?'

'Just sitting in the car,' Meg shouted back.

'Sitting in your car? It's three in the morning, you daft cow. What are you up to?'

Betsy's mind struggled to regain some semblance of control.

'Just drive, Bets,' Meg said.

'We're lost. Just checking the map,' Betsy said.

'Checking the map,' the man snorted with derision. 'Do one, copper!'

'We'll go. Sorry to wake you. Thanks. Thanks,' Meg croaked.

Betsy started the engine and aimed the car into the road. She looked back once. The man was still there, watching them go. His open front door hurled light onto the pavement.

'Christ,' Meg said. 'That tops off a thoroughly shit day.'

'I'm inclined to agree,' Betsy said.

They drove past the drop off point. No sign of Andrew Heath, or anyone else. Betsy continued to the junction with the cul-de-sac in which she had been parked last time she visited. Still no sign.

'Nothing this way,' Meg said, looking into the dead end of Wellspring Gardens.

Betsy turned right. After another hundred metres she was at the junction where she'd slammed on the brakes two days earlier. Facing the fence she looked left and right, searching for Andrew Heath. No sign.

'I'm on to you, Heath,' she said.

Betsy turned right, drove to the main road and then left, with nothing to show for the night's work but a racing heart.

*

Andrew Heath stood at an upstairs window and cursed silently. He was on edge enough as it was without the hullaballoo that had taken place when he'd crossed at the end of the street. Noticing a car driving slowly past, he wondered if it was responsible. The shouting and commotion had been most undesirable, especially when approaching the house of the woman with whom he was having an affair.

*

The Friday morning pick up had gone without a hitch. James had hidden the USB stick at the one point six mile mark, as convention dictated when he was dropping off, from the finish heading towards the start. The route of The Long Night was four miles long. ChipsWithMayo had been pleased to find the stick, stuffed under a brick in the gutter, half a mile further along the route from the location of two nights before.

At four o'clock in the morning, an hour after collecting the package, ChipsWithMayo plugged the new USB stick into a computer propped up on the bed. The computer ran a programme to ensure the stick contained nothing other than the folder labelled 'pictures'. Once confirmed free of viruses, ChipsWithMayo opened the folder and clicked on one of the three identical images. Each was of a beach scene on a stormy day. Crashing surf was highlighted against a bruised sky. A few hardy gulls floated just above the water. Two walkers in the middle distance paced the beach, raincoats pulled tight against bodies by the stiff breeze.

'James, you old romantic,' ChipsWithMayo said.

Chips clicked on the last of the three images and dragged it into an application, already open on the computer. The application presented the user two windows. The left window was labelled 'Input', the right 'Text'. It was a crude and unsophisticated user interface, but needed only basic functionality as it had been written specifically for Chips.

The programme finished translating the image and presented the words that had been hidden in the surf and sand. The text said: 'Last message corrupted. Send again'.

'You little tinker, James,' ChipsWithMayo said. 'You never were going to tell me you lost the stick were you? Bloody idiot. We've only got a week now.'

The USB stick was ejected and computer powered down. The bedroom light was switched off. Chips lay on the bed in the dark.

'All these lies,' ChipsWithMayo muttered. 'Doesn't anyone tell the truth any more?'

19.

Sébastien Bonal stared at the woman in the bed. Her eyes were closed and her hair had been brushed recently. Probably one of the fashion-conscious nurses in the tight blue tunics. Even coma patients have to look their best in the south of France.

The woman's chest rose and fell in time with one of the many blinking lights on the machine to which she was attached. She looked peaceful enough, but he could only guess what horrors were lurking behind her eyelids.

Concussion, fractured cheekbone, partially collapsed larynx, other less serious cuts and bruises. The doctor said she had been lucky; that if Bonal hadn't appeared when he had, golf club in hand, to smash her assailant's jaw and no doubt crack a few ribs with his follow-on swings, she would have been in real trouble. He'd always wondered why doctors thought such conditions should be described as lucky.

He knew nothing about her. Except, probably, that she had saved his life. When he had opened the door he had barely registered the unconscious man. Before he'd had time to take in the significance of the dark alcove, the woman had barked her warning. That had scared him. So had the look on the second man's face, illuminated by the light from Bonal's apartment.

A focussed determination to end human life. It had only been as he had leapt back inside that he had noticed the blood on the wall and, next to the body on the ground, the knife.

He had no idea who the men were or why they would want to harm him. Kill him, he forced himself to admit. They had wanted to kill him. The second man, defeated and grunting in clear pain after being set about by the 5-Iron, had ignored Bonal as he'd dropped the club to attend to the woman. Instead, body canted over to one side to protect his ribs, he'd staggered to the man on the ground and forced him to his feet. The two broken bodies had then shuffled off towards the road.

Bonal had barely been aware of their departure. Terrified, he hadn't wanted to lay hands on the woman fearing she'd shatter under the slightest touch. A tortured rasping told him air was being gulped through torn lips. It had not been a reassuring sound.

He looked again at her passport on the side table. Passport, wallet containing one card only and barely fifty euros in cash. All her possessions. Not even a mobile phone. Keys to a hire car, parked half a mile away from his apartment. Nothing in there either. Julianne Fieldhouse. British. His mysterious saviour, somehow appearing out of the darkness to floor two equally mysterious assailants. Assassins, he told himself. They were assassins.

The young policeman returned to the side of the bed.

'The Inspector said you can make the call, Monsieur. You will be able to supply more details and hopefully gain some information.'

Sébastien Bonal nodded, and smiled his thanks to the man.

'I will call her now and let you know straight away of anything I discover.'

Bonal picked up the passport again and opened it on the page listing the emergency contact. Mrs Betsy Trenmore-Halford. Godmother. Why not a parent, or – he looked again at the woman lying in the bed – a husband?

It was the middle of the night. He considered leaving it until later on Friday morning to make the call, but didn't want to give the Inspector a chance to change his mind. He walked to the empty relative's room and dialled the number for a British mobile phone.

*

'Well I won't miss this day,' Meg said.

She was leaning on the back wall of Betsy's house next to a bright red moped, resting on its stand by the kitchen door.

'This thing yours?' she called into the house.

'Sputnik?' Betsy replied. 'Yes, although I've not been on her for a while.'

Meg came in from the back garden and closed the door.

‘This will help,’ Betsy said, handing her a glass of whisky.

Meg collapsed onto the sofa in the front room, repelling Major Tom from the far end. She looked at the pictures on the wall. They were all similar to the country scene on the USB stick. Stout representations of classical Britain. The only one that wasn’t of this genre was also the only one she could identify. Meg had been deployed to the war in Bosnia earlier in her career. She wondered how the watercolour of the famous old bridge in Mostar was linked to Betsy’s past. Father was a diplomat maybe?

It was as she was looking around that Meg saw the gun. It was perched on top of a pile of papers. She was about to dismiss it as a replica – why else would it be so brazenly displayed? – but something made her pause. She observed her host, bustling around her armchair plumping cushions. She laughed at the thought that the one abiding characteristic about her friend, and the only thing she *really* knew about her, was her ability to surprise.

‘What’s so funny?’ Betsy said.

‘Is that a real gun?’ Meg asked, pointing to the weapon.

Betsy looked up from the cushions.

‘As real as it needs to be to hold my papers in check.’

Betsy twisted her armchair better to face Meg.

‘So,’ Betsy began, cutting off any further enquiries, ‘we do shifts tonight then you find other digs tomorrow. Sound reasonable?’

'We're splitting up?' Meg said

'Yes. I need to visit a couple of places,' Betsy said. 'Where will you go?'

'St Albans, I guess. To my daughter. Where are you off to?'

'Malaysia.'

'*Malaysia?*'

'Your suggestion, dear, if you remember. I've got to go and see for myself. Malaysia first, then Croatia.'

'What?'

Betsy's phone erupted into life, startling them both.

'A bit bloody late,' she said as she picked the phone up.

Meg swigged her whisky and watched Betsy's face pass from irritation, to shock, to anger.

'Yes, this is she…'

'…Bonal?...'

'…Yes, I'm her godmother…'

'…How?...'

'…Where?...'

'…*Where?...*'

'…What happened?...'

'…Who was involved?...'

'…Have there been any arrests?...'

'…Who have you told?...'

'…What the hell is Jules doing back in France?'

*

Betsy thanked Meg as she accepted the glass. She poked the ice in her whisky, which was a larger measure than the first one.

'It's very difficult for me to talk about this,' she said.

Meg refilled her own drink.

'But Jules in a hospital bed and Monsieur Bonal, no less, ringing me confirms it.'

'What's the connection?' Meg asked.

'Half drowned and nearly attacked in the street, but there are no flies on you are there?'

Betsy sipped her drink.

'No more talk of going to the papers,' she said.

'What? Why?' Meg said.

'There's a black and white certainty to journalism they won't be able to shake off. Spying is all nuance, as you well know.'

Betsy spoke with an almost maternal encouragement.

'Spies seek facts then build the analysis,' Betsy said. 'Journalists decide on the analysis then only use the facts that fit. We can't allow that to happen. We're up against professionals. The facts lead, we follow. Otherwise the opposition will win. They'll hide in the cracks. We'll never see them.'

'So what's the connection between France, Malaysia and Croatia?' Meg said.

'Three strange murders. Well, two, and an attempted murder. As I told you, I have it on very good authority that these people had been placed under surveillance by MI6.'

'Very good authority? You mean Jules told you?' Meg said.

Betsy looked at her and sipped her drink.

'You know more about my loved ones than anyone else on the planet,' Betsy said. 'You will appreciate how important anything Jules may or may not have done can go no further.'

'Understood,' Meg said. 'So, MI6 had something to do with the murders?'

'I don't know, Meg. The surveillance was both human and technical. And there's no telling where the product ended up. So, no, it's not at all definite MI6 killed them, if indeed they were murdered.'

'Any connection between them and the names in the steg, Gabriel Dubois and Tatiana Petrova?' Meg said.

'Impressive memory,' Betsy said.

'A hacker's knack for recalling detail. Besides, if my life is in danger because of them I should at least try to remember who they are.'

'Fair enough,' Betsy said. 'But no obvious connection. Keep checking around, but there's only so much we can do from here. First, I need to go to Jules,' Betsy added.

'Well the trip'll do wonders for your air miles,' Meg said, draining her glass.

20.

Betsy had gone to the coffee shop to calm down. She was absolutely livid with Jules and hadn't held back in letting her know it. To her credit Jules had taken it on what was left of her chin. She hadn't pretended to be tired, confused or in pain. Betsy was all of those things and more. She was still exhausted from the incident on the train. Added to that her hip was playing up again, even though it had only been a short flight from London.

She hadn't chanced bringing her cannabis oil vape, or any home made products. She had so far managed to keep Jules's name out of the hands of the French authorities. She didn't want to give them another reason to show an interest.

Upon her arrival she'd found a man with slick black hair snoozing in the chair next to Jules's bed. Police? DGSE? Betsy could really do without either, but reckoned the latter would be the most problematic. It wasn't that she – or Jules - didn't know anyone in the French equivalent of MI6. Quite the reverse. She was more worried that they would be recognised.

The man had opened his eyes at Betsy's approach. He immediately sprung out of the chair to stand at attention with his hand outstretched. If he had been wearing anything more substantial than espadrilles his heels would have clicked.

Taking the proffered hand, Betsy's 'Bonjour' had been met with a cocked head, raised eyebrow and a reply of 'British?' Betsy had said yes, then added 'French?' just because she was in that kind of mood. The man had thrown his head back at this and roared with laughter, seemingly oblivious to the fact he was standing in a hospital ward. He'd pumped her hand and bowed in exaggerated fashion. He'd then released her and said 'You must be Madame Trenmore-Halford. I am Sébastien Bonal. Bienvenue en France.'

A gushing and hurried report had followed of his miraculous escape from near certain death thanks to the heroic actions of the wonderful woman lying in the bed. His re-enactment of the moment he had floored the assailant with the 5-Iron golf club produced such flamboyant arm actions Betsy had worried he was going to disconnect the bed monitor.

The volume and emotion grated. Nevertheless, Betsy had been happy to allow Bonal's bombastic account of the action to flow uninterrupted. It had left only minimal room for her own input. She'd told him Jules had flown out a day ahead of her for a weekend break on the Riviera. He had presented his business card, insisted, again, that he was at her service and asked that she and Julianne join him for dinner when able. More bowing and hand shaking had followed. He had then looked down at Jules, sighed and patted the bed frame.

'Quelle femme,' he had said.

Betsy was sure she had seen the edges of Jules's mouth twitch at the words.

Bonal had then swept out, leaving only eddy currents of expensive cologne. Betsy sat and waited. Within a minute the anticipated theatricals had started. Jules groaned and stretched. An eye peeled open, scanned the room then snapped shut. She groaned again.

'You can cut that out for a start,' Betsy had said.

Jules had opened both eyes and sat up in bed.

'Aw'right, Bets?' she'd said, grinning.

A very British row had erupted. Near silent, but full of venom. Lots of hissing and pursed lips on one side. Rolling eyes and sighing on the other. After ten minutes Betsy had left to calm herself down in the coffee shop on the ground floor of the hospital.

Where she nursed her tea. She could feel her heart rate returning to its normal level as she flicked through the local paper, Nice Journée. Betsy had a passable level of French but was looking at the paper to stop thinking, not to actually read the news. One page had a photograph of a beach. The headline said something about local objections to a building project. She turned a page. A group of mainly elderly women were gathered outside a municipal building. Something about pensions? Betsy harrumphed her support for the women's cause and turned the page. A photo showed a woman in chef's whites smiling in front of a fish platter with a lobster as centrepiece. Betsy liked lobster. The headline read '*Première étoile pour Estelle Dubois'*. The text explained how a local chef, Estelle Dubois, had won her first Michelin star.

'Congratulations, Ms Dubois,' Betsy said.

She stopped reading. Something tapped the inside of her head. A thought, a memory. Just out of reach. She sat back. Sipped her tea. Take it slow. She'd learned to recognise the feelings. Her mind was trying to tell her something, trying to paint a hazy picture. Grab too hard and it will slip through your fingers, like one of the fish in the photo. The photo. Of fish. Lobster. Estelle Dubois. Her soul tugged again.

Estelle Dubois.

The name, Dubois.

Another name. Gabriel.

Gabriel Dubois.

She looked back at the article. Searched the text. There it was: '*…fille de Gabriel Dubois…*' '…daughter of Gabriel Dubois…'.

Betsy closed her eyes. Reached into her mind. Gabriel Dubois. One of the names hidden in the steg image on the USB stick. The tugging stopped. What are you doing here Monsieur Dubois?

'*…qui est devenu l'an dernier chef cuisinier au Kremlin.*' '…who last year became head chef in the Kremlin.'

Gabriel Dubois. A walk-on part in a steg image and now shown to be head chef in the Kremlin.

'Merde,' said Betsy.

*

Meg clambered out of a taxi and into the gravel driveway of a neat detached house in St Albans.

‘This is a nice surprise,’ Pippa Moon said, as she greeted her mother.

‘Where are my grandchildren?’ Meg trilled, dropping her bag and hugging Pippa.

Two small children ran out of the house and threw themselves around Meg’s legs. She cooed over them, gripping their heads and planting kisses on both cheeks of each child.

‘Right,’ Pippa said, ‘tea, tea, tea, tea, tea.’

Meg followed her into the house, an arm wrapped around each child.

Two men sitting on a bench in the park opposite the house watched the front door close. The surveillance detail from London had been easy. Following a target who was not surveillance-aware and whose attention had been split between reading the paper and staring out of the train window wouldn’t have taxed a bunch of rookies. It had been overkill to use a full team from the GRU.

*

The Kremlin. The spooky castle on the hill. The name itself was loaded with portent and mystery, whispered to young intelligence officers as part of bedtime ghost stories. What the hell was it doing connected to a man’s name hidden on a USB stick?

Betsy examined the angles. Gabriel Dubois was head chef at the Kremlin. His name was being secretly passed by persons unknown, but possibly the British Defence Secretary, to other persons unknown. A lot of effort had gone into hiding that fact. She and Meg had briefly discussed whether this whole thing was a training exercise, possibly even one conducted by a firm totally unconnected to the intelligence world. They'd both doubted that, but like good little officers they hadn't closed their mind to the possibility. But now, thrown into the mix, was the Kremlin.

Worst-case scenario: she and Meg were in the middle of a massive international espionage operation. One side, most likely one person, was talking to the other. But the name Gabriel Dubois was already out in the open as being connected to the Kremlin. You can't really hide a head chef, she told herself; far from it, they'd want to show off their new acquisition, that was the whole point. And she'd read it in a daily newspaper. The bit about Dubois being linked to the Kremlin wasn't being hidden, that wasn't the big secret.

So what was?

One suspicion sprang immediately to mind. And Betsy didn't like it one little bit.

21.

Betsy stared at the sign in the taxi window. The image of a round spiky object with a handle, or possibly a stem, at one end was contained in a big red circle with a line through it. Grenade? Did that even make sense?

The other images with similar red lines through them she recognised: stick thing with smoke coming off the end, no cigarettes; burger and cup, no eating or drinking; gun, well, no guns. Easy.

But the spiky thing eluded her. Must be the jet lag, she thought.

'No durian.'

The voice belonged to a smiling man standing behind her. The man lifted Betsy's half empty suitcase.

'Don't worry. If you don't understand, you won't have one,' the man said, still smiling. 'Into KL?'

Betsy blinked sweat out of her eyes. She'd only been outside the air conditioning for five minutes, only in the country an hour, and she was already struggling with the humidity. Should have drunk more on the flight, she told herself. Or less.

'Sorry?' she said to the man, who was now loading her bag into the back of the van.

'KL. Do you want to go into Kuala Lumpur?' the man said.

'Yes. Yes, please.' Betsy said.

'Good. Sliding door, madam.'

The man reached across Betsy and opened the door to the van. There was room for sixteen people inside but she was the only passenger. Most of the windows were hidden behind small curtains. Betsy winced when her damp shirt pressed against her back as she sat down in the air-conditioned interior. It was nearly ten o'clock at night. Betsy guessed it was Saturday but wasn't really sure anymore, the rushed flight from France having spun her internal clock.

'When does it get cooler?' she asked the driver.

'Ha, ha, it doesn't! First time in Malaysia, yes?'

'Yes.'

'Oh wow. Let me tell you - '

'Please, just drive the car.'

The silence in the cavernous taxi amplified the transactional nature of their relationship. Driver and client, nothing more. If it was an embarrassing silence Betsy didn't show it or care. She was still smarting from the row she'd had with Jules in the hospital. She sat back in the freezing interior of the van and replayed the conversation, searching desperately for evidence the botched attack on Bonal was not connected to the other incidents.

*

She had a name: Ravi Marimuthu. Occupation: academic adviser to the government. An address in the Ampang Jaya district of east Kuala Lumpur. Not a lot to go on, Betsy thought.

She'd left the colonial splendour of her guesthouse in favour of the shopping mall with its boringly delicious air conditioning. The heavy air sat on her like a bad memory. Just scuttling from the taxi to the automatic doors had made her break out in a light sheen of sweat.

She bought a coffee and a croissant and sat at a table staring through a large window at the hazy morning, already soup-like with humidity. The Petronas Towers reared up in front of her. The skybridge, almost half way up, made the columns look like two ballistic missiles nervously holding hands.

The Internet had so far yielded nothing.

Searching 'Ravi Marimuthu' when she'd had been waiting for the flight, after her row with Jules, had offered a few social media profiles and a link to the finance director of an oil company in Texas. None were remotely linked to Malaysia or a recent death.

'Ravi Marimuthu organised crime' yielded similar results.

'Ravi Marimuthu Malaysia crime drugs money'. Offered nothing.

'Ravi Marimuthu MI6 murder death kill assassinate'. More nothing.

Betsy finished her coffee and pushed her way through the soggy air towards the Royal Selangor Public Library, across a neat city centre park. By the time she reached the cool interior her blouse was discoloured in uneven sweaty blotches. After two hours of research all she'd discovered was that the Ampang Jaya district was popular with international organisations and foreign diplomats. A few Malaysian officials lived there also, but there was nothing to suggest Marimuthu's ownership of a house in the district would be out of the ordinary or any reason to be under surveillance by MI6.

Frustrated, Betsy left at midday and walked for three blocks to a covered street market. The heavy air smelled of fish oil, chilli and cooking meat. She queued at a stall for a box of noodles, then looked for a spare seat at one of the hundreds of tables crammed into the market.

A waitress cleared empty boxes into a black bin bag. Betsy hurried to claim the vacant space. The waitress wiped the table with a cloth, which was then tucked back in her apron. Betsy sat down. Her stumpy legs, protruding from beige shorts, immediately sealed themselves against the plastic chair. She ate her noodles. The hot food made her sweat even more than she was already.

She looked out at the street and saw two large statues opposite the market guarding the entrance to a brightly coloured Buddhist temple. Three backpackers in shorts and T-shirts were buying joss sticks to burn as offerings inside. Praying to the gods, Betsy wondered, or paying their respects to the dead?

The sudden realisation of how to track down Ravi Marimuthu exploded in her head as if she'd just bitten into a chilli. She rushed from the market, arriving back at the library ten minutes later in a sodden heap. She asked the receptionist for the five most important ministries in the Malaysian government, noting down the phone numbers. She then moved to sit near the library entrance, far enough from other visitors to be able to use her phone, newly acquired since her submergence in the River Thames, but still just within the welcoming chill of air conditioning.

She dialled the number for the Prime Minister's Office.

'I've been out of the country for a few weeks,' she told the official. 'I'd like to send condolences regarding my friend Ravi Marimuthu, I believe he was an adviser in your department.'

The official expressed sympathy but said nobody of that name had worked in the PM's office. Betsy got the same reply from the Ministry of Finance. She used the same line, and received an identical answer, when she tried the Ministry of Home Affairs. She called the Ministry of Defence.

'We were all so shocked,' the official said in answer to Betsy's query. 'He was a lovely man, I'm sorry you lost your friend.'

Betsy murmured an appropriate response, hoping she'd kept the relief and delight from her voice.

'Minister Badawi will be happy to receive a card for the garden of remembrance,' the official said. 'Ravi was his most important adviser, they were especially close.'

Betsy ended the call and hurried to a computer terminal at one of the long wooden desks. She logged on with the code given by the receptionist and searched for articles about Defence Minister Badawi. The most recent article, in the Malay Times, was dated four weeks previously. The headline read: '*No place for imperial Britain in Malaysia's future defence, says Minister, as White Paper is launched'*. The article explained how Mohamad Badawi, the Defence Minister, was calling for the scrapping of the Five Power Defence Arrangements, a historic pact signalling Britain's military commitment to the region.

A photo showed the politician brandishing a document over his head as he accepted the adulation of a gushing crowd. The caption under the photo said: '*Defence Minister Badawi and chief adviser Ravi Marimuthu attend Parliament to table the White Paper'*.

Betsy blinked at the page.

The name Ravi Marimuthu stared back at her.

The younger man was standing behind the Minister and smiling for the cameras. He was described as the intellectual power behind Minister Badawi's tub-thumping rhetoric. The White Paper, calling for a more assertive Malaysia and the ditching of defence links with Britain, was widely seen as his work.

Betsy considered the implications of Britain's military establishment being cut out of the region. Defence exports would go for sure, she reasoned. Political influence too, in all likelihood, if the treaty was scrapped by Malaysia. That wouldn't go down well in Washington. A very diminished Britain would be left creeping around the world stage like an unwanted guest.

Betsy examined her thoughts. Ravi Marimuthu had been the architect behind the White Paper. His ideas had threatened Britain's standing in the region and, perhaps, the world. He'd been under surveillance by MI6.

And now he was dead.

*

The traffic was as thick as the air. Betsy's taxi ground through clogged streets, inching towards the Ampang Jaya district. She'd bought an umbrella. Whether for the heat, although it was more humidity than sunlight, or the rain threatening from the clouds bubbling up over the city, she wasn't sure.

She fidgeted in the back seat of the car. She'd had sharp stabbing pains in her legs most of the day and guessed she must have tweaked a nerve on the flight. Too old to have sat for so long in one position, she admonished herself, but where else could she have gone? There are only so many laps of economy class you can manage before you have to make polite conversation with the woman at the back with the shrieking toddler.

The taxi cleared the city's ring road. The speed of progress improved the closer Betsy got to the address for the Marimuthu property. The Ampang Jaya district sat to the east of the city and was a little higher in altitude. It made no difference to the heat. As the road climbed between well-tended houses Betsy could see, out of the rear window, the Petronas Towers a few kilometres away, dominating the murky skyline. The taxi turned off the main road and passed a golf course.

Smart four-by-fours and executive saloons filled the car park. The driver turned left. Betsy saw a board by the road indicating they were heading into a housing development. One road led in and out. The houses within were located on a large circular loop. They drove past a sentry box. Without slowing, the taxi driver gave a cheerful wave to the uniformed man inside. The security guard waved back, both at the taxi driver and at Betsy in the back seat. The post didn't have a barrier and Betsy wondered exactly how much security was being provided by the little box.

The houses all stood apart from each other, with broad driveways up to carports, which were mostly double-width. The driver deposited Betsy outside a substantial dwelling made of dark Balinese wood. A large veranda faced the road. A swing chair pivoted on the veranda in the gathering breeze. Betsy could imagine Ravi Marimuthu relaxing in the chair after another day stifling British political ambition.

The house looked empty. Betsy knew it had been under surveillance by MI6 so was reluctant to walk up to the front door. Surveillance could be human or technical; she'd said that to Meg with a misplaced confidence, given her years of retirement. There was nobody about, although in the gathering darkness even Betsy admitted there could be eyes on her from a dozen places. A casual glance over her shoulder probably wasn't going to sniff out a bunch of MI6 spooks on a surveillance detail. She would just have to chance it. Anyway, technical would likely mean cameras, possibly voice recorders. Maybe even an IMSI grabber to get hold of the memory card in her new mobile phone, the last one being at the bottom of the Thames.

She decided to open the umbrella to hide from any cameras. If anyone was in, she wasn't sure what she'd say but guessed it would be something about rain coming, can't be too careful.

She pressed the buzzer. No answer. After two more attempts she concluded the house was indeed empty. She walked back to the road and was about to collapse the umbrella when the first fat drops of rain started to fall from a darkening sky. Like two or three other plots of land Betsy had noticed in the development, the one diagonally across from the Marimuthu house had not been built on. Some foundations had been laid and there were a few concrete blocks lying about. Betsy decided to take a seat while she considered her options. A low rumble of thunder rolled up from the city. The rain got heavier. Betsy hoped it would clear the air that was sticking the clothes to her back. A squally wind whipped the swing chair around on its hook. Her legs ached.

What am I hoping to find here, Betsy asked herself. A gardener with long-held suspicions? Someone in the house that would recognise the names on the USB stick? A career in espionage had taught her that heading to the centre of a story and asking questions often produced results. So she'd gone. But Ravi Marimuthu's death had been investigated and determined to have been caused by an allergic reaction to nuts. What was there left to discover from the vantage point of an increasingly soggy concrete block?

And if that place is under surveillance, what will they make of me turning up, Betsy wondered?

Who were they, anyway? Betsy had a collection of suspicions, but they were fragmented, like the pieces from multiple jigsaw puzzles muddled together. Some fitted, but that felt like luck rather than design. And Meg, usually so dependable and opinionated, had been vague regarding her thoughts on the opposition. That wasn't like her, Betsy realised. Old age? Lack of practice? Fear? Something worse - betrayal perhaps? As soon as the thought entered her head Betsy admonished herself. She shook her head. 'Meg's as trustworthy as they come,' she said to the rain, falling heavily on the umbrella. Even if the plea to involve the papers had been reckless, out of character. Somehow desperate. And somebody had tipped off the mugger to expect her, Betsy remembered. She shivered.

As for the man who had ended up a crumpled heap on Wellspring Gardens, did his actions really scream of being a member of MI6? Would such a person really be so cack handed as to actually carry a map on them during the pick up, Betsy wondered. But maybe he had come from Legoland. Maybe, Betsy thought, the man bouncing off her bonnet had right royally cocked things up. Things that needed to be un-cocked, fast.

Betsy was surprised at the speed with which the shower broke. Rain started hammering down in heavy lines from a black sky. The umbrella was in danger of being dragged out of her hands. Her feet, clad in sensible hiking boots, were in mud and her legs were soaked.

The Badger.

A flash of lightning lit up the trees in the Marimuthu property. They waved their arms in hard panicky jerks.

Where have you come from Badger, Betsy wondered. What are you doing in my head?

The umbrella was being pulled so hard Betsy struggled to keep it upright.

A conversation Betsy had once had with her friend swam back into her mind. Good spies assess impossible questions quickly and accurately, Badger had said. That's what they're paid for. They write a good analysis of what the problem is today.

Another flash, accompanied by a terrifying crack. Storm must be right on top of me, Betsy thought.

The Badger wasn't listening. He continued his speech. But great spies, he said, answer tomorrow's problem. If you want to be a great spy, Bets, you've got to get ahead of the pack, get in front of events. Work out what's going to happen in twenty-four hours time and put yourself there.

Throw your vision forward.

Betsy did as she was told.

'So who does it suit to have me cowering under an umbrella thousands of miles from home outside the house of a possible murder victim?' Betsy asked aloud.

We're up against professionals, her brain reminded her. Professionals probably didn't like mistakes. Probably liked to clear them up quickly, quietly.

They'll hide in the cracks, she'd told Meg. Which means I'll only see what they want me to see.

Spying is all nuance, she'd said that too. Which means they say one thing and do another. We lie, cheat and steal. Which means they get people to do their bidding, go where they want them to go. Had she been spouting all this to the very woman engineering her demise?

'I told her spies had given their lives for the truth. More have had their lives sacrificed to hide it. Have you been laughing at me the whole time, behind your oh-so solemn features, Meg?' she asked the black sky.

Betsy swore at her boots. 'She's still in the game, you bloody idiot!'

She suddenly felt very cold, despite the heat that was cloaking her, and thousands of miles away from a friendly face.

'What a fool I've been,' she told the sodden night.

The violent glare of a lightning flash illuminated two feet standing next to hers. A finger appeared under the rim of the umbrella and slowly started lifting it up.

22.

Kathryn Fieldhouse was worried about her sister. Her concern was not born of the fact Jules had just graced a hospital bed, although an inquisitor might have thought as much from the damned good show the MP was making of it. Kathryn considered Jules her intellectually inferior and uninspiring lesser half. But, she was family. And when a family member gets bashed up and hospitalised, it was natural to feel a certain amount of concern. The fact that amount had to be upped a bit to meet a level deemed acceptable for public consumption was, as far as Kathryn was concerned, neither here nor there. Besides, when it came to Jules it wasn't as if a bit of violence every now and again didn't come with the job.

The job, thought Kathryn. For reasons she'd never managed to understand, Jules had somehow followed The Badger into MI6. Not only that, but once there, she had happily wallowed as a footslogger. Not like Kathryn: full of drive in her pursuit of greatness, but seemingly never attaining the happiness her sister possessed. If Jules had any ambition at all, it had only ever been to get a tighter grouping on her range practices. The discrepancy had always struck Kathryn as slightly unfair.

So it wasn't for any bloody nose that Kathryn was worried. She was more concerned with the purpose of Jules's visit to France, rather than what had happened when she got there. Jules was not an impulsive woman; anyone close to her knew that. But Betsy had said her visit to Cheltenham had been on account of something Jules had put her onto. Of course, in her usual cryptic manner Betsy had supplied few details, a character trait that had always enraged Kathryn. But if Jules was in her professional capacity now helping an old spook with a colourful past, that was enough to worry Kathryn.

These thoughts tumbled around her head as, with an unwavering gaze, she pretended to listen to Trevor, one of the security guards at the Ministry of Defence. Trevor had rarely been out of uniformed service in his career, although he hadn't always been a Whitehall guard. For twenty-two years he had been a man of action in the army. The security job now paid the bills, and afforded him the opportunity to tell his old stories, but it was a bit dull. Which was why he had always enjoyed the visits from his old boss, on her way to or from the Commons. She'd kept him alive on his last tour in Afghanistan, kept him laughing, got him back to his family. He'd do anything for her.

Kathryn nodded a curt goodbye to Trevor, as if having just received a military briefing. She strode onto Whitehall. As she hailed a taxi to take her to the television studios, she pondered why she wasn't feeling more uncomfortable. For one, she'd been pretty much ordered to appear on the programme. Her disastrous radio interview the week before was still fresh in media memory and needed to be corrected. The invitation from the television company had been polite enough. They dressed it up as offering a voice to a newly elected female MP, of course. It didn't need particularly sharp political antennae though, to tell they just wanted another slice of roadkill. The party whips had left her in no doubt what was expected: say nothing substantial, mention World Wide Britain once, twice tops, and don't cock it up again.

Another worry was the fact it was TV. At least with radio you could surround yourself with notes. And the fear in your eyes was hidden. It was different with TV. She was literally in the glare of publicity. No hiding place. She was being interviewed by Tam Westminster for his Sunday morning television show. "Westminster Politics" was her chance for redemption.

Ten minutes in and all was going well. The review of the papers had been navigated with ease. She'd even got a laugh out of Tam Westminster by saying the Department for Transport's "war on potholes" was a perfect example of Keynesian economic policy at work.

'Speaking of war,' Westminster then said, 'in your former life you were a soldier, an intelligence officer I think?'

'That's right, Tam. A long time ago now, ha, ha,' Kathryn said.

'You must be overflowing with leadership qualities.'

Careful, a little voice in Kathryn's head said, danger ahead, remember what happened with Carole Aggerton.

'That was all a long time ago,' she said.

'But - '

'What I will say about leadership though, Tam,' Kathryn said, suddenly sitting forward in her seat, 'is that this government is showing that global problems don't go away by wishful thinking. It is too easy to be a spectator on the edges of world affairs.'

Kathryn could see a monitor to one side of the studio, just over Westminster's shoulder. She saw that the live camera had panned in for a close up of her face. She looked good.

'Britons have never shied away from tackling the big problems: rolling our sleeves up, getting dusty, taking a few knocks,' she continued. 'But it's only with vision, commitment and real compassion born of a strong and unwavering moral code that we can make things better at a global level. If you have values to which many in the most deprived areas of the world aspire, you have to be prepared to get out there and stick up for those values. And that's exactly what we're doing through the World Wide Britain agenda.'

Tam Westminster stared at Kathryn.

'Kathryn Fieldhouse, many thanks. Let's get the headlines.'

The red light on the live camera went out. Westminster smiled at Kathryn as she stood and disconnected the microphone from the front of her suit.

‘Great stuff. Really, wow,’ he said. ‘We should do this again.’

‘You know how to get hold of me,’ she replied.

‘One thing I’ve been dying to ask,’ Westminster said, ‘didn’t you once use a flag to annoy the Taliban?’

Kathryn’s defences went straight back up. No such thing as off the record with a journalist, even if the red light had gone out on the nearest camera.

‘Not really, it was an important mission to reassure the local population and use non-violent means to explain to those opposed to our peacekeeping efforts that we intended to see through our promises to the international community.’

‘Wow, you managed all that with a flag?’

‘Well, the village of Nahr-e-Puzeh was regularly subjected to intimidation and violence by the Taliban that lived there. I decided to send a message to them that we would not be deterred from our task of protecting the local people.’

‘As I understand it you led a team of soldiers at night through a minefield to leave a flag in the centre of the village with a note attached,’ Westminster said. ‘What did the note say?’

Kathryn thought back to her tour in Afghanistan, when she first discovered the ability to motivate people to put themselves in danger for her. That the power had come easily had been a surprise at first, but she soon got used to it. Not only that, she found she was quite good at it. The realisation had been no brief high, though, like a shot of caffeine or nicotine. It had had a lasting effect. As had discovering the moral fluidity to ask soldiers like Trevor to risk their lives on the altar of her career more than once.

'It was a long time ago, Tam, I can't really remember the details. Something about being there to help, I think.'

'"Your good friends up the valley," I'm remembering now from the official citation for your gallantry medal,' said Westminster, pretending he hadn't rehearsed the moment, '"want you to know that we are not going away and we are watching over you". Quite a message.'

'I can't remember all the details. Unlike you, apparently.'

Kathryn had slipped effortlessly through the ranks of the army, but had always been frustrated, always sought more. There was a hole inside her, carved out by her parents' divorce and her unconscious craving for The Badger's approval. No amount of success was able to fill it. Winning felt hollow. If she could achieve it, it wasn't worth achieving; he wouldn't be impressed. Only by failing would she have found a worthy cause and know what she really wanted. But she never failed.

'A message designed to reassure the locals and let the Taliban know you had them in your sights. Very clever. That's proper hard core. Something you bring to your politics?'

Kathryn noticed one of the cameras on the far side of the studio was pointing at her and still had a red light on. She stepped close to Westminster and put him between her and the camera.

'Something I bring to the balls of any journalist who tries to catch me out after the interview,' she said in a hard voice.

Westminster smiled. 'We'll be seeing more of you, I think,' he said.

Of course, the part of her that very rarely saw the light of day knew it wasn't true to say she'd *never* failed in anything she'd really cared about. But, like the colours on a flag snapping in the breeze of an Afghan village, the relevance of that knowledge had dimmed long ago, and it was quite easy to ignore.

*

'You don't see many hiking boots in this neighbourhood.'

Betsy looked up at the man. Fat rain fell into her eyes smudging what little vision she had.

'Mind you, you don't often see an old girl sitting in a field holding a lightning rod in the middle of a downpour either.'

'I guess not,' Betsy said, on her guard.

'You'd be better off holding a 1-Iron,' the man said. 'Not even God can hit a 1-Iron.'

'If you say so.'

'It's a joke, sport,' the man said. 'Geez, you poms need to lighten up, you really do.'

The rain continued its assault on Betsy and the man.

'So, I'm guessing you're not waiting for the house to be built around you?'

The rain had soaked the man to the skin, but he hadn't seemed to notice. The visitor wore white trainers, royal blue shorts and a yellow polo shirt. Have I ever known hitmen to wear polo shirts? Probably not. That's good, Betsy thought, but still no reason not to cast an eye around the building site for a potential weapon.

She needed to gain the initiative.

'I'm Betsy. A reporter. From London,' Betsy said.

The man looked surprised, and didn't try to hide his disbelief. 'A journo? Which rag?'

'The Sentinel.'

'Oh yeah? We used to get the Sentinel in Afghan. Kept it by the desert rose for spills.'

'Desert rose?'

'The pisser. A bit of plastic drain pipe buried in the ground for the blokes to piss in.'

Betsy nodded

'Just as much piss in the paper as on it, if I remember correctly.'

'Charming.'

The rain continued to lash down from the sulphurous sky, black and purple even though it was only late afternoon. The man waited. Betsy said nothing.

'Look, Betsy, reporter from London,' the man said, 'I love chatting and meeting new people, especially in the rain. It's kind of romantic. But I've gotta ask. What the fuck are you doing in my yard?'

Betsy felt vulnerable, staring up at the man standing over her. She needed to shift the advantage.

'Do you think he was murdered?' Betsy said.

'Who?'

'Ravi Marimuthu.'

The man fell silent as the storm continued to rage over their heads. Wrinkles appeared at the edges of his eyes as he squinted down at Betsy.

'Beer?' the man said.

Betsy stood up and folded the umbrella. It had provided no protection whatsoever and she was a bit nervous about the lightning rod comment. The man had already turned away and was walking through the mud towards the nearest house, opposite Ravi Marimuthu's property.

'I'm John Cobbett by the way,' he called over his shoulder. 'Nice to meet you.'

Betsy followed him, at a short distance, past a black Range Rover Evoque parked on the drive and into a garage. She immediately understood why the car was outside. The floor of the garage and much of the wall space was taken up with sporting and garden paraphernalia: kayaks, nets, hoses, bats, balls, helmets and enough boots, flip flops and running shoes to equip about six people. Betsy propped the umbrella against a chest freezer the size of a small car. John threw her a towel, grabbed one for himself and stood on alternate heels to drag his shoes off. He peeled off his socks and dropped them on the shoes. Betsy, with some difficulty, bent down and did likewise. John entered the main house through a side door. Betsy paused on the threshold and checked behind her.

'It's a long way to go home empty handed, dear,' she said to herself, then followed.

She was punched on the nose. At least, the rancid smell of bad drains and something, or possibly everything, dead was so bad it felt like a punch. She pressed the towel to her face.

'Oh God, she's on the bloody durian again,' John said.

Betsy followed him through a small utility room into a spacious kitchen. The house had been built in the same Balinese style as Marimuthu's. Sturdy columns of dark teak connected open spaces delineated by bookcases or other large pieces of furniture. As the man walked in a woman looked up from a chopping board on the central island in the kitchen. Her eyes were watering and her cheeks were flushed. Two large spiky fruit, each the size of a small football, were in front of her. She was chopping up a third. Betsy recognised the fruit from the sign in the taxi at the airport.

'I found a garden gnome in the plot next door,' John said as he opened a tall fridge.

'Best dressed gnome I've ever seen,' the woman said. 'I'm Sue.'

'Betsy,' she said.

'Here you go, Bets, reporter from London,' John said, as he tossed a beer can across the kitchen. 'Might be a bit cold for you, sport, but you'll survive.'

Betsy caught the can awkwardly and looked at it as if it might bite her. 'Thanks,' she said.

'Sorry about the smell. You'll get used to it in a minute,' Sue said.

'I found Bets outside playing with a kid's umbrella in the yard,' John said.

Sue looked blank.

'She's a reporter, apparently. Asked me if I thought Ravi was murdered,' John said.

John stared at Betsy and opened his beer can. He didn't take a sip.

'Okay, sport, that's the who. Now try the why again. I don't mean to be rude, but we both work at the Australian High Commission and have heard a few tall tales since we've been here. Although, no offence, they usually come from folks a lot younger. So why the interest in Ravi?'

Betsy was wet, tired and her legs were hurting again. If this was all a waste of time she figured she'd rather find out early and get home.

'Do you think he died from an allergic reaction?' she said.

John took a sip of his beer. Sue continued chopping the durian. Slowly.

'That's what the cops said.'

'What do you say?'

'I don't have to say anything, sport. Besides, we weren't here. We took the kids up to Bangkok for the weekend.'

'Goodness, that's got to be a hell of a drive.'

'Probably is. We wouldn't know, we flew. No way we'd drive that distance. You seen these guys on the road? Maniacs! We've been wiped out twice. Had to buy a dashcam just to make the claims easier.'

Betsy held her unopened beer.

'He didn't like you lot much though,' John said. 'Sorry, your government, not journos. Although we never really talked about the press. Let's give you the benefit of the doubt.'

Betsy looked at the can in her hand. She realised it was the only thing, other than coffee, that she'd had to drink since getting off the plane.

'That's why you're here, isn't it, Betsy?' Sue said. 'You knew he was all for giving your lot a knee in the shorts. You reckon they did a number on him, don't you?'

'He didn't eat any chicken bloody satay, that's for certain,' John said as he returned to the fridge.

'Babe?'

'Yeah, I'll take one,' said Sue.

Betsy stared at the beer can. She felt light headed and swayed against the kitchen island.

'You all right, Betsy?' said Sue.

'Yes, dear, yes. I've had these terrible pains since I got here,' she said. 'I think I sat poorly on the flight.'

'Sharp stabs in the legs?' said John.

'Yes! Exactly. How did you know?'

'Ha!' Sue exclaimed. 'It's bloody muscle cramps, mate. You're dehydrated. Catches us out too from time to time. It's the humidity. You forget it because it's not so hot, but the bloody humidity does for you.'

'Have one of these, sport,' John said, passing Betsy a glass of water.

'Thankyou,' Betsy said, 'and you're right. That's why I'm here.'

Two cans snapped open. Betsy drained her glass of water.

'My word,' she said, 'that's amazing.'

'So what's your plan, Bets? Or was sitting in a field getting piss wet through the best of it?' John said.

'What kind of dashcam have you got?' Betsy asked, placing the empty water glass on the counter and taking hold of her beer can once more.

'Dunno,' John said. 'A black one.'

'How long does it record?'

'Three hours, then downloads to my hard drive if it can see Wi-Fi or my phone, then starts again.'

'Always on?'

'Yeah, unless we disconnect it for holiday.'

'Did you disconnect it when you went to Bangkok?'

'No, it's okay for a weekend, we don't bother.'

'And do you always park your car like that in the drive?'

'Like what?'

'Facing out.'

'Yeah, why?'

'Because it's pointing right at Ravi's house,' Betsy said, and opened her beer.

23.

All three were leaning forwards, as if the image was magnetically dragging them towards the screen. In a way, it was. John had clicked the fast forward button. The black and white image was still, but for the occasional exaggerated flutter of the trees in Ravi Marimuthu's garden.

'Ravi left work on the Friday about six o'clock,' John said. 'He was supposed to play golf with some fellas on the Saturday but didn't show.'

A vehicle suddenly blasted across the screen. John stopped the recording and went back a few seconds to look at the car.

'Another taxi,' said Sue.

John continued reviewing the dashcam footage forwards in time. A streetlamp, out of shot on the boundary between the Marimuthu property and a neighbour, cast shadows of the trees across the driveway.

'Nobody got too concerned until he didn't show for work on the Monday. We got home to a load of cops in the street after they broke in.'

Betsy looked at the numbers in the top corner. They were still on the Friday night, racing through the evening hours. Nine, ten, eleven o'clock. Nothing but the occasional taxi and some animated foliage.

'I'm still amazed this has worked,' John said. 'I've never tried it before. We'll have to have another bash in the car now I know it records properly.'

They were reviewing the night hours first, from eight through to six in the morning.

'It's dry,' Betsy said.

'This was three weeks ago, Bets,' said Sue. 'It doesn't rain like this all the time.'

Midnight came and went without incident.

John said, 'I'll have to point the car over at the Spanish ambassador's place. Might catch his wife spraying on her evening dress.' This earned him a jab in the ribs from Sue.

One o'clock, two, nothing.

'This is good,' Betsy said, spooning another mouthful of durian from the bowl she was holding.

'Still bloody stinks,' said John. Another jab from Sue.

Betsy was strangely energised, and not just by the fruit. She hadn't done this sort of thing for years and was loving every moment. Would she rather they find something on the recording, or find nothing? She wasn't sure what was more concerning: that she realised she was hoping for trouble, or that she didn't feel in the least bit guilty about it.

There was a sudden ripple on the screen, as if the digital image had momentarily broken down in one small area. John went back a few seconds. He played it forward in real time. The image hadn't pixelated. It had altered with the arrival of a figure, alone, wearing a dark padded jacket. The time read: 02:57.34. The figure entered the screen from the right, with no vehicle visible, and walked from the road directly towards Ravi Marimuthu's front door. Stepping onto the driveway, the figure casually checked over a shoulder.

'Can you see his face?' Betsy said.

'Keep it going,' said Sue, 'we'll come back.'

The figure approached the front door and removed something from a jacket pocket. The picture was too dark to see what it was. After a few seconds the door opened. The figure stepped inside and the door closed gently.

Nobody spoke.

After two minutes John clicked the fast forward button. Almost immediately he had to stop and rewind the recording as the figure had reappeared from the front door. The time read: 03:01.15

The figure walked straight down the drive, looking around. It turned left, exiting the screen the same direction it had arrived.

'Go back,' Betsy said.

'Hang on a sec,' said John.

He clicked the fast forward button and let the recording play out for another five minutes. With nothing significant added he returned to three o'clock in the morning.

On cue, the figure left the house, softly pulling the door closed. Striding down the driveway, hands in pockets, the figure was momentarily lit up by the streetlamp, glancing at the camera. John clicked the stop button. He used the computer keyboard to zoom in on the figure's face. The edges of the head were blurred, but to Betsy it was unmistakeable. She stared at the screen, and the same round face she had last seen being thrown off her bonnet stared back.

*

Dmitri Goncharov licked his fingers and dipped them back in the bowl on the table in the secure room.

'These are good,' he said, through greasy lips, 'you should try them.'

He dug around for another pelmeni, slathered one in sour cream and shoved the tiny meat dumpling into his mouth. He wiped his fingers on his trousers.

'Okay, start the briefing,' he said.

'Trenmore-Halford spent just twenty-four hours in Kuala Lumpur,' Misha Niechenko said. 'She had an open ticket so was able to switch to an earlier flight to come back.'

'Why so little time? What did she find?'

'The security guard at the diplomatic apartments says she visited the Marimuthu property in a taxi.'

'Is he sure?'

'Yes. When we saw the woman's flight details we sent our asset the latest image. He's sure. We don't know what she found but with her early departure we assess she has uncovered some evidence.'

'Where is she now?'

'Dubrovnik. Just landed from the overnight flight. She'll be looking into Marko Babić.'

'Who have we got there?'

'Viktor and Tomas. They left as soon as Trenmore-Halford flew out of Malaysia.'

'And the USB sticks?' Goncharov said.

'Our last drop off was completed but we still don't know where the lost stick is. The signal has died. It was only a small battery.'

'Or it has been read and is now being shielded. Come on boy, don't think in straight lines.'

Misha Niechenko flushed.

'The other woman, this Clover woman?'

'Still in St Albans. She's not moved.'

Goncharov looked at his deputy for the first time since the briefing had begun.

'What do you advise, Misha? Send a message to Mrs Trenmore-Halford by interacting, shall we say, with her friends? Or are we beyond messages? Should we just take advantage of her being alone right now?'

'I think we should let the operation run for a few more days,' Niechenko said.

'We haven't got a few more days!' Goncharov exploded. 'Operation Meadowland is a fixed date. I sometimes wonder if you have the stomach for this work.'

He shoved the bowl of pelmeni across the table towards his deputy. It tipped over, spilling dumplings onto the table.

'Take one. It will settle your nerves. I've decided what we're going to do.'

24.

The Monday morning sun shone bright in her face. Betsy's white shirt was already starting to stick to her back. She was more out of shape than she'd realised. Every laboured breath screamed at her as she climbed what seemed like the thousandth step on the walls surrounding the old town of Dubrovnik. At least the walk had shaken off any residual tiredness. She'd barely slept on the flight. She was too wired, jumpy. There was a murderer out there somewhere who knew Betsy's name, face and address and had a reason to hold a grudge. Sometimes the world felt a very small place.

The old town had clearly had a facelift in the thirty years since the war. Polished stone and gravelled courtyards echoed to the chatter of tourists. Rubberised soles slapped up and down ancient stairs, unsure and uncaring about their destination. Catholic churches reared up and stretched in the sunshine, reminding locals and visitors alike of their pre-eminence.

The Adriatic Sea threw a million points of light into the sky. She could imagine herself enjoying the view, except she was sure Marko Babić had been murdered here. And if the opposition could reach this far, what else would they be prepared to do?

Betsy had wanted to find facts then build an analysis. Well, now she had a round face on the dashcam footage and an adviser stymying Britain's global ambition. Betsy knew another murder had occurred here, she just had to find out why. The thought was like an invisible shadow hanging over the otherwise perfect scene.

A whoop and shriek drew her gaze to the left, further round the walls towering over the old streets. A boy in tight red trunks was briefly highlighted against white stone as he flew through the air. A splash and more whooping from a group of teenagers watching told Betsy the boy had plunged safely into the water almost a hundred feet below. That must be where Marko Babić jumped, she thought.

Climbing yet more steps she walked round to the place the boys were hurling themselves over the edge. A dozen stone steps, flanked by warning signs, led six feet down in a curve from the main path to a small flat area. This square piece of rock had posts supporting a chain-link rail running around the outside, overlooking the drop into the sea. In the far corner between two posts about three feet apart, the metal chain could be unhooked to allow access for the next feat of machismo. The rock was full of teenage boys, some leaning on the metal chain. Betsy felt queasy just watching them. She couldn't tell if diving was encouraged or not. The effort put into constructing the platform suggested it was. The warning signs indicated otherwise. Either way, it wasn't deterring the gang crowding the launch point. Betsy had to turn away when the next boy leapt through the gap.

Once he had disappeared from view, the boys rushed off the rocky platform and back up the steps, moving as uniformly as a school of spooked herring. They were laughing and joshing each other as they pushed past the old woman.

For the first time since she had started the walk around the walls, Betsy found herself alone. She stepped cautiously down to the platform and paused on the bottom step. She wanted to look over the edge but knew she wouldn't be able to proceed unless she gripped onto something for as long as she was on the platform. The logical thing to do would be to hold onto the metal chain, but that would mean being close to the edge the whole time. Betsy was frozen with indecision.

The sound of two people coming down the steps shook her into action. She crossed the square rock to the launch point in the far corner, hoping her fear was not obvious. She felt her throat tighten when she saw that the boys hadn't fastened the chain across the gap before dashing off. With one hand digging into a post and the other squeezing the chain she peered over the edge. The wide blue sea stared back, a long way below. In the couple of seconds she allowed herself – she could already feel her legs starting to shake – she took in quite how far off to the side the rocks started. They lay against a wall supporting a path that led from the main city battlements to a lookout point. Someone intending to jump into the sea wouldn't have covered the distance to the rocks on the far side after an accidental slip. The humiliated diver might have been met with derision by the crowd, but would also have been met with water at the bottom. To leap across the distance needed to smash onto the rocks Marko Babić would have to have departed the exit gate at full sprint. He must have really wanted to kill himself. Or, Betsy acknowledged again, someone else must have really wanted it.

She left the platform to the tourists, grateful to be back on the main path. She walked for another five minutes before arriving at a bar overlooking the sea. Betsy took a seat and was happy to pay the inflated prices for a bottle of water and a sandwich. She exhaled loudly. A man and a woman, seemingly in their sixties, ran the café. Betsy guessed they were married, or possibly siblings, the way they bickered. The woman came to take her order, addressing her in English, as the man piled crates of empty bottles at the side of the building.

As she ordered her meal Betsy asked the woman if she knew of Marko Babić. She didn't get a chance to respond.

'Is definitely Russians,' the man said from the doorway.

Betsy said nothing, but saw the woman roll her eyes.

'Not Russians,' she said, 'he always says Russians. Anything bad, is Russians.'

'Is Russians!' the man said again, shrugging his shoulders and throwing his hands in the air. 'You think

Marko just jump on rocks. For what? For fun? Is Russians, for sure.'

'You don't think it was an accident?' Betsy said.

The man blew air through his lips.

'Accident. What accident? Marko dive here every day. Very good diver.'

'You knew him then, Marko?'

'For sure,' the man said, 'he drink coffee here every day. Where you sit now. Working, always working. Tap, tap, tap on computer. Pen, pen, pen on paper.'

'So not an accident?' Betsy said.

'No accident. Why you ask about Marko?' the man said.

Betsy decided to try the story she'd invented in Malaysia.

'I'm a journalist,' she said, 'From London. I don't think it was an accident either.'

'London,' the man said, 'why you think it no accident?'

'I'm not really sure,' Betsy said, 'just a hunch from a friend.'

'Hunch?'

'A feeling,' Betsy said, 'a guess.'

'Well, no guess,' the man said. 'Is definitely Russians.'

'Not Russians,' the woman said, returning inside the café.

Betsy sat in the warm shade trying to think of reasons why the British government, a troublesome foreign adviser and Russian assassins might be connected. She indulged herself by looking for an innocent explanation. Nothing came to mind. With a frown she gave up the search, a feeling of dread gnawing the pit of her stomach.

*

ChipsWithMayo was putting the finishing touches to the next steganography signal for James Easton. In a window on the computer, under the tab labelled 'MESSAGE IN CLEAR' were the words "Operation Meadowland. Date/time: no change. Sell: Gabriel Dubois. Tatiana Petrova". The Minister, however, had insisted an additional name be added. This extra detail was placing great strain on ChipsWithMayo's moral compass, jaded though it was. It was an unusual and unwelcome feeling.

The cursor sat next to the last name, blinking an almost petulant demand. Chips sighed, typed five more words and pressed enter.

A line of code immediately scrolled down the screen. The usual notifications appeared: "Building image", "Compressing", "Converting".

An audio chime and the notification "Complete" announced the image was ready. Chips clicked on a tab marked "Preview". Another screen opened next to the code. Chips tapped the tab marked "Export to USB". The new screen showed a picture of a bright red kite struggling in a stiff breeze, the line pulled taut against a menacing backdrop of purple and brown clouds.

'I know the feeling,' ChipsWithMayo said.

25.

Betsy closed her eyes and let the warm sea breeze flow over her. She tried not to think about the likely endpoint to which her discoveries were drawing her. It was increasingly hard to concentrate though, to force her mind onto the task at hand. There was a weariness stretching from her bones to her soul. It was more than mere age, she knew that. A sneering voice – hers or another's, it mattered little – laughed at the old lady's attempts to hang onto her past. You're not up to this, it said. You're ancient, past it, a relic from a bygone age. You're only fooling yourself. It kept dragging her thoughts back to the likely danger she was willingly striding towards. Striding, with friends and loved ones following.

She was running on adrenaline alone, and knew there wasn't an inexhaustible supply of that. She'd felt a physical reaction when she saw the man's face frozen on the screen from the dashcam. It wasn't an exact image, but that hadn't stopped every fibre of her being jolting with alarm. She'd been more shocked than scared when the man had chased her car down the street. Cold fear had seeped into her only later. Then the train. The lottery of life had taught her not to worry about the violence. She was either hit by debris or not.

Almost the same as stubbing a toe. So completely out of her control there was no point worrying about it. But her time in the dark, tapping the glass, that had been different. Black water, with tiny plastic bottles of air. No way of getting out. That fear had taken a grip on her soul and, finding it a comfortable and plentiful accommodation, had settled in like an unwanted lodger.

She had the connection she'd been looking for. She knew she should feel pleased about that. There were many questions still to answer, but she had a link between the USB stick and Ravi Marimuthu's murder. She had a possible motive, to boot. So why was she feeling lousy?

Because the closer she felt herself getting to the answers, the harder it was to deny she was too old for the confrontation to come.

She needed to push things on.

She'd never liked slivovitz, the Croatian plum brandy, but had used it in the past to gain a confidence or build a friendship. The camaraderie usually lasted only until the end of the mission, at which point it had been ditched as unwanted and soiled goods. She'd always been fine with that. She thought she should try the same trick now, as a way of ingratiating herself with the couple to ask more about Marko.

Her sandwich arrived. She asked the woman if she and her father – big smile - would join her for a glass of slivovitz. The woman smiled, said, 'Ivano, yes,' and called to the man. Betsy started on her sandwich. The man joined her.

'I'm Betsy,' she said.

The man touched his chest, said 'Ivano,' shook Betsy's hand and, indicating the woman now bringing a tray with two small glasses of almost clear liquid, said 'Marija, my wife.'

Betsy raised her glass.

'Marko,' she said.

Ivano said the name and touched his glass to Betsy's. They drank. It hurt. Better get a move on, Betsy thought. I can't handle many more of these.

'You don't like Russians?' Betsy said.

Ivano pulled a face.

'I had bar in Cyprus. In Limassol. Lots of Russians. Dirty money. Anything bad happen, always the Russians.'

'Not Russians,' Marija said, as she wiped a nearby table.

Ivano said, 'ach' and waved a hand at the woman, then 'Marko was good man.'

'He liked diving?' Betsy asked, miming with her hands.

'For sure,' Ivano said, 'always diving. Very good.'

Betsy wasn't sure if this last comment was directed at Marko's ability to dive or the slivovitz. Either way, Ivano leant round and beckoned Marija to refill the glasses.

'You like diving? Ivano said, smiling, now with his palms pressed together as if about to launch into the water.

'Me? Oh goodness, no. I can barely swim. I hate the water,' Betsy said.

The woman approached the table.

'What was he working on?' Betsy asked.

'Work, paper, who knows?' Ivano shrugged.

'I know,' Marija said.

'How you know?' Ivano said, 'you just make him coffee.'

Marija poured more of the sharp-smelling liquid into the glasses.

'He give me paper one day, to block hole where mouse run around. You never know this because it called hard work.'

She smiled at Betsy and returned inside the building, leaving the bottle.

Ivano had raised his glass. Betsy did the same. As she poured the drink into her mouth she watched Marija kneel down behind the counter and work a piece of folded paper loose from a hole in the floor through which a pipe descended.

'Ha, ha ha,' said Ivano. 'Is good, yes?'

'Yes,' Betsy managed.

Marija smoothed the folded paper against her dress as she returned to the table. She handed it to Betsy and she scanned the page.

'He was a human rights lawyer,' she said, frowning.

'Mmm, yes,' Ivano said. He clearly hadn't understood a word.

Betsy raised her eyebrows to Ivano whilst pointing to the bottle and, having received a hearty 'yes, yes' from the man, poured another two glasses.

'Members of the Council of Europe, reaffirming their profound belief in those fundamental freedoms which are the foundation of justice and peace in the world – I'm quoting now, from his draft letter to his boss,' Betsy said to Ivano, who happily nodded along, 'find that British military actions in Iraq and Afghanistan failed to meet the standards expected of an effective political democracy, and that the British government should be subject to the full force of European Law for the wilful contravention of Article 3, namely the prohibition of torture.'

Betsy tucked the paper in her pocket.

'To two thorns in the side of the British government,' she said as she raised her glass. Without waiting for Ivano she drained her shot and banged the glass down on the table.

And saw, across the battlements, a man with a very round face staring straight at her.

26.

Betsy threw some money on the table and stood up, fast. A bit too fast, given the slivovitz. She stumbled backwards, knocking over her chair. Ivano laughed and said something that Betsy couldn't understand. He stood to help steady Betsy. She grabbed his hand, pumped it up and down whilst saying, 'thankyou, thankyou,' and started running for her life.

She headed back the way she had come, towards the dive platform. She chanced one look back. The man was running towards her, still fifty metres short of the café, where she could see Ivano and Marija looking at her with blank faces. Her shoes slapped against the flat stone as she ran. The sound made her suddenly aware how empty the path was. No point shouting for help. Her hip protested and she knew she wouldn't be able to keep running for long. She tried to remember how far back it was to the next exit point from the wall-top path. Her eyes watered as she squinted into the light. She saw the next exit. A few turns, no more than a hundred metres and she'd be able to descend into the city and lose herself in the crowds.

Another man, similar T-shirt, cap and sunglasses, was running towards her from the front. Betsy felt her stomach lurch as she realised the second man was between her and the exit steps. She glanced over the city side of the wall. As expected it was a long drop onto rock. She wouldn't make it. She looked over the wall on the other side at the even longer drop into the sea. She swore loudly and rushed forwards to the steps leading down to the rocky square where the boys had earlier been jumping. She groped her way down, her hands running over the rough stone for support.

She scanned round for any sign of help or deliverance. The city walls were smooth; no chance of climbing down, and no loose rocks either, or anything that could serve as a weapon. She grabbed one of the metal poles holding the chain. Tugged at it, hard. She knew it was more out of hope than expectation. The pole was cemented firm. She looked over the edge and felt sick. If she jumped she'd land in the water, the rocks at the base of the city walls were well off to the side. Even so, there was no way she was jumping.

The two men exploded down the steps. They were ten feet away and didn't stop running when they reached the platform.

So Betsy jumped.

About a second later, so did one of the men.

*

Pippa Moon stood with her hands on her hips.

'Bloody kids,' she said, looking at her car.

'What's up, darling?' Meg said, as she pulled the front door closed.

'They've pulled my windscreen wipers off. I'll have to get a new pair now.'

Meg looked at the car. It was facing the garage door at the end of a long driveway.

'Pretty brazen,' she said. 'It's not as if they just whipped them off as they walked past. They would have had to come all this way from the path.'

'Probably drunk,' her daughter said. 'Or on something, you know. I'd like to bloody well catch the buggers.'

'Not sure that's a good idea, Pip. No offence, but you've never been a scrapper.'

Pippa extended her eyebrows.

'I've done boxersize for three years.'

'Just don't go looking for trouble,' Meg said.

Her daughter threw a couple of mock punches into the air.

'Boff, boff! Life in the old girl yet, mum.'

They separated at the retail park. Meg went to the supermarket while Pippa headed for the car accessories shop, thankfully open on a bank holiday Monday. When they regrouped thirty minutes later the car had new wiper blades.

'You took your time,' Pippa said.

'I'm beginning to agree with you about the kids of today,' Meg said.

'How so?'

'Twice during that trip my trolley went missing while I was off picking stuff up. It was full of shopping on both occasions so whoever took it couldn't have thought it was spare. Both times I found it parked in the next aisle. Nothing missing, just left there. Must have been kids mucking me about.'

Pippa tossed her head and said, 'kids,' to her mother, grateful to have an ally.

It was only later, at home as they unloaded the shopping, that Meg found the folded note someone had dropped in one of the bags.

Say hi to Pippa, the note said, and those lovely children of hers.

27.

Betsy hit the water like a rag doll tossed by an angry child. She was vaguely aware of something else landing nearby. Her arms and legs flailed under the water in uncoordinated mayhem before she managed to subdue her fear. Her head broke the surface and she took a lungful of air. She dipped below the water again. Held her breath. Forced her head up once more. Remembered a line from an old training course: the worst thing to do in water is panic.

She saw some rocks a few metres away and started flapping towards them. Back under the water. Back on top. Snatched breath. Slow progress, but the rocks were getting closer. She could feel a dark terror waiting for her, biding its time. It was hovering close by, but so far she'd managed to stop it crowding her mind.

Above the sound of her frantic splashing though there was something she hadn't expected: from behind her, a sharp howling. One of her feet hit gravel. Then the other. Flapping became wading. Her breathing slowed. She coughed violently and looked behind her, to the source of the rasping cries. She saw that she'd made it from the centre of the dive pool to the side nearest the city walls, stretching above her. On the far side of the deep circular landing area she saw more rocks abutting the wall leading to the lookout point.

Lying on his side on the gravelly sand next to the rocks was a man. Betsy saw that one of his legs was cocked at an unnatural angle.

Betsy guessed the injured man was one of the people that had been chasing her. Looking up, she saw a round face wearing a cap and sunglasses peering over the edge. The man lying on the sand must have jumped off the platform at such speed he had flown almost completely over the water. Betsy figured his life had only been saved because he had altered his direction slightly at the last moment and had landed in a few feet of water.

'Who are you?' Betsy called across to the injured man. 'What do you want?'

At this the man, clearly in a lot of pain, dragged himself back into the water. He started powering across the pool. He'd lost his sunglasses and cap, an action that had freed up a head of thick hair; matted and stringy now it was wet. Betsy saw muscular tattooed shoulders coming towards her surrounded by a blizzard of white foam. She realised she was still waist deep in the water. Turning, she waded desperately towards the rocks. The man caught her and dragged her down. She cried out. Betsy's head dipped below the water. She was met with the immediate taunting of her panic. Her hand dug into the gravel and she pushed herself up with a new and brutal strength. She lashed out, more in fear of the water than the man, but was relieved to feel power flowing through her arms. She realised she was clasping her phone in her right hand. His assailant was propped up on the sand, trying to grab Betsy's neck.

She wriggled free and smashed the phone into the side of the man's head, relishing the meaty contact. She followed this up with a couple of ineffectual punches, the sudden release of adrenaline filling her with a wild excitement. The man grasped at her again, unconcerned by the puny fists aimed at his head. Betsy kicked out, connecting heavily with the man's shattered leg. He yelled and flinched back. Betsy kicked again, harder this time. She aimed at the man's leg, knowing the advantage it would give her and wanting to cause pain. The man pushed her away and curled into a ball, moaning through gritted teeth. Betsy found her hands on the man's face, delighting at the sight of her nails biting into the pockmarked skin. She was overtaken by a violent urge. She was on top of the man. All the fear and anger that had been building up for the last week had finally found a release. She forced the man's face into the sand. Water and gravel flowed into the man's mouth. An inhuman sound filled the air, whether from the man in the water or from herself Betsy couldn't tell. The man was trying to grasp Betsy's arm, but there was no strength in his fingers. Betsy continued to push, watching her knuckles bulge with the effort. Ragged breathing forced spittle from her mouth, down onto the man's face. The man was choking. He was spitting water and sand onto Betsy's knees. She continued to force her weight down. Her right hand slipped and lost its grip. Her fingers, wrapped in the man's hair, dug into the sand. She remembered the feel of the woman's hair on the train; her limp body pressing against hers, and her hair tangled around Betsy's fingers. She drew her hands back sharply. The man didn't move. Betsy's chest heaved as she stared down. The man's face seemed frozen in a grimace. Betsy grabbed the man by his T-shirt and dragged him until his head was out of the water and on dry gravel. Betsy could feel a chill spreading through her body and realised she was exhausted. She became aware of the screaming pain from her hip, forcing its way through the adrenaline. The man was propped on the sand, lying still on his side. Betsy pressed her fingers into the man's neck, but they were too wet and covered in sand to feel anything. She looked up. The round face was still there, but now with a phone pressed to an ear. Betsy scuttled backwards out of the water. She clambered over rocks and through an arch, leading into the city. Her hiking boots spat water at tourists as she hobbled off, leaving the image of the man on the sand far behind her.

*

She was on a pre-determined path, she knew that now. No deviating left or right. No going back. She had to keep straight on, until the end, whatever that may be. Had she started this thing, willingly invited it in after years of stagnation? Could she have stopped it before decoding the stick? After? Could she stop it now? Now they knew she'd been to Malaysia and Croatia? They'd tried twice to stop her, with a finality she had experienced rarely even when she did this stuff for a living. At the same time she'd felt a strange thrill hurting the man in the water, as if she was taking action, taking charge of the situation, not just passively accepting whatever came her way. Refuting the years of irrelevance and sterile torpor. In the quiet moments, between the cars driving past as she approached her house – damn the risk, it's my home, she thought - she accepted that deep down she'd enjoyed it.

28.

Betsy walked past her house. She'd checked all the cars from the tube station for the number plates she had memorised and any sign of strangers sitting in their vehicles. She'd seen none. She continued scanning for the hundred yards of street beyond her front door. She knew there was no plausible reason for acting in this way, less still for a sudden about-turn, but figured if there was anyone out there in the dark waiting for her, they'd know by now she was on to them anyway. She had to take the risk.

As she approached her house for the second time her eyes darted towards movement coming from bushes in an alleyway on the far side. A figure dashed across the road towards her. Betsy flinched and braced for an attack.

'Meg!' she exclaimed, 'what are you doing here?'

'Inside! You're clear, I've been here two hours, but we've got to get off the street,' Meg said in a rush.

Betsy did as instructed.

'No lights, no noise,' Meg said.

The women blundered through the house in the dark to the kitchen at the rear. Betsy checked the back garden was clear then turned to her friend, the light from a nearly full moon illuminating the lines on Meg's face. Betsy was about to speak when Meg raised a finger to her lips, pointed at Betsy and directed her to a kitchen chair. Betsy sat down as instructed. Meg swung a backpack off her shoulders and reached inside. Betsy couldn't make out what was pulled out of the bag, but it fitted neatly into Meg's hand. A thin accessory, about six inches long, was screwed into the top of the device. Meg then plugged in a cable attached to a set of headphones, which she stretched around her head. She twisted a dial. Betsy heard a click. A faint green glow bathed Meg's face. Meg leant over the kitchen table and placed her mouth next to Betsy's ear.

'I'll clear the house, make sure there are no uninvited eyes or ears. Stay here, don't move, don't speak.'

Meg moved slowly around the kitchen, lifting the electromagnetic scanner from floor to ceiling. She looked to Betsy like an airport security guard screening travellers. Meg silently moved a chair and climbed up to sweep the top of the kitchen cupboards, out of reach from floor level. Satisfied, she moved to the hallway, dining room and sitting room. She then started up the stairs. Betsy sat alone in the dark for a quarter of an hour, tracking Meg's slow progress by the occasional creak of a tell-tale floorboard.

Meg returned to the kitchen and dismantled the equipment in the dark.

'The house is clear. All the electrics are doing what they should and there's been nothing added as far as I can tell. We should keep the lights off though and mustn't change the external appearance of the house. The curtains stay as they are.'

Meg sat at the kitchen table.

'Why did you come back?' Betsy said.

'They followed me to my daughter's house,' Meg said. 'Left a note in my shopping bag. My family were in danger. Because of me. Because of us. I had to get away. And do it in a really obvious way.'

'A note?' Betsy said.

Meg leant over the table.

'They threatened the kids!' she hissed.

'The kids? Oh my goodness.'

'I didn't see them but made a big show of leaving the house. Lots of hugs and kisses. Made it obvious I'm not going back. Then spent the afternoon shaking invisible tails. I'm not as good at it as you, I was always indoors on the computers, wasn't I?'

Even in the dim moonlight Betsy had never seen Meg look so old and vulnerable. She felt a stab of remorse for questioning Meg's loyalties earlier.

'I tried calling you to warn you but your new phone's switched off.'

'Full of water again, I'm afraid.'

'Water? What happened to you?'

She ignored the question. 'I know why they were killed. Marimuthu was an adviser to the Malaysian defence minister. Babić, a human rights lawyer. Both were making things hard for the British government to get the World Wide Britain treaty over the line.'

As she spoke Betsy rubbed the knuckles of her right hand, as if they were about to betray the violence they had visited upon the man in the water. There was tension in her voice as she worked the joints, squeezing out the fear. Major Tom arrived on her lap in one confident leap.

'Are you all right, Bets?' Meg said.

'They attacked me in Dubrovnik. I just ran. Got the first flight out to anywhere. Brussels as it happens, then got the train back here.'

Betsy could feel her heart pounding as she spoke. Part of her wondered if she'd known all along there had been an inevitability to the events she was describing. Another part wondered if she was strong enough to see it through.

She hadn't realised Meg was holding her hands until she spoke.

'Bets, we've been friends for, what, twenty years?'

Betsy said nothing and just stared at her liver-spotted hands, tracking the route of the raised veins as if they might lead to an answer.

'I've always known there were demons in your past, but I never asked. You didn't in our line of work, did you? But this is different. What we've discovered has threatened my life and the lives of people I love.'

She released Betsy's hands and threw her arms up in dismay.

'And I don't even know what the bloody information means!' The laugh she tossed out was quickly smothered. She leant back on the table, palms flat to the wood.

'So you need to give me a damn good reason not to walk out of here right now and take my chances with the police.'

Betsy pushed the cat off her lap and brushed away hairs.

'One of the names on the stick, Gabriel Dubois, is head chef at the Kremlin,' Betsy said.

Meg didn't alter her position, but the hard shell of her face broke, scattering wrinkles around her eyes as she frowned.

'The Kremlin?'

'Yes.'

'That wouldn't be a secret,' she said.

'No.'

'So the secret wouldn't be who he is.'

'No.'

Meg thought for a moment.

'The secret would be what he is.'

'Yes.'

'A spy.'

'That is my assessment,' Betsy said.

'Someone's warning the Kremlin they've got a spy in the camp.'

Betsy pursed her lips and nodded.

'The other name?' Meg said. 'Tatiana Petrova?'

'No idea,' Betsy said, 'but I imagine she's in a similar position.'

Meg sat back in the chair and smoothed her hair. She leaned forward again and her face hardened once more.

'Okay,' she said. 'That would be of great interest to my journalist friends, but why is it to you? You're retired, aren't you? Isn't this more your goddaughter's business?'

Betsy smoothed her skirt.

'As a young girl, Meg, what did you want to be when you grew up?'

'I don't care. Get on with it, I'm past playing games,' she said.

Betsy raised her face, defiance written across her features.

'As a girl, I always wanted to be an astronaut,' Betsy said. 'Of course, we called them cosmonauts.'

A pause.

'Cosmonauts,' Meg repeated.

'The first woman in space was a lady called Valentina Tereshkova. We shared a surname. And a love of science,' Betsy said. 'When I was twenty they said I was bright enough to join the space programme. Of course, I was thrilled. I took test after test, some of which bore only passing relevance to space travel as far as I could tell. I had to undergo resistance to interrogation training as a means of showing whether I had enough mental resilience for the isolation of space, apparently.' She laughed. 'Sounds funny now, to say that. I never found out if the whole space programme thing was just Party bullshit. A year after I started my so-called cosmonaut training, they congratulated me and said I'd joined the KGB.'

Betsy stared at Meg, waiting for a reaction.

Meg spoke very slowly, as if mulling the words over, even as they left her mouth. 'KGB. And yet now you live here and I've been calling you Betsy for two decades. Carry on.'

'I'd forgotten some of this until I saw you with that McDonald's meal last week,' Betsy said. 'I'd made my choice many years before the first restaurant opened in my country, of course. On the bridge in that watercolour in the front room, actually.'

'Mostar?' Meg said.

Betsy nodded. 'The rot didn't suddenly set in; it had been there from the start. I hated the system even before I knew it existed. By the time the McDonald's opened I'd spent about six years passing secrets to The Badger.'

'The Badger?'

Betsy's face brightened a little, the way a marble headstone over a fresh grave can shine in the rain.

'My British friend,' was all Betsy offered. 'A white flash through his wonderful black hair.'

'Another spook, I take it. Go on,' Meg said.

'By then, though, I'd known for some months that I was under suspicion. I wasn't willing to take any more chances, even in Mr Gorbachev's sparkly new Soviet Union. I used the Big Mac box for my sandwiches and raved about the quality of the food. I figured that by being so brazen my colleagues would think, well, she can't possibly be up to anything,' she said. 'Hiding in plain sight.'

She stared into the darkness of the hallway, allowing the ghosts of her past to swim before her eyes.

'Did it work?' Meg said.

Betsy smiled and shrugged.

'It bought me a few more days, a couple of weeks, maybe. Enough time to send the emergency extraction signal to The Badger.'

Meg stood and fumbled her way to the cabinet in the dining room. Betsy heard a clink of glass on glass. Meg returned with two large whiskies.

'How did they get you out?' she said, as she placed the glasses on the table.

'Finland,' Betsy said. 'Last few miles in the boot.'

She took a glass as Meg reclaimed her seat.

'We paused at the border. I could hear the voices, muffled, of course. I still don't know if we'd been discovered, but they suddenly said they wanted to look in the boot. The Badger accelerated. He'd picked the border post with the least infrastructure. We got through the gate. But then they opened fire. I can still hear the bullets clattering into the back of the car. One blasted through the number plate and into my hip.'

'Your hip,' Meg said. 'It still hurts, doesn't it?'

'It's manageable, with my potions, but always there,' she said. 'You look pained, Meg?'

'Seems a harsh reward.'

Betsy chuckled.

'Spies don't work for the glamour, Meg, despite what Hollywood says. Defectors, traitors – two sides of the same moral coin in the intelligence business – do it for what one side sees as a higher calling and the other as petulant narcissism. Soldiers get the parades, Meg. We spies, if we're lucky, get shrugs. I didn't want public recognition or photographs. All I got was two medals. The first was the Companion of the Most Distinguished Order of St Michael and St George, I got that one from the Queen, no less, bless her.'

'And the other?'

'A shiny red weal on my hip; a neat 7.62 millimetre circle. I got that one from a conscript's assault rifle.'

*

ChipsWithMayo closed the front door and walked the short distance to the car. In this part of London it was almost impossible to get a parking space directly outside the house. Anything less than a hundred metres from house to vehicle was counted as a win. Having undamaged wing mirrors on arrival was an added bonus.

The route to Mayfair was easy enough. Even the location for the drop-off was well known to the car's sole occupant. The only possible snag would be any one-way systems in the immediate area. For that reason ChipsWithMayo had left extra time for a good nose around to find a parking space. Time spent in reconnaissance is seldom wasted, various uniformed voices whispered from the past.

The sports car slipped easily into central London, even with strict adherence to the speed limit. No sense drawing unwanted attention from a bored police officer at this time of the morning. No speeding up on the approach to traffic lights. No need to be an amber gambler. Not tonight.

ChipsWithMayo drove on, past the gargoyles on the Natural History Museum. They leered down as if registering the darkness creeping past. Chips's hands trembled slightly on the steering wheel. Bad tarmac or something else? Sticking up for plucky old Britain, bravely forging ahead in the wide, wide world, was one thing. It was quite another to spend one's spare time arranging murders.

*

'Did you ever go back?' Meg asked.

Betsy had finished her drink and was once again staring into the past.

'There was no going back for me,' she said. 'It was fifteen years before I saw my parents again, until they were allowed to leave the country. My father never truly accepted it. He'd fought in the war, the Great Patriotic War, they called it. He didn't think I was being very patriotic. We never properly saw eye to eye again before he died. And it cost me the closest friends I have ever had: Anatoly and Svetlana Niechenko, fellow KGB officers. Their careers never recovered from the suspicion that they'd known all along.'

'Had they?'

Betsy shook her head.

'So, you took a new name,' Meg said.

'Katya sticks out somewhat in suburban London,' Betsy smiled.

'And the exotic surname?'

'Rivers,' Betsy said. 'A slight bastardisation of Trent, Mole and Helford. The three beautiful rivers I would walk next to, in between debriefing sessions at grand country houses when I first came over. I threw a lot of worries into those rivers.'

Meg studied her.

'Why are you telling me this?' she asked.

'Because you have a right to know, as you said. And also because we're nearing the end game, Meg, and I need you in my corner.'

Meg sipped her drink.

'So what happens to defectors?' she said.

'It depends how you play the game.'

'What do you mean?'

'There's an understanding between spies,' Betsy said. 'You can take an interest, you can meet old friends, reminisce, that kind of thing. No problem with that. It's fine. That's tolerated, expected even.'

Meg pointed her glass at her.

'But you've done more, haven't you? You're still on the pitch, and you're worried that one day your name's going to appear in a steg image. Close enough?'

'Close enough,' Betsy said. 'I used to brief the new recruits on the intelligence officer course at Legoland - I can't bring myself to refer in any other way to that boxy monstrosity in Vauxhall. After a few years of building trust they let me do a few other bits and pieces.'

'That must have been when we first met,' Meg said. 'These bits and pieces, they cross the line I take it?'

'It would be deemed too active,' Betsy smiled. 'If someone is surrendering MI6 assets to the Russians in return for removing obstacles to Britain's glorious future, my scalp could be a very good prize.'

Meg exhaled loudly.

'I won't say you should have told me, because I understand your reticence now,' Meg said. 'But, by fuck, I wish I'd known this a week ago.'

'Would you have stuck around if you had?'

Meg looked at her.

'We don't know it's the Russians,' she said.

Betsy looked at her and snorted. 'You're not even convincing yourself.'

'We'll know after the next drop off,' Meg said. 'Have you checked for any movement between Chips and James?'

'I've got no phone to check - we'll have to use yours,' Betsy said.

Meg searched Twitter.

'Shit,' she said. 'Another message, sent earlier today, actually,' – a quick glance at the watch – 'yesterday. Monday. They're meeting again, Chips dropping off at three in the morning, I guess. That's two hours from now.'

'We need both ends,' Betsy said. 'The traitor, Chips, dropping off and confirmation of whoever is picking up, although I'm willing to bet James Easton is a Russian.'

'We need help,' Meg said.

'Well, she got us into this,' Betsy said. 'She can bloody well help get us out of it.'

'Who?'

29.

'Whoo-hoo! I knew I was right!' Jules shrieked.

She jumped off the chair and started to dance around the kitchen, pretending to do a goal celebration. She pulled up, sore, and held a hand gingerly to her ribs. Meg stared at her from the other side of the dark room.

'My family are in danger and you're taking the piss. You'd better be as good as she says you are. And stop shouting, they could be outside listening.'

'Sorry,' Jules said.

'Right,' Betsy commanded, opening a large ring-bound street atlas of London, 'I'll do the ground brief.'

She flicked to the pages covering Waterloo and the Thames, illuminated by torchlight.

'The war walk Theatreland Under Attack starts here at the Old Vic theatre just south of the river,' Betsy said. 'It then goes over Waterloo Bridge and meanders around Covent Garden, Soho and Mayfair.'

Towards the end of the walk Betsy had marked a cross on the atlas.

'This is Shepherd Market in Mayfair. This is where the drop off will take place. It's exactly one point six miles from the start of the walk.'

'One point six?' Jules said.

'Yes. I found the number on a map.'

'Mile one point six,' Jules said again. She smiled and shook her head.

'What do you think?' Meg asked.

'Good routes in and out. Good arcs of vision. Plenty of options to get off the main track,' Jules said.

'Meg and I will cover the drop off location and impose surveillance on whoever picks up the package,' Betsy said. 'She's brought a hard drive to download the stick, as we won't be able to take it.'

Meg patted a black box on the kitchen table.

'Jules, you take Chips, the dropper-off, away from Mayfair in your car. We'll use my moped.'

'Sputnik? She's still alive?'

Betsy ignored her. She stared at the map, tapping a finger on her lips.

'How certain are we that we've seen all the traffic between ChipsWithMayo and James Easton would you say, Meg?

'Pretty sure,' Meg said. 'Why?'

'Because we might already know what's being traded tonight. If there's been nothing else sent from Chips to James Easton, tonight's message may well be just a repeat of the one I bumped into last week.'

'Yeah, I buy that. So?' Meg said.

'So if there is some sort of trade going on, the names on that stick might soon be in danger. Gabriel Dubois and, who was the other one?'

'Tatiana Petrova,' Meg said.

'Yes, thank you,' Betsy said. 'Mean anything to you, Jules?'

The younger woman shook her head.

'I need to make a call,' said Betsy.

She dialled a number. After a long wait it was answered.

'Hazel? It's Betsy. Yes I know it is. Sorry but this can't wait. Yes, everything's fine, sort of. Well if you let me speak I'll tell you. Of course I do, it's just gone two o'clock.'

Meg looked at Jules. She shrugged.

'No, it can't, I said that,' Betsy continued. 'We need to meet first thing in the morning. All right, second thing. When the morning properly starts. You know what I mean. Hazel please, this is important. You've got something running. I don't expect the details and I'm sorry this is on an open line but Gabriel Dubois and Tatiana Petrova are in danger.'

Betsy paced the room.

'Yes you do. You do. You do, Hazel. Just make the calls then meet me at seven at the Portuguese café. Yes you can, you have to. Sorry to wake you, dear. Bye, byebyebye.'

'Who did you call?' Meg said.

'An old Legoland friend. She owes me a favour.'

'Can you trust her?' Jules said.

Betsy gave the question serious thought.

'Almost certainly. But quite frankly, we're out of options. It's a risk, but I really think we have no choice.'

Meg sank her head into her hands.

'Listen everyone, I know this all feels completely beyond our control. It mostly is, but that's espionage,

I'm afraid. We're still very much in the game though,' Betsy said.

'Doesn't feel like a game to me,' Meg said.

Jules stared at her, then gave a thumbs up to Betsy.

They left ten minutes later, progressing quickly through empty streets. Few traffic lights hindered them. They approached and then crossed the near-deserted bridge outside Parliament. Lights from the Palace of Westminster, more used to bouncing off the bonnets of VIPs' cars and the attendant police motorcycle outriders, shone down on the little group, stationary at a pedestrian crossing. Big Ben marked half past two. They drove up Whitehall and paused only briefly at the lights on Trafalgar Square.

'Nice pizza restaurant down there,' Meg said, over the sound of the moped's engine. 'Italian ambassador says it's the best outside of Naples.'

Betsy looked over her shoulder at her.

'Sorry,' she said. 'A bit nervous.'

The group moved on, past the statue of Eros. Vivid colours from the billboard screens splashed over the road. They turned down an empty Piccadilly. The dark hulk of Green Park loomed into view on the left. Betsy turned off the main road, slowing as they entered the tight streets of Mayfair. She steered the moped to the side of the road. Jules pulled up alongside.

'Meg and I will leave the bike here and head into Shepherd Market,' Betsy said. 'Jules, go round to the other side.'

Jules moved off and the sound of the car's engine died as she turned a corner.

'Ready?' Betsy said.

Meg nodded. The women climbed off the moped as softly as they could. Meg followed Betsy's dark shape down an alley, a backpack containing the hard drive hanging limply from her shoulders. Buildings climbed three storeys on either side. To the left, a solid brick wall. To the right a bookshop silently became a florist's then a barber's. Red security lights twinkled in mirrors and seemed to move around in the dark as they passed. Betsy could just make out photos on the walls. Ahead, a pool of light indicated the small square of the market, in reality a no-through road. Before they cast their first shadow Betsy held her arm out, across Meg's path. They stopped.

'The one point six mile mark is in front of us, on the north west corner of the market, between that pub and the restaurant.' She didn't whisper but spoke in a low volume, her sonorous voice soaking into the dark bricks.

Betsy could just make out silhouettes of hanging baskets indicating, along the wall to her right, a pub hunkered in the darkness. A French restaurant, bathed in a murky yellow glow, faced them a little further on in the square proper. Meg nodded. It didn't seem to bother Betsy. She was already in another place. Possibly another time too.

'Of course, we've no idea how exact their map reading will be so we need somewhere that can cover the whole square. And we need to be in position quickly, it's quarter to the hour. We can risk one passage through the market.'

They resumed their movement and broke out into the relative light of the square, cast by two lampposts working hard to lift the gloom. Two other alleys emptied into the top half of the square. Meg swivelled her head round, searching for other visitors.

'Don't, Meg,' Betsy said. 'Straight ahead, just in case.'

They walked through the square. Nothing moved. Cardboard boxes surrounded overflowing bins. Windows were closed. Those that weren't covered by curtains or shutters were black. They walked past a pharmacy, a fish restaurant and a newsagent. A clown grinned out at them from a poster in the last window. Betsy had never liked clowns. She could feel her heart beating fast but found the sensation strangely welcoming.

Betsy steered Meg towards double doors at the far end of the square, set back from the pavement and surrounded by tall metal trolleys stacked with empty boxes. The light from the square had barely ventured this far, preferring to stay away from the edges of the market.

'This will do,' Betsy said.

She stepped with care over a pile of rubbish snaking towards the kerb and stood behind the trolleys. She backed into the doorway.

'Good,' she said.

Meg joined her, treading with equal caution. She didn't speak, but wrinkled her nose at the high stench of urine emanating from an unseen source.

'We're in position,' Betsy said softly.

Betsy looked out at the square, the target of her surveillance mission. She smiled into the semi-darkness. How many times had she stood in the shadows watching out for movement, she wondered. She realised with a thrill that even though she was squeezed between bins and standing in piss of indeterminate origin, she hadn't felt so alive for years.

The low drone of an engine, some streets away, forced itself through the darkness. It abruptly cut out.

'Someone's coming,' Betsy said slowly. Whether the comment was meant for Meg or just herself, neither woman knew.

*

ChipsWithMayo parked the car outside the market. It would have been possible to drive into the dead end and quickly drop off the package, but that was too risky. Impossible to see, from the low confines of the sports car, a sleepy spectator on their way to the loo glancing out at the rumble of an engine. Better to kill the sound and walk the last bit in silence, ears straining for voices or footsteps.

The path, although covered in paving slabs, was wide enough for a vehicle. Perhaps it had been a road once, Chips thought. It made little difference. There were few lights to betray a pedestrian with an elongated shadow, especially with a hood up. Even before Chips had broken into the dull light of the market a suitable drop off location had presented itself. A bin, rammed with fast food boxes, was on the corner outside the French restaurant Chips had frequented many times. Chips briefly considered stuffing the newspaper page containing the USB stick into the bin, to make James, or one of his minions, search through the muck. Why not? He'd lied about the last stick being corrupted. He'd understand the raised-middle-digit symbolism of making his people dig through a stinking bin.

But that would add time and noise. Think to the finish. The operation wasn't over until James had the stick, had converted the code and read the message. As satisfying as it would be to rub their noses – or at least their hands – in the dirt, Chips knew it couldn't happen.

Stepping into the light of the market Chips quickly glanced around. There were an unnerving number of alleys leading off, more than memory had suggested, and not much cover. Maybe James's man was already here, watching from the darkness, Chips thought. No way of knowing, not without making it obvious at any rate.

It was a stupid place for a drop off, Chips accepted that, but it had been important to keep to the routine. Her ego had demanded it. If she was going to pass on state secrets from the organisation that had turned their noses up at her application for employment, she was damned sure she'd allow herself a little giggle in the process. So, mile one point six it was. And, not for the first time, as she hid the paper with the USB stick inside, the punch line slipped from the lips of Kathryn Fieldhouse.

'Fuck you, MI6.'

30.

Whatever it was, sibling rivalry was too simplistic a term. The relationship between the twins had always been testy. Even before the squabbles for their father's attention, when The Badger and their mother had divorced, Kathryn Fieldhouse and her sister Jules had never really seen eye to eye. That had not exactly been unexpected. The parents would shrug as if to say, twins, well, must be tough for both of them. If the deterioration in their relationship had even been noticed, it was tolerated and explained away.

From their early teenage years though it became clear Kathryn was developing another, altogether darker, character trait. What had been an endearing haughtiness as a young girl had morphed into an expectation of reward and gratification. The Badger and his wife had smiled as they had watched four year-old Kathryn organising her teddies for teatime. A few years later the teddies had been replaced by school friends. Her matronly habit of running the show at birthday parties had drawn smiles from parents. But then the charming bossiness became coercion, and then manipulation. By the time that was added to a pin-sharp intellect, even The Badger – no stranger to bending others to his will – could tell they had a problem.

The army hadn't helped. It had taught her how to mould the talent and effort from a disparate group of people and use it to her advantage. But she knew all along where the real power lay.

So to politics she turned. But first there had been a Jules-shaped itch to scratch.

Kathryn had applied to MI6 as an intelligence officer. The job would be fun, a good stepping-stone. Not only that, but it would be one in the eye for her sister. The Badger had encouraged her. Betsy though, godmother and spiritual guide in more ways than one, had been hesitant with her support. Kathryn had put this down to Betsy being old and past it once the game had become too real for her.

Application tests? A doddle. Interviews? Paint by numbers. Assessment Centre? She'd felt sorry for the other attendees with no life experience from which to draw examples of strategic thinking and resourcefulness. She'd been given a provisional offer of employment, pending successful security vetting.

Provisional.

The vetting officer had spent hours building rapport, chatting, laughing. But always noting, in that little pad of hers. Always watching, as the questions hung in the air, ready to catch the tell tale giveaways of duplicity.

First memory of loss? Scribble, scribble. Most difficult decision? Scribble, scribble. When had she first seen her parents as flawed human beings? Scribble.

Kathryn failed the vetting process. No reason given. No chance of appeal. She had already resigned from the army. Her last six months before discharge had been tainted. She'd felt ashamed and angry and had had no one to turn to. Posted to a meaningless desk at Nato headquarters in Brussels she presented the world an agreeable but impenetrable outer skin. She vowed to trust no one but herself ever again.

She'd struck up a friendship with a diplomat from the Russian embassy. The fact it was unwise had been the whole point. Misha Niechenko had been a minor functionary on the Nato-Russia Council. He was exactly what she needed. Even so, it had been humiliating to be told to end the connection.

Asking her father to help had been just as galling. The Badger couldn't get her rejection from MI6 overturned, but he could get a glimpse at the vetting report. It had left him cold. True to form though, she had bent him around her little finger, until he could resist showing her the report no longer.

> Fieldhouse displays many of the character traits of narcissistic personality disorder. She confuses manipulative behaviour for resourcefulness or sees it as a measure of her ability to appeal to princes and paupers.
> Access to her affections - and her body - is brokered on strictly transactional terms as reward or inducement. On the plus side though, she is scrupulously fair in ensuring this policy is

conducted on an equal opportunities basis for both sexes.

Constraints on her behaviour are not applied by reference to any external source of authority. Instead it is she that decides where and when to stop. Of course, any limits are constantly reviewed and adjusted as her needs dictate. Boundaries, such as they are visible in her world, are simply targets to be exceeded.

She believes that rules are for fools: a guide to the weak and a challenge to the strong.

Fieldhouse is not awarded developed vetting status.

The failure was erased from history, of course. All energy was thrown into politics. Getting selected had been easy enough when the charm was switched on. Getting elected had been even easier. Once sitting on the green leather benches she'd wasted no time making her ambition obvious. The hierarchy quickly noted her name and background. Female, smart, attractive, gallantry medal; the party bigwigs fell over themselves to offer her jobs. She'd had a choice of positions. She chose the one underneath the Minister, albeit with very limited kissing.

The World Wide Britain agenda was her big opportunity. That MI6 had been tasked, quite legally, to spy on politicians and advisers from around the world with whom Britain was negotiating was a fact known to a small number of people. That the Minister was ruthless enough to want to see those opposing Britain's plans permanently removed from the process had been known only to him, until loose pillow talk doubled the number in the know. Kathryn's access to MI6 secrets through Sarah, another useful possession acquired along the way, made it possible to build a bargaining position strong enough to make the Minister's vision a reality. Voicing this suggestion had surprised them both, but then ambition can make people do the strangest things.

*

The unwelcome thoughts always rushed back after a drop off. The humiliation and bewilderment of her failure still shocked Kathryn. She decided another session in the boxing gym before work would be necessary to release the tension.

She kept to the shadows as she made her way back to the car, a different route to the one she had taken into the market. Never set patterns, never tread the same path. Afghanistan had taught her that, among other things.

'I knew it would be you,' the darkness said.

Kathryn stopped. She was in shadow, so the owner of the voice would not be able to see her face.

'I knew it would be you as soon as I heard the stupid reference to mile one point six,' the voice said from the next doorway, set back from the street.

They were alone. The street was empty and the doorway was not overlooked by residential properties.

Kathryn knew the owner of the voice would have picked a location away from any CCTV too.

'Sister, dear, how are you?' Kathryn said.

'As if you care,' Jules replied, invisible in her hiding place.

'Actually, you're right, I don't really care,' Kathryn said and made to walk past the shop.

The darkness erupted. It extended black tentacles and took physical form. Kathryn had expected the move, but not the speed. Jules punched one shoulder, spinning Kathryn round just enough for a shove on the back to have her suddenly face up against the wall. Jules pressed her weight into her sister and twisted an arm up her back.

'Good to see you, sis,' Jules whispered into an ear.

Kathryn tried to kick backwards, but Jules was ready for it and had her legs far enough apart. She twisted the arm higher. Kathryn gasped in pain.

'I heard you were around,' Kathryn managed, angered by the pain obvious in her voice. 'Telling tales out of school? Won't look good at the next vetting review.' She inhaled sharply as her arm was forced higher up her back.

'Whatever you think you're doing, you need to stop it now,' Jules said.

'And what if I don't want to?' Kathryn said.

Jules released the arm and threw Kathryn into the doorway.

'Then you'll fucking burn,' Jules said.

Kathryn leant against the window, angled in from the street, and bit her lip to mask the pain. She rubbed her shoulder, grateful for the lack of light that obscured her face. She forced her body to calm down.

'I don't get it with you, Kat,' Jules said. 'What is this obsession with power? I'm presuming that's what this is all about? Some psycho plan to get you up the greasy pole?'

'There's no point even trying to explain it to you,' Kathryn said. 'You don't get how the world works. You just like sitting in your little car watching it happen to other people.'

'Try me.'

'Alright, but do keep up, I'm only going to say this once.' Kathryn flinched as the darkness closed on her. She heard Jules snort, and sensed her back away.

'Afghanistan did it for me. I thought Iraq was bad enough. Embroiling the country in one senseless war could be forgiven as exuberance. Doing it twice was criminal. You wouldn't understand, you're happy to take whatever orders they throw at you. To change it though you need to get to the real power, and that's where I'm going.'

'Ah, the old can't-make-an-omelette-without-breaking-eggs argument. Murder was just a small inconsequential moral compromise on your way to the top, I take it? They were all making noble sacrifices were they, the people you killed? Shame they didn't get a choice though, eh?'

'You're right, Jules. The few lives lost getting the right person in the right place are more important than the millions of lives that will be saved by not starting pointless wars. Do me a favour. And there will be more pointless wars, even you should be able to see that.'

'What I see is a sociopath on an ego trip. Call it off, Kat. Whatever it is.'

'I said you wouldn't understand.'

The squeak of wood on wood reached the sisters, as a window was opened somewhere along the dark street.

'Oh, don't get your armoured knickers in a twist, no one else is going to die,' Kathryn said, 'it's just a question of politics now. Nothing for you to risk your wonderful career over.'

'She's onto you, you know,' Jules said.

'Betsy? She hasn't got a clue.'

Her words sank into the body in front of her, somewhere close.

'She's got a lot more than that. She's got your stick and the message in the steg.'

Kathryn played the only card she had.

'Betsy can't do anything. Where did I get the names from, Jules? Betsy doesn't know who to trust in Six and if she goes looking for someone, that's you fucked.'

'Other people are involved now. Kids are in danger. Do these words mean anything to you?' Jules said.

'They mean you could have been on the team, Jules, but I guess you've just not got it in you.'

A fist jabbed into Kathryn's stomach. She doubled over, sucking air in big gulps. It took some effort, but she managed to laugh.

'The funny thing is, you actually believe all that shit, don't you?' Kathryn said. 'Betsy could have stopped all this years ago. But she encouraged me – and you – to stand on our own feet. If it hadn't been for her, neither of us would have got where we are. The Badger just wanted us married off. Betsy was the only one pushing us. She's not worried about what I'm doing. She's just worried I'll get caught.'

Quite how much Jules had heard, or how long she'd stayed after punching her sister, Kathryn had no way of knowing. The darkness didn't say anything more and when Kathryn, stiffly, walked out of the doorway and back onto the street, Jules had gone.

31.

'That wasn't the Defence Secretary,' Betsy said.

'Any ideas?' said Meg.

'No. Couldn't see the face.'

The figure had arrived in the square, dropped something next to the overflowing litter bin and disappeared. That had been a minute before. The market had returned to murky stillness.

'Was it the same type of procedure?' Meg asked. 'Quick, practiced, very self-confident?'

'Yes,' Betsy said. 'Actually a bit slicker than last time. No faffing about looking for a hiding place.'

Betsy nodded her head as she watched the square.

'Let's go,' she said softly.

The pair stepped carefully over the line of cans and discarded newspapers trickling towards the kerb. They walked back into the square and hurried across to the rubbish bin. Betsy took up a vantage point from which she could see up the three alleyways leading into the square. She nodded to Meg, who knelt by the rubbish bin and swung the backpack from her shoulder. She reached out for the ball of paper left carefully by the visitor. Meg unpeeled it slowly as if it was a live grenade that could go off at the slightest touch. Inside was a USB stick.

'Oh boy,' she said.

She looked at Betsy. The older woman nodded frantically and beckoned rapidly with a hand, telling Meg to get a move on.

Meg grabbed the backpack. The sound of the zip opening was like a klaxon. She pulled out the hard drive. Pressed the power button. A reassuring blue light appeared. She inserted the USB stick into a port on the side. A small amber light next to the port started flashing.

Betsy could feel her heart pounding as she kept watch. She felt hot and could hear her own shallow breathing as she looked over at Meg with the USB stick. The light continued flashing amber. Betsy checked over her shoulders. The square seemed brighter, bigger somehow, more dangerous. If anyone appeared she would say, what? She had no idea. There was no plausible reason she could give to explain why two old women were crouched next to a bin fiddling with a rucksack at three in the morning. Betsy felt sick.

'Meg,' Betsy whispered. The meaning was obvious: hurry up.

Meg nodded. The amber light continued flashing.

Looking up the alleyway they had used to enter the market, Betsy saw a vehicle drive past on the road. She heard it stop and a door open and close.

'Ten seconds, Meg,' Betsy said.

The flashing amber light changed to steady green. Betsy's stomach lurched. Meg ripped the USB stick out of the port.

'Got it, Bets,' she said.

Betsy moved back to Meg.

'You go,' Meg said.

'No,' said Betsy.

Meg shoved the USB stick back in the newspaper. She squeezed it as hard as she could into a ball and placed it back on the ground. She grabbed the rucksack and rammed the hard drive inside. Didn't bother zipping it up. She and Betsy set off, back across the square to their hiding place. Betsy quickly started hobbling. Her groans were muted, but obvious. Meg put a hand under her forearm. Betsy didn't resist. Neither dared look back. They reached the mess of cans and liquid on the floor, stepped over the trail of litter and reclaimed their hide. Betsy held her body at an odd angle. She no longer tried to mask her whimpers. She was breathing hard and could feel her body shaking, although she knew she was neither exhausted nor cold.

A figure entered the square. A bearded man came from the alleyway the women had used. He walked slowly forwards, all the time twisting left and right. He was looking down at a bulky device in his hand.

'That's them,' Betsy said.

She saw Meg nod.

The man was a dozen steps from the litter bin. He continued to stare at the device, all the while weaving around as if drunk. The man stopped by the bin and checked over his shoulders. He faced the women's hiding place straight on, but they were the far side of the square and in darkness. As long as they stayed still he wouldn't notice them. The man bent down and rummaged through the take-away boxes crowding the bin. He unwrapped the crumpled piece of newspaper. Betsy saw him pick something up and place it in his pocket.

The man stood up and started walking back the way he had come. No weaving now. His hands were stuffed into his jacket pockets and he moved with purpose.

'Let's go, Meg,' Betsy said.

They broke out of the hide. As quietly as possible they moved swiftly back through the square to the alley. At the corner Betsy stopped. She pulled out a new phone, selected the camera function and reversed the direction the picture would be taken, as if preparing to take her own photo. Making sure her body didn't go further than the edge of the wall she held the camera on her phone into the alley. The image on the screen showed the far end, perfectly lit, with no silhouette of the man.

'It's clear,' she said. 'Let's go.'

They turned the corner and hurried to the far end of the alley. Looking left they could see the man climbing into the passenger seat of a black executive car. It immediately drove off.

'Come on, Meg,' Betsy said.

They climbed back onto the moped. Betsy started the engine and pulled away from the kerb.

'He's gone left at the lights,' Meg said.

The lights were red by the time the moped arrived. Betsy looked around the junction then, seeing no other traffic, revved the engine and drove on.

The women sped past a museum, set back from the road behind black iron railings. The rear lights of the car were visible ahead, travelling fast. It reached the main road and turned out of sight.

Betsy slowed at the junction and turned.

'Middle lane,' Meg said, 'just passing that bus.'

'Got it.'

The black car was moving around Hyde Park Corner. Betsy followed a few car lengths behind. The roads were not empty, but offered little by way of cover. They followed west into Knightsbridge. They skirted the edge of Hyde Park. The huge Albert Memorial stared down at them from the darkness. The eerie silence of the park came to an end. Just as shops and restaurants crowded both sides of the road once more the black car slowed and turned right.

Betsy followed the car into a road with embassies on both sides. She'd been here before, although never at this time of night.

'I've got a bad feeling about this,' Betsy said.

The car slowed. Betsy allowed the distance to close.

'Careful, Bets, they might double back,' Meg said.

'I don't think they're going to do that.'

The car stopped at the far end of the row of imposing buildings. A set of electronic gates slowly opened in front of the last embassy. The car drove in.

Betsy continued past and turned right at the next junction.

'Confirmed?' Meg said.

'Confirmed,' Betsy replied. 'They went into the Russian embassy.'

*

Betsy's mobile phone started vibrating.

'It's Jules,' she said, steering the moped to the kerb to answer the call. She crammed the phone inside her helmet, nodded a few times then said, 'I see. We'll meet back at your flat. We're up against the Russians. Yes, they've just driven into the embassy. We can't trust my place anymore.' She hung up.

'Don't bother,' Meg said.

'What?'

'She lost Chips, didn't she?'

'It would appear so.'

Meg exhaled loudly and for a few seconds rested her head on Betsy's back. She sat upright only as she felt the moped move away from the kerb. They continued cruising back into central London. Betsy looked over her shoulder at the ragged body clinging on behind her. She felt mercifully released from the confines of having to keep an open mind. The opposition had revealed themselves. They had one end of the mystery and a motive. All in all, not a bad night's work.

'Good job tonight with that stick,' Betsy said. 'I was worried you - '

'So that's it then!' Meg declared, gripping Betsy's waist tight. 'That's the last of your precious fact stones in place. It's the Russians! Doing MI6's dirty work! There's your analysis.'

They drove along the north side of Hyde Park towards the bright lights of Marble Arch. There were no other vehicles on the road. Betsy stretched her back but said nothing.

'We're just a bunch of amateurs, aren't we?' Meg said. 'You're broken, I'm out of my depth and the only one of us who does this for a living turns out to be pretty shit at her job. Pull over here.'

A garish oasis loomed out of the dark, signalling an all-night petrol station. Betsy eased the moped onto the forecourt.

'She's not bad at her job,' Betsy said.

'Could've fooled me,' Meg said.

Stationary, Meg struggled off the back of the moped and walked towards the attendant behind the glass.

'I wasn't saying it as a defence,' Betsy said to the silent petrol pumps. 'I was saying it as a statement of fact. One that raises many questions.'

Meg spoke briefly through the glass to the night attendant. The man reached behind him and selected a packet of cigarettes and a lighter. Meg paid and shuffled back to the moped.

'I didn't know you smoked,' Betsy said.

'Used to. Long time ago,' Meg said. 'Now seems a good time to start again.'

They crossed the river on Vauxhall Bridge. The boxy green hulk of the MI6 building squatted in front of them on the south bank.

'Always a bit too male for my liking,' Betsy said, over the sound of the engine.

'What, the staff?' Meg said.

'Oh crikey, they were easy to handle. No, I meant the architecture. All thrusty shoulders and power stance.'

'Who did you call earlier?'

'An old friend, a colleague. She'll be clocking on in that building in a few hours time. As I said, she owes me a favour.'

They continued for a few minutes in silence, until Meg let out a long sigh.

'It's the treaty, isn't it? World Wide Britain. It's being signed tomorrow. That bloody reception's tonight,' Meg said.

'We'll have to go,' Betsy replied.

'Of course we will. Well, you will. But without any evidence we won't know what we're looking for. We're dead in the water.'

They pulled up outside Jules's flat, having spent twenty minutes clearing the road for any signs of surveillance. They'd been gone for just over an hour. Nothing had changed in the street. Everything had changed in the two women.

'One step at a time, Meg. Let's check that hard drive,' Betsy said as she forced herself from the seat.

'Wait,' Meg said, 'I need to clear the flat.'

Betsy strode up to the front door of the apartment block and reached for her keys.

'We haven't got time and I'd welcome the attention,' she said as she punched the door code into the keypad by the front door. She entered the communal hallway.

'Besides, Jules is already here,' Betsy said. She indicated a battered old car, parked in a residents' parking bay next to a collection of rubbish bins. 'It's number nineteen, upstairs,' she said.

Meg stayed outside and caught the door as it swung to. She wedged a doorstop into the gap, pulled the packet of cigarettes from her pocket, took one out and lit it. Meg leaned back against the brickwork and pulled hard on the cigarette. Finished, she flicked the stub of the cigarette onto the small area of paving between the communal garden and the apartment block and went inside. She came out a moment later and rooted around in the pitch black. Meg retrieved the cigarette butt and threw it in a bin next to the door.

'Were you born near a barn?' Betsy called from inside the flat, as Meg mounted the last of the three flights of stairs. 'Either come in or close the door please.'

Meg entered Jules's flat and moved towards Betsy's voice.

'It's "in a barn",' she said.

'Pardon? What is?' said Betsy.

'The expression is "were you born *in* a barn",' Meg said. 'If you were a native of this country you'd know that.'

Meg heard Jules laugh from the room she was approaching. As Meg entered Betsy looked up, aghast, from the kitchen table. Meg grinned, but Betsy could tell it took effort.

'I'll have to work on that,' Betsy said.

Meg connected the hard drive to a computer on the table. The machines woke up and started winking at each other. Meg took a seat next to Betsy. As in the market hide, she noticed the years had fallen from Betsy's face once more.

'So these things should just talk to each other?' Jules said.

'Should do.'

The computer emitted a tinny beep and a window appeared on the screen. It was split in half. The window on the left showed an image of a red kite fighting against a storm. The window on the right displayed the word "Confidence" and a figure next to it. Betsy watched as the figure climbed rapidly from '37%' to '56%' where it paused.

'What does that mean?' she said.

'Anything over sixty-five per cent means the computer can see there is hidden text, but has to work through the least significant bits to reveal it,' Meg said.

'How long will that take? Jules said.

'Ah, that's where my expertise runs out. Could be anything from minutes to days. We'll just have to wait.'

Betsy filled the kettle from the sink and switched it on. She opened a window and retrieved her vape pen from a pocket.

'How is it?' Meg said.

'Painful. Running through the market didn't help. Sometimes I feel very old, dear.'

Jules arranged cups and tea bags. Betsy stared at her as she sucked on her vape pen, blowing the steam out of the window. The edge taken off her pain, she put the device on the kitchen cabinet and shuffled past Meg towards the bathroom.

Jules finished making the tea as Betsy heading back into the kitchen.

'We're in business,' Meg said, then, 'oh.'

She stared at the message on the screen:

"Operation Meadowland. Date/time: no change. Sell: Gabriel Dubois. Tatiana Petrova. Buy: Sarah Archer. EXTREME URGENCY."

'Who the hell is Sarah Archer?' Betsy said. 'And I don't like the sound of extreme urgency.'

32.

General Napier stared down from his plinth at the white van, stationary at the traffic lights. The green light illuminated and the vehicle, the only sign of human life navigating Trafalgar Square at this hour, pulled away into the dawn. General Napier went back to staring at the tarmac and waiting for his first pigeon of the day.

The van cruised down empty Whitehall and turned towards the Ministry of Defence. The building, all chunky grey blocks and lifeless windows, slouched by the river like a sulky teenager. Don't go expecting any fun here, the building seemed to say. An access road, blocked by a red and white barrier and guarded by a sentry box, sat to one side of the imposing walls. Beyond the thin layer of security the small road sloped down to an underground delivery area. The government-issued walls, road, barrier and guard box, including the sentry inside, were functional, unimpressive and completely predictable.

The van stopped at the red and white pole and the driver leaned out of the window.

'Good morning, Trevor,' the driver said, holding up a vehicle pass.

'Early start to a Tuesday morning for you two,' said the guard, as he gave the driver a clipboard with a form attached.

'Yes, drilling today, big noise. Got to finish before eight,' the driver said.

He scribbled on the form and handed it back.

'Well, I wish our lot had your attitude to work. Don't know what we'd do without you Polish,' said the sentry. 'Check the back?'

'Sure, sure,' said the driver.

'I always do the first one, gets the day off to a good start.'

'Yes, for sure, I know. Danny, open up the back.'

The passenger hopped out and opened the van's rear doors. The guard peered in at a pallet holding a dozen bags of cement and an assortment of tools.

'Messy business cement,' Trevor said. 'I did the patio last year. Nice job but bloody awful to work with.'

The passenger nodded along with the man's words but said nothing.

'Okay, boys, all good. One minute on the door down there please,' Trevor said. 'Enjoy your day. And mind that fancy wall.'

'Yes, good,' the driver said. 'Danny, let's go.'

The passenger closed the doors and got back in the front. The driver waved to the sentry, who waved back, and drove down to the empty underground delivery area. Security cameras watched the van descend the slope. The driver reversed towards a set of doors and switched the engine off. He held his pass against a sensor on the wall. A small red light turned green. The men propped the doors open with two bags of cement and unloaded the remaining sacks onto a platform trolley. The man answering to the name Danny, in the back of the van, handled the cement bags with extreme care. Likewise, the driver placed them delicately onto the trolley, with the concentration of a parent laying a sleeping toddler in a cot. Neither man wanted to split a bag and have cement powder pour onto the floor. Of more pressing concern though, and the reason for such tenderness, was that they had both forgotten which bag had been modified to hold the bomb.

*

'They're panicking,' Betsy said. 'If extreme urgency means what I fear it does, it means they won't have time to plan it properly. Something's spooked them. They're clearing up before the main event. I'll meet Hazel at seven and after that we'll be able to go for whoever's calling the shots.'

'How can you be so sure?' Meg said.

'This deal, this unholy alliance, the Russians aren't stupid, they wouldn't move unless they had a gold-plated deal. And that sort of thing doesn't come from MI6.'

'A politician?' Jules said.

'Yes. The sort of clout needed to set this up comes from those elected to office, not appointed,' Betsy said. 'Andrew Heath's top of the suspect list right now.'

Meg nodded.

'I'm not going to sugarcoat it,' Betsy said. 'This is a dark place. And right now we are the only lights. That's scary. I'm scared.'

'You're scared?' Meg said.

'Absolutely. I have, as you said, skin in the game – mine.'

'That is strangely reassuring.'

'It's meant to be,' Betsy smiled.

'I've put my family in danger, haven't I?' Meg said.

'The opposition have done that, not you. After I speak to Hazel I think I'll ask them for a chat,' Betsy said.

'Is that safe?' Jules said.

'I'll take precautions. Just to be sure though, will you call me each half hour from, say, twelve thirty onwards?'

'Sure,' Meg sighed.

'You've got a voice, Meg. You, me, that hard drive. It's not much, but it's real. It's a stepping-stone through the minefield,' Betsy smiled again. 'We can build on that.'

'My voice really isn't very loud, Bets.'

'It's the only one Ravi Marimuthu and Marko Babić have now. I'll deal with the opposition, you go to a public place until we decide what to do. And take a power cable. Jules, carry on at Legoland as normal, but work on those names: Petrova and Archer. Check in every hour.'

'Okay, but I need some sleep first,' Meg said, then to Jules: 'sofa?'

'End of the corridor. I'm going to grab a shower,' Jules said, lumbering out of the kitchen.

The first light of dawn edged past the neighbouring tower block and broke through the kitchen window. It splashed across the table and highlighted the sharp edges of the hard drive, still connected by a cable to the computer. Meg stood and started for the door to the hallway. Betsy stayed where she was.

'There is something else though, dear.'

The sound of the first plane of the day drifting over London broke into the room.

'In Croatia, when I had that fight,' Betsy said.

'Yes.'

'I think I hurt him.'

'Well it sounds like you needed to, Bets. It sounded like a very traumatic situation.'

Betsy nodded. 'It was,' she said.

'His people will sort him out.'

Meg turned to leave the room.

'I enjoyed it, Meg.'

The younger woman stopped and turned, but said nothing.

'I enjoyed the power. The control I had. The first thing I've been in control of since this whole bloody thing started. I hurt him and I enjoyed doing it.'

'Bets -'.

'That's not me, Meg. I don't do that sort of thing.'

Meg sat back at the table.

'Bets, you were in real danger. We do what we have to do to protect ourselves in those situations.'

'I know, but normal people don't enjoy it.'

'Stress works differently in all of us. Less than a week ago you nearly drowned in a train. Yesterday you fought off a Russian assassin. These are extreme events, Bets, there's bound to be a reaction. You wouldn't be human if there wasn't. Feelings of fear and remorse are both perfectly logical responses. They show me your emotional and moral compasses are still working correctly.'

'Maybe,' Betsy said.

'No maybe about it. Come on. I'll burn you some toast for the road.'

Meg started searching the near empty kitchen for bread.

'That's carcinogenic apparently,' Betsy said and smiled at her friend.

Meg patted her shoulder.

'The jam makes it all fine,' she said, with a smile that collapsed the moment Betsy turned away from her.

*

Trevor and boxes. Not the sharpest tool in them, couldn't think outside them. But he loved his little guard box at the top of the access road by the side of the Ministry of Defence. His personal fiefdom. His own small patch of Britannia. What he said, went, even if he was the only one around to comply.

And it was his place to think. Not a regular pastime, but necessary every once in a while. Right now he was thinking about the Polish builders. Actually they were Russians, he'd known that for a while now. The news had come as a surprise but Kathryn Fieldhouse had told him to play along. So play he had. He'd assembled a platoon of tiny covert cameras to cover the part of the renovations the Russian boys had chosen for their bomb. During each shift, alone in his box, Trevor would download the product, make a cup of tea and settle down to watch the show.

He could still remember the thrill of being asked back on one last mission. The fact it was a secret he was ordered not to tell anyone, not even his colleagues at the Ministry of Defence, made it all the more intoxicating. Can't risk anyone else knowing they're Russians, she'd said. Keep mum, Trevor, loose lips sink ships, and all that. All a bit odd, he'd be the first to admit; disconcerting to go to the office each day to wait for a bomb to be delivered, but even the small cogs have to do their bit if the great big machine is going to work. So he'd planted the cameras to record the builders hiding the device behind a bit of plasterboard. He'd made sure a few other areas were covered too and saved the product well away from the scene, ready to hand over to the subsequent investigation. He'd blame it on an outbreak of personal initiative.

Trevor watched the film of the men gingerly placing the device in the area of the newly revealed wall. They'd certainly taken advantage of their good fortune. The unexpected discovery of a centuries-old wall right next to the wine cellar offered perfect cover for their deadly package. They spent twenty minutes erecting the new plasterboard. Trevor reviewed this section of footage at sixteen times the normal speed. He liked his DIY, but watching two blokes slap on a bit of plaster would have been about as interesting as watching the paint dry, not that they were ever going to get round to the decorating.

He knew what they were going to do. He knew where they were going to do it. With a sigh of relief he could happily report now that the task of securing the footage had been accomplished. The way Trevor saw it, that was Phase One completed. He had a few hours until Phase Two commenced. When he'd first been brought into the plan he'd had a question at this point: what plausible reason could a man have, even a guard at the Ministry of Defence, to start smashing through new plasterboard walls? No matter that hello-ello-ello, he'd discover a bomb, without a decent reason for all the muscles, questions would be asked.

So he'd asked his question, but he hadn't worried. Trevor didn't do that sort of thing. The army had taught him how to keep calm in stressful situations. It had also taught him how to spot a good leader. A good leader thought of everything. The best leader he'd ever followed had told him to carry a big stick one night, when they'd snuck into a village in Afghanistan. Why carry the stick, he'd said, there's bound to be something to tie the flag to and it keeps poking me in the arse. Carry the stick, she'd said, just in case. She'd been right, of course. Without the stick the mission would have failed. She'd earned his respect on that tour, big time. As a boss, she was one in a million. So he wasn't worried about asking his question. And of course she'd had an answer ready. An anonymous tip-off called into the main switchboard would get everyone on shift searching for a bomb; all the cover he'd need to start tearing the place apart.

He watched the image on the tiny screen of the two men shuffling about in their baggy jeans. He chuckled, clicked the power button off and went back to being master and commander of his little sentry box.

*

Betsy was scared. She'd not lied to Meg about that. She had skin in the game, she'd said. That had been a truthful but incomplete description of her situation. Her concerns for herself were not insignificant; she'd long ago decided every new dawn was a bonus and if not exactly expecting her story to come to a swift and unglamorous end, she knew it was a daily possibility and that her continued good fortune was, to a certain degree, mortgaged to the whims of others. She had come to accept the limitations of her ageing and damaged body. It irked her, but she had also come to accept society's assumptions about the role and value of an old woman. It wasn't just the skin she had in the game that nagged at her though. It was also her identity. She'd left her first one behind when she was spirited out of Russia. She'd lost a second when her husband had died. Married five years after her defection, their happy ever after had lasted only another four, before Barry was snatched from her. No time at all. A few memories and some silly stories of plans for the future. "B and B's B & B" in Cornwall with special rates for ex-spooks being the most ridiculous. Still, they'd laughed at the thought, happy, finally, to allow themselves the indulgence of planning for a life outside the shadows. But shadows have a way of creeping over you when you stop moving. Barry had found that out the hard way. Betsy had had to live with the knowledge ever since, her life consigned to wondering what might have been and toasting her husband's memory with his favourite drink: Old Fashioned, with extra ice for American guests, just as Barry had taught.

Recently though, and more worryingly, Betsy had felt the identity she'd invented along the riverbanks start to slip through her fingers too, like a favourite old coat was beginning to sag in the wrong places. She wasn't sure who she was anymore, what her purpose should be. It was as if her past had caught up with her and was asking questions to which she had no answers. She remembered her last trip to the dentist. 'We'll have to take a couple of X-Rays,' the impossibly young man had said, 'to chart the rate of decay.' Betsy had scoffed at the thought. 'You don't need an X-Ray to tell you that,' she'd replied.

'Tell me again about Shepherd Market and the drop-off,' Betsy said, joining Jules in the kitchen having checked on the slumbering Meg.

'Wow, easiest debrief ever,' Jules said. 'I didn't see anybody. Simple.'

'It's not that big an area,' Betsy said. 'Not so many ways in and out on your side to have eluded a professional.'

Jules cocked her head to one side.

'So, I'm either no good at my job or on the inside, is that it?' she said.

'Oh don't be so melodramatic. I'm surprised, dear, that's all,' Betsy said, watching closely as Jules shuffled through unopened mail. 'Quiet night, no other traffic. I'm just surprised.'

Jules put the letters down and turned her attention to the limited contents of her fridge.

'Well this game is full of surprises, you know that better than anybody,' she said.

Betsy looked at her goddaughter. 'Don't I just,' she said, as she took another puff on her vape pen.

33.

Hazel Muir, Director of Covert Operations at MI6, was grumpy and tired, and it was only Tuesday. The coffee she'd inhaled prior to leaving her house had yet to give her the buzz she needed to kick start the week. Or maybe it had. Maybe, compared to the jolt to her system Betsy's phone call had caused, the coffee had no way of competing.

'Sorry I'm late, dear, the busses must still be on the bank holiday schedule,' Betsy said as she shuffled towards the table.

Their embrace was business-like, but Betsy added a back rub as a reminder of the friendship she was about to play on. They sat alone in the café. An enormous photograph along one wall, taken from the sky, looking down on Lisbon, dominated neat tables laid for the day. The picture stretched over one entire side of the building. The opposite wall was mostly mirrored. Diners were treated to the impression they were flying over the Portuguese city.

'It's been too long, Betsy, you look well,' Hazel observed, as the waitress laid out menus on the other tables.

A cool start, Betsy thought. Non-committal, shows her guard is up. Good. She needed Hazel to be at her professional best the moment the waitress disappeared with the order for two coffees.

'Gabriel Dubois and Tatiana Petrova,' Betsy said. 'I don't know and I don't care, but get them out.'

Hazel winced at the names. Hearing them outside the tight confines of the fourth floor of the office was alarming and surreal.

'I don't know who - ' she attempted.

Hazel stopped talking. Betsy was glaring at her.

'When I came over from the other side, I had to do my time in the wilderness,' Betsy said. 'I was then allowed to eke out my career for a few years, some of it trying to keep you gainfully employed if you remember?'

Hazel remembered.

Working on a case to an insane deadline a decade before, Hazel had taken a document graded secret from her MI6 office to read at home. She'd been so busy she'd forgotten a colleague was having engagement drinks at a local pub. Hazel had dashed into The Black Cat as she passed, just to show her face. She'd showed a lot more when she left her copy of the day's newspaper next to her table containing the secret document. It had taken her two hours to get home, panic, remember where the document was and return to the pub just as it was closing to grab the paper. Quite what the bar staff thought of a crazy lady demanding to be let back in to the pub to retrieve a newspaper, she never explored. But she had told

Betsy of the possible compromise. Betsy had let her sweat overnight – an expected but no less unnerving wait – before informing her the next day that she would not be taking the matter further. Could have been a career-ender, that one. Hazel had never forgotten it. Neither, evidently, had Betsy.

'How the hell do you know about them?' Hazel hissed.

Betsy fired information: Intercepted USB stick; communication between two people on twitter; Operation Meadowland; investigation of suspicious deaths ('What made you look at them?' Hazel had tried, to no response); discovery of Dubois's identity; Kuala Lumpur; Dubrovnik; the World Wide Britain Treaty; Shepherd Market; Russian embassy.

Hazel had always looked up to Betsy. She had steered her career as an intelligence officer, if not actively manipulated it to take advantage of opportunities as they arose. So she knew better than to dismiss her revelations out of hand. In the silence after Betsy finished talking, Hazel pursed her lips and stared longingly at the peaceful streets of Lisbon.

'You've given me a hell of a morning,' Hazel eventually said. 'I had to wake up the Resettlement Team leader and call a possible Operation Congraze, in readiness for an emergency extraction.'

'Two extractions,' Betsy said, 'and nothing possible about it.'

'I then had to brief the head of the Russia desk,' Hazel continued, ignoring Betsy. 'I've warned off the Chief's outer office and have to give an operational update in,' a check of the watch, 'thirty-five minutes.'

'Oh, the resettlement bean counters are only interested in the money. Cost of new identities and home security kit, you can ignore them,' Betsy said.

'Thank you for the advice,' Hazel said.

'You can't ignore this though Hazel,' Betsy said, 'you have to convince them. You're the only person who might listen to me. I know they'll want to try and sweat it out, keep the agent in place and not draw attention. But it's beyond that now.'

'Is it?'

'Yes,' Betsy said. 'I know it will confirm them as assets and that may compromise other operations, but get those people out.'

The women stopped talking as the waitress approached with their drinks. They dismissed her enquiry about food orders as quickly and politely as possible.

'It's not that simple,' Hazel said, once the waitress had returned behind the counter to stare out at the street. 'It took years to get them there. One of them was the Chief's personal work. He won't want to risk that on the say so of a ghost. No offence.'

'None taken,' Betsy said, without conviction.

'They're delivering really good stuff. One especially,' said Hazel.

'Dubois?' said Betsy. 'The chef, what does he know?'

Hazel ignored the question.

'Actually it's the other one doing the real damage,' she said.

'Petrova? Who is she?' Betsy said.

Hazel did her best to smother the smirk of professional pride that broke out across her face.

'Putin's personal dog walker,' she said. 'Hears everything, especially at the dacha.'

'My word,' said Betsy, 'what a scalp. Well done indeed.'

'Thank you,' said Hazel.

The women sipped their coffee, Betsy first raising her cup to Hazel in mock salute.

'I have friends in danger, Hazel. I'm not interested in your business, but I need to stop whatever's happening. How's Goldhawk?'

Hazel stopped smiling. She stared at the photograph of Lisbon and wished she could be down there, on the warm streets.

'I brought Irina Sokolova into the building, if you remember. Kept you in there as well,' Betsy said.

Hazel sighed and rubbed her eyes.

'I didn't know there was a use-by date for loyalty,' Betsy continued. 'What other qualities might I have to get rid of before they turn sour? Trust? Friendship?'

'We shouldn't be having this conversation,' Hazel said.

'But we are,' Betsy said. She leant over the table. 'Someone has been trading Legoland assets for favours with the Russians in a bid to derail the World Wide Britain treaty. It's due for signing in a little over twenty-four hours and there's a target-rich environment gathering tonight for canapés in the Ministry of Defence. So pardon me for giving a modest amount of shit about it.'

Hazel stared hard at her companion. Betsy sat back in her chair.

'You didn't used to swear.'

'You didn't used to let bureaucracy get in the way of doing your job.'

Neither woman spoke. Hazel checked her watch. Thirty minutes to the operational update with the head of MI6.

'Look,' Betsy said, 'the Russians are very good at this game, that's what makes them so much fun. But they know how to handle risk. There's an elected official somewhere in this.'

'I agree,' said Hazel.

'So I ask again, how's Goldhawk?'

Hazel sighed, but stayed silent.

'Events are moving now at a speed you cannot match from a standing start,' Betsy urged. 'Plus, of course, there's the inter-agency treacle you'd need to wade through if you wanted to motivate the cousins on the north bank to launch an operation inside the UK. I'm up to speed, and unencumbered by protocol and misplaced optimism.'

Hazel started speaking, but so quietly Betsy had to strain to pick up the words.

'About six months ago Goldhawk reported that her boss, the FSB Resident - she's been promoted since you left - had gone on a very secret meet with a new contact,' Hazel said.

'Who is the Resident?' Betsy said.

'Dmitri Goncharov,' Hazel replied, not meeting Betsy's eyes. 'Goldhawk said normal procedure hadn't been followed. He'd logged nothing, drove himself. We think he only shared the new contact's name with his deputy, Niechenko.'

'Not Misha Niechenko?' said Betsy. 'Former GRU? Good hair, winning smile? Used to be based in Brussels on the Russian team at the Nato-Russia Council?'

'Yes, that's right. Know him?

'Only as a baby. I know his parents,' Betsy said. 'Knew his parents,' she corrected.

Betsy's face darkened. The waitress appeared at the table to ask if they needed anything else. Betsy didn't answer and seemed not to notice the woman's presence.

'No. Thankyou,' Hazel said.

Betsy shook her head. 'The wheel turns again,' she said.

'Goldhawk reported Goncharov met the contact on November fifth, she remembered it was firework's day,' Hazel said. 'Now that's all I can tell you. I have to get to this meeting.'

Hazel stood. She pulled a ten-pound note from her purse and tucked it under her saucer.

'I'll make some calls about the treaty business and I'll get our people out,' Hazel said.

Betsy hadn't moved. As if a switch had been flicked she suddenly looked up at her companion.

'What? Oh, yes, dear.'

Betsy suddenly gripped Hazel's arm.

'Oh my goodness, I nearly forgot,' Betsy said. 'One more name. Sarah Archer. Know her? I think the Russians are going to take action against her imminently. The stick said extreme urgency. That can't be good. Who is she?'

Hazel's face sagged, her mouth hung loose.

'Sarah - '

'Sarah Archer,' Betsy insisted. 'Who is she?'

'She's one of my admin staff. She knows the identity of every agent we've got running. What the hell has she got herself into?'

'Worry about that later,' Betsy said. 'She's in danger. Where is she now?'

*

The park was filling up with people enjoying the break in the recent bad weather. Sarah Archer had stuck to the paths – impossible to negotiate soggy grass in white trainers – on the way to her favourite café by the canal. It was her day off and she needed a slow start and a strong coffee to gather her thoughts. She knew her relationship with Kathryn Fieldhouse was toxic, one-sided and bad for her. But she couldn't stop. She'd never been that successful when it came to romantic relationships and had been as shocked as she had been thrilled when the MP had made it clear she sought more from her than just the odd briefing in MI6. As a member of the Intelligence and Security Committee Kathryn had visited regularly. She and the other parliamentarians had received briefings at the highest level. Sarah had administered the meetings and she and Kathryn had exchanged glances, smiles and knowing looks over the years. As a lowly admin clerk Sarah had been flattered to receive the attention Kathryn had poured over her. She knew she shouldn't really be talking about work outside the building, but figured Kathryn was on the committee so it wasn't like she was blabbing to a total stranger who didn't have security clearance. At first she'd felt a bit uncomfortable discussing the actual names of agents MI6 had running around the world; real-life identities of such people being the crown jewels of the intelligence business. But as Kathryn's affections had blown hot and cold Sarah had found dropping those juicy titbits into their conversations had been the only way to keep her interested.

She eventually found herself by the canal. The gentle current wafted reeds towards a small weir, bubbling under a pedestrian bridge. Unlike the main park, clogged with dog walkers and caterwauling children, the stretch of water was empty. She started along the towpath, only slightly less muddy than the park, towards the café. Sarah was happy for the ten-minute's silence it would take to get there. The narrow track was flanked by long grass and a high hedge. A man slid down the muddy bank next to the bridge up ahead. He had to grab the wall to stop himself toppling into the canal. As he did so his short jacket rode up as he threw out an arm for support. Sarah saw a black lump tucked into his waistband.

Before she had a chance to shout, the man was pointing the gun at her. He advanced, arm outstretched, skin pulled tight across his clenched jaw. Sarah looked from his face to the gaping black hole at the end of the barrel. She tried to walk backwards but her foot slipped and she stumbled. The trip served to electrify her from panic into action.

'All right, chief, no need to be hasty,' she said, a hard edge of confidence in her voice, honed in the training camp.

Sarah strode forward, hands up, as if in an old war movie. The gunman was five feet in front of her but she kept walking.

'Just take it easy, chum,' Sarah said as she closed the gap to the man. Her hands were pointing straight up, fingers clenched tight as if in a salute. The man had stopped walking but hadn't lowered the gun. His blue eyes were fixed on the young woman, inexplicably walking slowly, but with purpose, towards the firearm. Sarah kept moving until the barrel was almost touching her chest.

'Kids near, sonny,' she said. 'Don't be an idiot.'

Her mobile phone started ringing.

*

Hazel had had to walk for about ten minutes after leaving Betsy before making the call. Standard procedure said no mobile phone calls were to be made anywhere near the MI6 building, as if hooking to a mast a few hundred metres away would make any difference. If the opposition were tracking phone data to the extent they could detect cell tower usage, they would be good enough to pick out which phones always seemed to go dark around Vauxhall. Still, rules were rules.

'Sarah, it's Hazel Muir. You are in danger and are to initiate Operation Hudson immediately,' Hazel said into the voicemail, giving the instruction for Sarah to move to a designated safe place and call into the office as soon as possible.

Hazel had walked as far as Kennington to make the call. She quickly stopped in at a building supplies warehouse for a colour chart of house paints to cover her immediate return to Vauxhall via the same route, hoping the time spent disassociating from her office wouldn't make any difference.

*

Sarah stood in front of the man with the gun. The phone in the pocket of her jeans had stopped buzzing.

'No need for this, chum' she said.

The man didn't move. Neither did the gun. The man had adopted a classic shooter's stance: feet level and shoulder-width apart. His arm was extended and he held the weapon tightly in his right hand. The fleshy pad of his index finger rested on the trigger.

Sarah looked at the man's face, than at the black metal lump pointing at her chest. Her gaze came to rest at the man's wrist and didn't shift from there. In one swift and violent motion Sarah chopped her hands across the front of her body. Before the gunman had time to react Sarah's right hand punched into the wrist supporting the weapon. The sudden blow to the tendons in the man's arm made the digits on his right hand involuntarily jerk. His index finger could not bend far but came off the trigger and snapped into the curved metal guard of the pistol. At the same time, the tight grip the man had on the body of the weapon was released as his thumb and remaining fingers twitched. A fraction of a second later Sarah's left hand slammed into the foresight at the end of the barrel. With nothing left to support it the weapon flew from the gunman's grasp into a clutch of stinging nettles by the side of the path.

The man's face registered alarm. Whether by the explosive action to disarm him, or by the heels of both hands that then cannoned into his chest, propelling him backwards into the canal, Sarah couldn't tell, and didn't care.

She ran. As fast as she could, arms half pumping, half steadying as her trainers slipped on the greasy surface of the towpath. She heard no shouts from the man in the water, but wasn't about to turn and check on him either. A young couple were approaching from the direction of the park, arm in arm. The look on Sarah's face obviously shocked them because they stopped in the middle of the track, staring at the woman hurtling towards them.

'Police, get back!' Sarah yelled, knowing most people responded almost robotically to a command from the law.

The couple didn't move. They were rooted to the spot. Sarah cursed and bundled into them, wrapping her arms around their shoulders to try to steer them away from the man who had attacked her. The couple both wore bulky wet-weather jackets. The thought briefly crossed Sarah's mind that such clothing seemed an unnecessary precaution for the slightly inclement weather, but who was she to judge? Given the lurid colours they were probably a throwback to a ski holiday in the eighties, she figured. Sarah almost laughed as an awkward dance ensued when she tried to spin the bulky forms round on the sticky path and push them back towards the park. She felt a scratch against her wrist and drew her hand back sharply. A tiny red dot of blood smudged against her sleeve. Must have caught on an old zip, Sarah thought. The couple were turning, but slowly, seemingly more interested in Sarah than any effort to run.

'P'lice,' Sarah shouted again, 'gerraway.' Was that her voice? Her lips felt numb, legs weak. Her head swam and her back prickled, almost to the point of pain. She felt sick, drunk? No, how? The question itself didn't make any sense. What was happening to her? She wasn't pushing the couple any more, she realised, she was now clinging on to them as she fell forward, her legs refusing to execute the command her brain had sent. Which was what? She couldn't remember, couldn't think straight. Her whole face had seized, legs and arms too. The pain in her back was overwhelming. She wanted to scream, call for help, but no words came out. Two faces were staring at her. The couple on the towpath. Are they here to help? The woman was taking her clothes off. What? No, just the jacket. Turning it inside out and donning it once more, the exterior now black. The man smiled. Why? Can't he see I'm in pain, Sarah thought. She felt herself lifted from the floor and guided by the pair. The man spoke. 'Enjoy the Fugu,' he said, 'happy fishing.' A shove, falling, water. Fugu, she remembered with possibly her last conscious thought. The Japanese fish, more poisonous than cyanide. Can kill a human if not treated immediately then disappears from the system, leaving no trace. The scratch at her wrist. The man in Malaysia. She rolled in the water, eyes open to the murk. She was still conscious as her paralysed body involuntarily started gulping water, desperate for air.

34.

The younger man paused at the top of the steps and placed his coffee cup on the stone wall. He answered the phone that was ringing in his pocket. Ten seconds later he hung up without saying a word. Picking up his cup again he followed the older man down into the ornate garden. The windows to the summerhouse on their right were thrown open to receive the sunshine streaking across the length of Hyde Park. It was too good a day to sit indoors the older man had said, so a stroll around the manicured grounds to enjoy the rare thrill of a brilliant London summer sky had been ordered. Plus, of course, there were no microphones outside.

'That was the team. It's done,' said Misha Niechenko.

Dmitri Goncharov smiled. He pulled the stem of a rose towards his nose and inhaled deeply. Niechenko waited patiently for the power play to run its course.

'And the other thing?' Goncharov said.

'The device is in the wall, directly next to where the speeches will be made.'

'The saddest part of being a gardener is the need to cut the heads off beautiful flowers after they bloom,' Goncharov said. 'They still have much to offer, yet we cruelly chop them down regardless, thinking only of the future.'

Niechenko said nothing, preferring not to flatter his preposterous boss with words of encouragement.

'What a wonderful summer it has been,' Goncharov mused.

The men strolled through the gardens of the Russian ambassador's residence. Pastel coloured stones crunched underfoot. The older man sucked on a cigarette between theatrical gestures with petal and leaf, attempting to show his appreciation of culture.

'We have the old place eating out of our hands and the sun is shining on us, in more ways than one,' he said.

In reality, as Misha Niechenko knew full well, Dmitri Goncharov was a dangerous thug. Not that thugs can't appreciate culture, just that Goncharov was that type of thug who didn't, but pretended he did, and looked poorly on anyone who pointed out the difference.

'Even history smiles on us Misha. The stonemasons that built that wall five hundred years ago had no idea it would be providing such a service all these centuries later.'

Goncharov stroked a leaf hanging from a low tree branch, then frowned and wiped his fingers on his suit jacket.

'Buying up those building firms and waiting for the call to come was a smart move. I've made sure your efforts have not gone unnoticed.'

Niechenko dipped his head and smiled in gratitude. He picked up the casual slight, the easy put down. The whole thing had been his idea, his contact and his plan, but that hadn't stopped his boss claiming it as his own when it started producing top grade product.

'Today will be a good day,' Goncharov said.

Although he detested his boss, Niechenko was careful around him. He was only too aware of the man's power and fragile ego; a combustible mix. Plus, this was Niechenko's first tour on promotion. So he courted his senior, never overstepped the mark and even admired and envied him on a certain level.

'What time is the speech tonight?' Goncharov said.

'Eight o'clock,'

'That's the time you've picked for activation of the device?'

'Yes.'

'And the power management intervention?'

'Quarter to. The St Petersburg factory will play around with the system but leave enough power so they don't cancel the event. The lights will stay on, for example. But there will be enough clues for tomorrow's investigation to suggest a gas leak and fire.'

'Good. And what time will our asset leave?'

'They will both be attending. The Minister will leave just after seven on urgent business. The woman will leave half an hour later.'

'Bring all our timings forward forty-five minutes,' Goncharov said.

Niechenko paused. He could see the trap laid out in front of him, as if his boss had scraped his heel in the gravel right by his feet. Even so, he didn't like so obviously contradicting his superior.

'Sir, we have no way of informing the assets of the new timings.'

Goncharov sucked his cigarette, sniffed at another rose and exhaled smoke over the plant.

'The Minister will still be clear, it is not a problem.'

Niechenko's neck felt hot. Hotter than it should have, given the weak forenoon sunlight.

'Sir, the other asset will still be in the building. You can't -'

'I can't what?' Goncharov said, turning to face the younger man.

'Sir, I meant, wouldn't it be better to run her as an asset? She's well placed.'

Goncharov arched his eyebrows.

'No. No I think we stick with the new plan.'

Niechenko could see one of the FSB team walking from the stateroom onto the balcony. He was scanning the garden, evidently looking for the two men. He spotted the Resident and Deputy and raised his hand in acknowledgement. He then started down the stone steps. Niechenko estimated he had twenty seconds to talk to Goncharov before the man reached them through the winding path, ending the discussion and any chance of talking his boss round.

‘Sir, please, I really think -’

‘You really think what Mikhail Anatolyevich Niechenko? That we just let your tart wander into our business and go about as she pleases. You’re new to this boy so I’ll forgive you this once, but don’t ever question me again.’

Niechenko dropped his head.

‘I’m sorry Sir, I regret my actions.’

‘Not at all, Misha,’ Goncharov said, tapping the young man on the elbow. ‘An Englishman once gave me a piece of advice that I’ve found very useful over the years. Actually, it rhymes in his mother tongue, which is how I’ve remembered it,’ he said, stepping closer and lowering his voice. ‘If it fucks, floats or flies, it’s better to rent than to buy.’ He leered at his deputy, displaying nicotine-stained teeth and a mouth ulcer on the inside of his lower lip.

The man approaching down the path slowed as he reached the Resident and Deputy.

‘Alas, it is as I say,’ Goncharov said, speaking louder and moving away from Niechenko to continue his wandering, ‘we cut the heads off beautiful flowers when they still have much to offer, thinking only of our future.’

The man addressed Goncharov.

‘Sorry to interrupt Sir. We have a technical development.’

Goncharov waved a hand at Niechenko and turned back to the roses.

‘What is it? Niechenko demanded.

'Our technical device,' the man said, 'the one that was intercepted a week ago.'

'What about it?'

'It's appeared again. An hour ago. It has been geolocated.'

'Where is it?'

The man pulled a piece of paper from his pocket.

'The team have it static in number 72 Hollett Road.'

'Who lives there?'

'One occupant only. A woman. Betsy Halmore-Trenford. No, Trenmore-Halford. Yes, Betsy Trenmore-Halford.'

'A woman?' said Niechenko, 'Trenmore-Halford?'

'Yes sir. I've sent Viktor to retrieve it.' He handed over the piece of paper.

Niechenko was silent for a moment, staring at the name.

'Tell him not to harm the woman. I'll go there now.'

'Sir?'

'Just do it,' Niechenko snapped. 'And tell him to be careful.'

'Of course sir, but he won't need it. She's just an old woman.'

*

Thirty minutes after Betsy removed the USB stick from the signal-proof bag and gave it a much-needed boost of power from her computer hard drive, she noticed the same car pass her house for the third time. It was a big risk returning to her house, but one she knew she'd had to take. She unlocked the back door. The armchair next to the fireplace was shifted to cover both the dining room and the doorway into the front room from the hall. Betsy prepared herself, sat and waited.

Five minutes after the hall clock had marked eleven o'clock the back door creaked. Betsy heard someone step into the kitchen. From the armchair she watched a figure slowly emerge from the hallway into the dining room next door. The man was short, thickset. As he entered the room Betsy could see he was the same man she had encountered on her car bonnet and on the ramparts of Dubrovnik. He was carrying a hand-held radio frequency detector, identical to the one Betsy had relieved him of as he lay broken on the pavement.

The pair stared at each other.

If the man was disappointed to see her, his face gave nothing away to Betsy. He would have been hoping to find the house empty, she knew that, but as a professional he would be quite accustomed to small hiccups like this during an operation. Betsy was, however, delighted to note a slight squaring of his shoulders. It told her that even if the man had anticipated finding someone in the house, he certainly hadn't expected to find an old woman sitting in an armchair pointing a gun directly at him.

35.

‘Where is the stick?’ said the man.

‘Call your boss, the deputy. Tell him to come here,’ Betsy said.

‘Now you listen,’ said the man, ‘where is the stick?’

For all his bravado though, the man hadn’t moved from the dining room. Betsy hadn’t moved from the armchair either. The Nagant revolver hadn’t moved from her hand.

A side table occupied the space where the adjoining wall had once separated the dining room from the front room. On the table sat a large glass apple-shaped lamp with an equally big shade. A soft light glowed through the cream material. The man laid his left hand on the light and drummed against the glass with sausage-like fingers.

‘You give me stick or this light go through your head,’ he said.

‘Sorry, dear, I don’t follow. I do what or you’ll what?’ Betsy said.

‘I say, you give me stick or -’

The glass dome of the light exploded. The gun returned to its level position, a thin trail of smoke rising from the barrel. The bulb remained illuminated and collapsed, still inside the shade, to land at the man's feet. His hands had snapped to his ears.

'Call Niechenko,' Betsy said. Whether the man heard her properly or not she had no idea. Her ears were ringing so much she'd barely heard her own voice. She'd only registered her words from the inside, the name echoing around her skull like an accusation.

The man seemed to understand. He slowly lifted a mobile phone to his ear and spoke quietly into it. Or he could have been shouting. Betsy had no idea really.

Neither person moved. The gun was still, the brief twitch as the bullet erupted from the chamber just a memory for them both.

'I would imagine we'll have to wait a while,' Betsy said. 'Unlike some who enjoy breaking into old lady's homes, I consider myself to be possessed of proper manners. So ordinarily I'd invite you to sit down. But I'm not going to. You can stand where you are now you've made my lamp break.'

The cat stalked into the room, as if checking up on what all the noise was about. It ignored the man and hopped up instead on the sofa. Betsy picked up the remote control for the television. She selected a radio channel.

'Do you like classical music?' she said.

The man did not reply.

'Very well then, classical it is.'

Heavy piano chords thumped into the room.

'Ah, Rachmaninoff, how appropriate,' said Betsy.

After one news report and two advert breaks Betsy heard a car pull up outside the house.

'Is that him?' she asked the man.

He craned his neck to see out of the front window. Betsy watched the folds of his skin stretch and smooth like an unspooling hose. He nodded.

'Be a good boy and go and let him in,' she said.

The man did as he was told. Betsy moved to the front window to check only one other man entered the house. She heard the front door open and two sets of footsteps approach on the varnished floorboards. She reclaimed her seat in the armchair.

A man appeared in the sitting room doorway. He was in his mid-thirties, smartly dressed with a wonderful sweep of black hair.

'Misha, dear,' Betsy said, standing and tucking the gun into a pocket of her cardigan. 'I've not seen you in years, you probably don't remember me.'

The man flashed a brilliant smile and approached her.

'Of course I remember you,' he said.

They embraced and kissed three times on the cheeks.

'Mrs Trenmore-Halford, I am so glad to see you again,' said the man.

'Betsy, dear. Sit down,' Betsy said as she turned the radio off. 'Tell your man to make us some tea then leave us alone. He knows where the kitchen is, I left the door open for him so he wouldn't bugger up my lock.'

Misha Niechenko spoke quickly to the other man without smiling. The man hesitated then slowly walked along the hallway to the kitchen at the rear of the house.

'So, how have you been since Brussels, dear,' Betsy said. 'Tell me everything.'

'Ha!' Misha accidentally released. He immediately regretted his lack of discipline. He plumped a cushion at the end of the two-seater sofa as he composed himself. The sudden activity made the cat jump off the other end.

'Let's say I'm very happy to be in London,' he said.

'Catching up with old friends,' Betsy said flatly.

Misha shrugged and deployed the smile again.

The clock in the dining room sounded half past midday. Betsy's phone started ringing.

'Hello, dear,' she answered. 'Yes, all fine. Just as I expected. I'll call you in thirty minutes.'

Misha nodded his understanding. 'It's good to have friends looking out for us,' he said.

Betsy knew her life was in danger, even with the precautions she'd taken by arranging the 'operations normal' calls with Meg every half hour. But she needed information from the man sitting opposite her. Plus, she had to convince him that she wasn't a threat that needed dealing with right now.

‘I always knew you’d go far,’ Betsy said. ‘What are you now, deputy resident?’

Misha self-deprecatingly nodded.

‘Oh that is good news,’ Betsy said. ‘Really good. No more ambassadors pushing you around now, eh? I like to see energetic and talented people get on in this world. I suppose it’s something to do with age. My golden years are behind me, but I can still take pleasure watching the next generation come on.’

‘Watching *over* the next generation as they come on, perhaps?’ Misha said, still with the smile.

‘Perhaps.’

The man appeared from the kitchen carrying two mugs of tea. He sheepishly looked for somewhere to set them down. Betsy moved a side table from next to her chair into the middle of the room.

‘Thank you,’ she said, ‘you can go now.’

The man put the mugs on the table then looked at Misha who nodded towards the door. As the man passed the sofa he spoke briefly and quietly to his superior. Betsy heard the front door open and close, and saw the man walking down her path to the street. The padded cells in his jacket caught the sunlight. They looked to Betsy like the thick coils of a python.

‘He said you tried to shoot him,’ Niechenko said, looking at the lampshade on the floor, surrounded by broken glass.

'Misha, dear, I may be old but I'm not past it. If I'd wanted to shoot him then shot he would be.'

The room fell back into silence. Major Tom hopped back onto the sofa next to Misha.

'My friend doesn't like the attention you are paying her and, no doubt, her family,' Betsy said.

'I must say, I am not drawn to that aspect of the work' Misha said. 'Those idiots can't think for themselves.'

'Then someone needs to think for them,' Betsy said, 'Sugar?'

'No. Thank you.'

The mugs sat untouched. Steam rose towards the ceiling.

'It seems rather an odd reaction,' Betsy said.

'All games have rules, Mrs Tren -, Betsy,' Misha said. 'Stakes can be high, but there must be rules. Without rules we can't talk.'

'Oh, I agree. It is good to talk. Is there anything you'd like to talk about, Misha?'

'Such as?'

'Well, when I run, sorry ran, little errands, I liked to keep things balanced. Made everything easier to manage. So I would only allow behaviour that matched the gravity of the situation. For example, if we were just after a bit of tittle-tattle -'

'Tittle-tattle?'

'Sorry, dear,' Betsy said, 'Saucy seaside photos, nooky letters, adults who should know better playing husbands and wives with other people's husbands and other people's wives, that sort of thing. You'd know it as kompromat.'

'Would *we*?' Misha said, emphasising the last word.

'Well, that stuff isn't worth much,' Betsy continued, ignoring the retort. 'Not going to win any medals. So I wouldn't allow my people to go over the top. No nasty business. No fisticuffs. Do you understand?'

'Yes.'

'So to actually go as far as to threaten women and children, I would say you're playing for very high stakes indeed. Idiots or otherwise.'

The steam from the mugs drifted towards Misha.

'And are you still playing? I thought you'd retired.'

'Misha, dear, retirement is the busiest time of our lives. Ask your parents.'

'My parents?'

Betsy felt a lurch in her stomach.

'Sorry,' she said. 'Figure of speech.'

She felt herself flush and was annoyed for it. When she was his age she would have been able to control it.

The mugs still sat on the side table. The steam floated towards Betsy.

'If someone is in danger of overreacting I trust you'll take the appropriate action,' Betsy said.

'I don't always have the, what did you call it?' Misha smiled, 'the balance? Sometimes even I cannot muster enough weight on the scales. Even if it is necessary.'

There are not many people in an embassy the deputy resident of the FSB could not push around, Betsy thought. In fact, she could think of only one.

'And other people?' Misha continued. 'Sometimes they are so driven they can't be balanced, no matter how much I'd personally like to.'

He stared at Betsy. Neither touched their drink.

Interesting choice of word, Betsy thought. *Personally*. Is he hinting at Kathryn?

'Well, we can only do what we can,' said Betsy. 'I remember I had a boss once who used to drink at work. Not normal drinking, although I hear that's now dying out. Bloody shame. No, this chap really went for it. He could function, but we all knew it wasn't good. Nobody did anything. Silly really. Nothing bad happened, but I always knew he could have been so much better if he'd only lay off the bottle. I always regretted not saying something, to him or to anyone else.'

She stared at Misha.

'It's tough when it's your boss,' she said, 'and you know he's gone too far.'

'Ha! Well there is no danger of that from my boss,' Niechenko said brightly. 'He never goes too far. The furthest he ventures is South Mimms service station. A complete waste of a very smart Range Rover. He says he loves the burgers.'

'Oh how funny,' Betsy laughed.

'His favourite is called the Inferno. Only available on Fireworks Night. He goes to get one every year.'

'They must be very addictive,' Betsy smiled.

They both reached for their tea.

'So what keeps you busy these days? Misha asked lightly.

'The garden mostly. And looking after him.'

She pointed at Major Tom, curled up on the sofa.

'He's getting on a bit now. We both are. Legs aren't what they used to be,' she said. 'His not mine.'

'So you're still active? You used to enjoy badminton I remember.'

That's a neat trick, Betsy thought, digging further into her current level of activity by introducing a game.

'Oh yes, and I still dabble a little now and then. Nothing serious, of course, those days are long behind me. I still like the game, but it's not worth risking a serious injury at my age. But I like to keep my hand in if I can. For my friends and those closest to me.'

'Ah yes, the girls. Kathryn and -' Misha pretended to search his memory, 'Gillian?'

'Julianne. Jules. Both well, thanks. Jules is still in private banking and Kathryn is now a politician. MP for Westminster no less.'

'I was always very fond of Kathryn. Even though we couldn't speak that often when she was in

Nato, we used to bump into each other around the Brussels circuit.'

'Yes, she said you used to bump into each other,' Betsy said with a grin.

Misha smiled back.

'And I had heard she was an MP. That's very good news.'

'Is it?'

'Of course. Our countries may have differences of opinion now and again, but that doesn't mean we can't care for each other on a human level.'

'Do you still care for her?'

'I knew we could never be together, but I always wanted what was best for her.' He stared hard at Betsy and added, 'I still do.'

'Well I know she's very junior, but you make it sound like she needs looking after,' said Betsy.

Misha smiled and shrugged.

'Well, Betsy, it's been delightful catching up but I must leave you,' Misha said.

They stood and embraced.

'Misha, dear, it's been a real pleasure,' Betsy replied. 'If you're ever at a loose end in London you should pop by again. It would be nice to stay in touch.'

'I'll do that.'

She led him into the hallway.

'Oh, I nearly forgot,' Misha said. 'I think you have something for me.'

He held out a manicured hand.

'Oh yes, how silly of me.'

Betsy retrieved the USB stick from the pocket of her cardigan and handed it over.

'Look after yourself, dear,' she said.

'You too. And those lovely girls. Goodnight, Betsy. Stay safe.'

36.

It had been a harrowing journey. Betsy gratefully aimed her moped towards the roundabout exit marked 'services'. She was pleased to be away from the noise and traffic. If she hadn't already formed a strong opinion of the selfishness of the average British road user, she would lay good money they had coordinated their efforts this afternoon to scare her witless.

The sun was low in the sky as the day shuffled towards dusk. She couldn't remember the last time she'd gone so far on the moped and was thankful Sputnik had made it without complaint. The car would have been preferable, of course, but she no longer trusted the number plate to flash up on any number of vehicle registration databases without causing eyes unknown to take an unhealthy interest.

She'd never been to South Mimms service station before, but seeing it laid out in front of her in all its splendour she was fairly sure it would be a once in a lifetime opportunity.

Betsy was grateful to the Russians, in a way, for allowing her this foray back into the old days; a chance to prove she still had what it took to be useful, to be a threat. Or at least divert her mind for a short time. So, yes, she was worried for herself but overall content, all things considered, to be active once more.

Flying free, after years of allowing her wings to gather dust. Of greater concern were the girls. Betsy knew Jules was more than capable of taking care of herself in a fair fight. No, what really had her cold, adding to the chill seeping into her bones as the day died, was Kathryn.

Betsy hadn't mentioned the USB stick or the deaths overseas of MI6 surveillance targets to Kathryn, fearing her industrial ambition would sniff an opportunity for self-aggrandisement. It was a persistent but manageable concern to be accounted for during Betsy's current investigations. That was until Misha had delivered his message. He'd been very clear: his feelings for Kathryn were personal, he cared for her on a human level and he still wanted what was best for her. That was bad enough, given their history and current professional positions. But Kathryn was too driven to be balanced, Misha had said. It was the purpose of this drive, given everything else that was going on right now, that Betsy most feared.

Betsy didn't know what she was going to find at the service station. Come to that she had no idea what it was even possible to find there, given the passage of time. But she had to go. Misha had dropped enough clues. Betsy had been careful to seed their conversation with tantalising bait. He'd nibbled straight away at the mention of their respective bosses. If an operation was being planned at the scale she feared it was, it could only be with the express say so of the FSB Resident. So let's talk about Dmitri

Goncharov, she'd decided. And like the burgers his boss supposedly loved so much – but only on fireworks night - Misha had been happy to chomp down hard on that one.

Misha couldn't just come out and tell her, of course not. She wasn't so long out of the game to expect him to so easily drop his guard. There was professional pride to consider after all, on both sides. Messages can be passed in plain sight, for players worthy of the test. Laid on the floor for those in possession of a spy's second sight to recognise. Pick them up, they're yours, if you can see what's right in front of you. And if you can't? Then you don't deserve to be in the arena and should probably head home before the rough boys turn up.

Betsy had passed the test. 'He never goes too far,' Misha had said of his boss. 'The furthest he ventures is South Mimms service station.' Nice bit of language that; passing the detail of the location whilst making it sound like a joke. Then another message dropped as a humorous aside: 'a complete waste of a very smart Range Rover'. So, now she had a date, a location and a vehicle. The rest is up to you, Misha might as well have added, I'm not going to do all the bloody work.

So, to South Mimms then. Located on the M25 motorway circling London it was a good place for a meet. Offering a steady flow of vehicles and a plausible reason to be there, Goncharov and his contact would be able to cite any number of possible onward journeys if challenged. Betsy could have sat at home thinking the problem through. Maybe even tried Hazel again, although that might look a bit needy. But nothing really compares with actually going to the scene yourself. Feeling the wind, taking in the sights, hearing the sounds, noticing all the oddities. Don't guess the route of the sentry patrol, one of her instructors back in Moscow had once said; you've got to smell the piss on the tree. Somewhat coarse, but the lesson had stuck with her.

She passed a huge sign at the entrance to the service station advertising the delights awaiting the weary traveller. Fried food and coffee mainly, judging by the brands displayed. She was behind a green saloon car. As the two vehicles approached the car park an information board burst into life. The green car's number plate was illuminated in a window underneath the word 'Welcome' and above the words 'please enjoy 2 hours free parking'. A digital clock at the top of the board showed 17:26. Betsy pulled over next to an information panel in the car park. For probably the first time in its unglamorous life, the small print took centre stage.

The car park was owned and managed by Hermitage Business Services, headquartered in Northampton, a division of Hermitage Group International, Betsy learned. Two hours free car parking subject to the following conditions. She read the conditions. Car park patrolled by plain clothed employees of Hermitage Business Services. Good for them. Charges may be incurred for overstaying. Why would anyone want to overstay here? CCTV cameras installed for safety and security. Oh yes, there they are, she thought, checking the crowded car park. For full terms and conditions see the following website. No, thankyou very much. Comments and complaints should be sent to the following address. Betsy read the address, realised it was in the service station and looked around. To one side of the main complex housing the restaurants, such as they were, she could see a smaller double storey building. It reeked of administration. That must be the office running the site, she thought.

She'd never liked the expression, but the thought did make her chuckle. Standing there next to Sputnik, reading the information board of South Mimms service station, Betsy, literally and metaphorically, could very definitely smell piss.

37.

The Chief Whip and Minister without Portfolio tapped the end of the blade with the pad of his left thumb. He looked up accusingly, as if the Defence Secretary had personally drawn his blood.

'That's sharp,' Passmore said.

'Gurkhas use it to slit the throats of their enemies. Being sharp is the general idea. You should try it sometime.'

The three Ministers had gathered in Andrew Heath's office on the fifth floor of the Ministry of Defence. He needed a chat before they descended to the basement for the World Wide Britain reception.

Heath was at his desk finishing the day's paperwork. Passmore hopped around the office cooing as if in a military museum. Patrick Evans, the Foreign Secretary, stood silently at the windows along one entire wall, staring out into the river.

'Done,' said Heath, casting a letter into a wooden tray with a flourish. 'Thank you for another thrilling visit to somewhere I can't remember to be shown something I don't understand.'

'If only the squaddies knew how much you care,' said Evans, without turning from the window.

Heath stretched and rubbed his eyes with his palms.

‘Oh I care, Patrick. The Foreign Office may be all sundowners but never forget, the last six inches of defence policy are made of steel.’

‘A tank?’ said Passmore.

‘Bloody small tank,’ said Heath. ‘No, a bayonet. And I never forget that it takes a human hand to shove it into someone’s guts.’

‘You are a man of unmatched principle,’ Evans said.

‘Indeed,’ Heath said, ignoring the insult. ‘That’s why I asked you both to come.’

He went to a cabinet running along the internal wall and pulled out a whisky bottle, three glasses and a small jug of water. His elegant fingers arranged them delicately on a tray.

‘Sorry gents, no ice,’ he said.

Heath carried the tray over to a low table between a set of easy chairs at the end of his office.

‘So what was so important?’ Evans said, turning from the window.

Heath closed the door to the office and sat in a chair facing the long window. Passmore joined him, sitting to Heath’s left and opposite a large oil painting on the end wall showing a group of soldiers in red tunics surrounded by near-naked tribesmen wielding spears. It clearly depicted some sort of desperate final stand. Evans sat with his back to the last decent light of the day streaming in over the river.

‘Sunlight has not come through,’ said Heath, as he poured the whisky.

‘We know that,’ said Evans, waspishly.

‘It’s time to take extreme action,’ Heath continued. ‘When we last spoke you both suggested you had options. David, you were talking about a backbench revolt. What are the numbers?’

‘Ah,’ said Passmore. ‘Good numbers, very good. Not quite there yet but I’m hearing lots of encouraging noises.’

‘The only encouraging noise you’re capable of producing is through your arse,’ said Evans. ‘He’s signing tomorrow. Have you actually got anyone onboard?’

Passmore swirled his drink.

‘Well, it’s a question of, we need to be in a position to, you know, strike when, ah - ’

‘I’ll take that as a no. Patrick? You said you’d leak the worst of the opposition’s negotiating positions gleaned by the Vauxhall vampires.’

‘I would do, but the civil service watchdogs have got the place wired so tight I’d be found out before you could say “scoop”,’ said Evans.

‘So still harbouring political ambition then Patrick?’ said Heath. ‘What happened to going down in flames for old Blighty?’

‘Oh grow up,’ said Evans. ‘I did what I could. Took more risks than either of you two. But the treaty was a done deal weeks ago, only a fool would pretend otherwise. Our only hope now is to keep our best players on the pitch.’

‘Our best players? You self-serving little shit,’ said Heath.

‘And your magnificent contribution is?’

'That,' the Defence Secretary said, indicating the oil painting looming over them.

'What is it?' Passmore said.

'The battle of Isandlwana. Zulu war, 1879. The plucky last stand of the first battalion, twenty-fourth regiment of foot.'

'Rorke's Drift?' said Passmore.

'Back to the history lessons, David. The company at Rorke's Drift were the lucky ones,' said Heath. 'That came after. If they'd not been sent off from the battalion they'd have been in this picture.'

'Fascinating, I'm sure, but your role in all this is?' said Evans.

'Self-sacrifice,' Heath said.

Passmore snorted and smiled. He looked quizzically at the Foreign Secretary.

'Go on,' said Evans.

'I heard a while ago, on very good authority, that Sunlight had collected another trophy,' Heath said.

'What, public speaking?' said Passmore, happy to play the fool.

Evans shook his head at the man to his right.

'How ever did you get selected?' he said. 'I think Andrew is suggesting the PM has been having another affair. Am I correct?'

'You are.'

'Who is she this time? Communications consultant? Arts ambassador?'

'Online media editor,' said Heath.

'Of course she is. And scribbling for?' said Evans.

'Russian Future,' said Heath. 'You look genuinely shocked Patrick, I didn't think you cared where the assassin comes from.'

'Pardon?' said Evans. 'She's an assassin?'

'God no,' said Heath. 'Now you're sounding like a dolt. It's a figure of speech. She'll be his downfall, that's all. But she is Russian. Or Ukrainian, maybe Moldovan. Hard to tell the accents apart really.'

'You've met her?' said Passmore.

'Yes. That's the tricky bit. I just wanted to convince her to spill the beans on Sunlight. To discredit him and buy us some time while we chose a new leader.'

'Oh no,' said Evans.

'What?' said Passmore.

'Will you tell our slow friend here, or shall I?' said Evans.

'She and I started a relationship,' said Heath.

'Printing your speeches in Russian Future, that kind of relationship?' said Passmore.

'You bloody idiot,' said Evans, 'and you.'

'Yes that was about the level of support I had expected,' said Heath. 'Anyway, look, what's done is done, but I'm prepared to cough to it, take the flak with my wife and spend some time in the wilderness.'

'She's a honey trap you bloody fool. The Russians must be laughing into their vodkas. First she snares the PM, then the Defence Secretary,' said Evans.

'I'll admit it will take something to come back from this one, but we don't know she's Russian intelligence.'

'Where did you meet for your trysts? Actually, romps. The red tops will go for romps,' said Passmore.

'Rotherhithe,' said Heath. 'We don't know she's a spy,' he finished in a weak voice.

'You're done, Andrew,' said Evans. 'Rotherhithe? Christ. At least the Profumo affair had decent architecture.'

'But I'll make sure Sunlight goes too,' said the Defence Minister. He can't hide from this one. We've got the world's press downstairs. I'm going to tell Sunlight that unless he stalls the signing I'm going to get them all to cover me breaking the whole story tomorrow morning.'

*

'Are you in a safe location?' Betsy said.

'Yes. Waterloo Station. I'm all set up, what do you need? Meg answered.

Betsy outlined the plan: Hack the computer belonging to Hermitage Business Services that logged the number plates of vehicles arriving at South Mimms service station. Block the outgoing request for technical support. Call the office next to the car park and inform them an engineer would be with them shortly. Send her in to find the entry time of Goncharov's Range Rover on the evening of the previous November fifth. Search the CCTV archive for footage of his car next to another. Correlate that second car against the Driver and Vehicle Licensing Agency database. Establish the identity of the official selling secrets to the Russians. Go to the drinks reception hosted at the Ministry of Defence to confront the traitor.

It had seemed plausible when it had existed only as an idea floating around her head. Saying it out loud however, and even Betsy's resolute inner voice had started to quibble on a couple of points.

'Blimey, is that all?' Meg said.

'Can you do it?' Betsy said.

'Of course. Question is, can you bluff your bit?'

'Yes, absolutely,' Betsy said, with a touch of indignation.

'Ha. You're so easy to wind up, Bets,' Meg said. 'But we've got to make you look like you're at work. What are you wearing?'

'Scruffs,' Betsy said. 'Tweed suit, silk scarf, brogues.'

'I think you'll scrape through an inspection.'

'Fair enough.'

'I'll get cracking. You go and sort out your identity card. Let's call it Clover Technical Solutions. I'll let you know when you can go in. Back in the game, Bets.'

'Back in the game, dear,' Betsy said.

Betsy parked the moped in the bike area and entered the service station. Her senses were immediately assaulted with chip fat, bright lights and drudgery. Absolutely nobody seemed to be enjoying their Tuesday afternoon experience. A young man in a yellow high-visibility jacket pushed a mop around a puddle of thick liquid. A small plastic yellow triangular sign had been placed near the spill. It said: 'Caution! Cleaning in progress'. Betsy went into the newsagents. She found a self-service machine that made business cards. She designed one for Clover Technical Solutions and added a few details suggesting it was an identity card. She left a large space on the left-hand side of the card. She bought ten, the minimum number. She then picked up a roll of sticky tape and a pair of scissors, paid and walked quickly to an empty booth in the centre of the complex. The tables were either empty and covered in the detritus of a recent meal or occupied by people in the process of eating. Nobody paid her any attention. She pulled her driving licence from her wallet and held one of her new business cards against it. Judging how much of the card to remove, she cut away a section so her photograph fitted neatly alongside the other details. Checking she was unobserved she then dropped the business card face down on the floor and pushed it through the muck with her shoe. Examining her work she saw that it was too smudged with fat and dirt to be plausible. She cut the same shape out of a second business card and repeated the process, but this time with less gusto. Better, but not there yet. Third time lucky. You make your own luck in this game, she told herself. Perfect. The third template was laid over her driving licence. She cut neat strips of sticky tape, placed them gently over the new card and trimmed the edges. Not completely foolproof, but good enough with a bit of confidence. Which was the one thing Betsy wasn't short of.

The man cleaning up the spill walked past Betsy carrying the mop in a bucket. He had left the warning sign in place over the wet floor by the entrance. Betsy's phone buzzed in her jacket pocket. A message from Meg read: 'You're on'. Betsy manoeuvred herself from the seat and cleared the belongings into her bag. She knew it was time to get into character, to focus on the mission in front of her. But before she could march over to the administration building she had to clear a niggling doubt from her mind. Misha had done a very good job, the boy was certainly talented, Betsy had to acknowledge. After finishing the Goncharov business, with a stare he had gently but firmly warned Betsy that Kathryn was out of her depth. About what, he hadn't divulged. 'I always wanted what was best for her. I still do,' he'd said. He'd spoken in the present tense. He'd been very clear about that. Some people are so driven they can't be balanced, he'd thrown in for good measure. Betsy paused outside the entrance to the service station. What the hell was that girl up to now?

38.

The woman behind the front desk glanced at Betsy's fake identity card and handed it back.

'They normally send a young lad,' she said. 'Just look at the camera. Thanks.'

'New contract,' Betsy said as her picture was taken, 'we're freelancers.'

'The IT in here is always going down,' the woman said. 'Enough work for both of you I reckon.'

'Let's hope so,' Betsy smiled.

The woman printed out Betsy's picture and stuck it on a pass with a red lanyard.

'James here will take you in,' the woman said.

Betsy followed a middle-aged man up a flight of stairs and through a set of doors into a large open plan office. Most of the desks, set out in long rows, were occupied. Nobody looked up from their screens. The man led Betsy to a room on one side of the building and said 'sorry for the smell.'

'It's an external system so doesn't get used often,' he continued. 'We saved the main room for our lot. This is our kitchen paradise.'

Betsy stepped into the small rectangular room. A single-paned window on one of the long sides looked out over the office. It was the only view on offer. A desk faced the window. It supported two computer terminals covered in dust and a microwave layered in organic matter of unrecognisable origin. A single high-backed swivel chair faced the desk, with foam missing from the arm supports. The other three sides of the room were covered in boxes of paper, one directly behind the door so that it could not open fully. The room was littered with take away food cartons, some in a bin, most on the desk or on top of the boxes. At the far end, nestled between cardboard towers, was a small fridge. Behind the fridge was a door with a push-handle bar across it. A large sticker on the door was just visible disappearing behind the fridge. Betsy could make out the words: 'Fire Exit. Do Not Obstruct'.

'I'm sure that's not supposed to be there,' she said, indicating the fridge.

'Don't worry,' said the man, 'the lock's on some sort of magnetic system wired to the building. We could never get it to work properly so we had another fire exit installed at the far end of the office. Any probs, head over there.'

He pointed to the end of the long room, across the ranks of soulless office workers. Betsy could see another fire exit. The door was currently propped open by a metal bin. She saw two people on the gantry outside smoking cigarettes.

The man started the computer and entered a log on code when prompted. He clicked on an icon named "system management". A new window opened asking for a user name and password.

'All yours,' he said. 'Shout if you need anything. Sorry about the smell.'

'No problem,' Betsy said, 'you should see my house.'

The man smiled and left. Betsy closed the door and gently eased the lock across. The man looked back at the soft click as the bolt moved into place. Betsy smiled and waved through the window. He waved back, but didn't smile. Betsy wrinkled her nose and set her bike helmet and bag on the desk in a clear space between a burger wrapper and a box holding a cigarette lighter. She connected an earpiece to her phone and called Meg. She lowered the seat so that the computer screen hid her from most of the office.

'I'm in,' she said. 'It wants a user name and password.'

'Okay. I've set the user name to S-M-I-M-M-S,' Meg said. 'Password is big burger world, no spaces between words. Replace the letter i with a 1 and put an exclamation mark on the end. That's as much as I can do from this end.'

Betsy did as instructed. The screen showed a page headed Hermitage Business Services Technical Area.

'Look for something saying vehicle registration archive,' Meg said.

Betsy clicked on an icon.

'Right, it's asking me for search parameters. I'll say November fifth last year, between 16:00 and 23:59.'

The screen was replaced by a spreadsheet with five columns: time of entry, vehicle registration number, make/model, colour and time of exit. Betsy watched as the indicator in the scroll bar to the right hand side of the screen shrunk to a tiny dot.

'There must be thousands. Any chance of refining the search to Range Rovers?' Betsy said.

'Hang on,' said Meg.

Betsy glanced around the side of the computer screen into the office. Nothing had changed. She looked back at the list of vehicle details.

'Is there an icon for search parameters?' Meg said.

Betsy hovered the cursor over the icons at the top of the page.

'New search, print, settings,' she read, 'format, freeze screen, advanced document search.'

'Try advanced document search,' Meg said.

Betsy tapped on the icon. The search parameter box opened again, but this time had additional windows for make, model, colour and vehicle registration number.

'Great, great, yes,' said Betsy. 'I'm searching for Range Rover.'

A new screen appeared. The indicator on the right hand side elongated.

'Must still be dozens,' Betsy said.

She looked around the side of the screen. The man that had walked her through the office was looking over at her and talking on his phone. She became aware of Meg speaking.

'Sorry, dear, missed that,' she said.

'We'll have to be bold,' Meg said. 'Change the search timings from five to ten o'clock and select the vehicle colour as black if you can.'

'Yes, I can do that,' Betsy said.

She changed the search criteria.

'Three vehicles,' she said. 'First one at 18:22:07, next at 20:05:45, last one at 21:36:29.'

The man on the phone stood up. He was still looking at Betsy.

'I've written those times down, Bets,' Meg said. 'Now hit home and look for the CCTV archive.'

'Yes, here it is,' said Betsy. 'There are a lot of cameras.'

'Find the entry camera. Set the date and search from 18:22:04.'

Betsy selected the camera marked "entry/welcome". A new window opened. She scrolled through to just after 18:22 and pressed play. She watched the digital display click through to 18:22:07. A Range Rover drove past the camera. Betsy paused, clicked back a short way and watched again.

'No, that's a woman driving,' she said.

'Try 20:05:40,' Meg said.

Betsy scrolled along to the time. The few seconds until the vehicle arrived felt like an eternity. Eventually a Range Rover passed the camera.

'No, one man, but it's not Goncharov,' Betsy said.

'Try 21:36:25,' Meg said.

Betsy saw the man in the office, still with his phone in one hand, talking to a colleague, who looked over in Betsy's direction.

'Anything?' Meg said.

'Sorry, dear, what was the time again?' Betsy said.

'21:36:25.'

Betsy dragged the time cursor.

'Damn, missed it.'

She managed to get the cursor to 21:36:23 and pressed play. After two long seconds a black Range Rover came into view.

'Well I never,' Betsy said. 'It's him. Goncharov. I'd recognise that lizard anywhere.'

'Excellent,' said Meg. 'Take a snap on your phone then check the cameras again. Search the main car park for Goncharov's vehicle. He'd probably have headed for one of the corners.'

Betsy captured the image of Goncharov's arrival on her phone. She clicked the home button, then reselected the CCTV archive.

'Main concourse,' she read.

She selected the camera. It showed the general car park area from the roof of the main complex. She dragged the cursor as close to 21:36:25 as she could. She watched a large black vehicle drive in and slowly take the form of a Range Rover.

'Got him. I've got him,' she said.

The vehicle cruised around the car park like a shark choosing its prey. Eventually it went static in a far corner, pointing away from the camera.

‘He’s stopped at,’ she checked the time, ‘21:36:56,’ Betsy said.

‘Find him on a camera that’s closer,’ Meg said.

Betsy could see a third person had joined the discussion with the man who had showed her to the computer. The two newcomers looked over at her.

She clicked on the home icon and selected ‘CCTV archive’ for the third time. She selected a camera named ‘car park south’. She dragged the scroll bar through to 21:36:56. She didn’t have to click the play button. She could tell immediately it was the wrong camera.

She clicked again on ‘Home’ then ‘CCTV archive’. She selected ‘car park north’. Dragged the scroll bar. Wrong place.

‘Come on,’ Betsy said under her breath.

The man started walking towards Betsy’s side office, accompanied by another man and a young woman.

‘Home’. ‘CCTV archive’. ‘Car park north west’. Scroll bar. Wrong place.

‘You okay, Bets?’ said Meg.

‘Quiet please. They’re coming,’ Betsy said.

‘Home’. ‘CCTV archive’. ‘Car park north east’. Scroll bar. Wrong place.

There was a knock on the door. Then a harder knock. Then the door handle was tried.

‘Excuse me, can you let me in please?’ a voice said from outside.

'Home'. 'CCTV archive'. 'Car park south east'. Scroll bar. Wrong place.

'We need to come in. Can you open the door please?' the voice said again.

'Home'. 'CCTV archive'. 'Car park south west'. Scroll bar. Black Range Rover parked, surrounded by empty spaces.

'Got him,' said Betsy.

'Right, go forwards in time. Look for another vehicle joining him,' said Meg.

'Open this door now,' said the raised voice from outside.

The door handle was tried again. Then, after a couple of seconds, the door was thumped, hard. Betsy clicked on the scroll bar and dragged it to the right. A couple of cars flashed past but nothing pulled in next to the Range Rover. The door was hit again and faces appeared at the window. Betsy hunched down but could not completely escape their gaze.

'Open this door, right now,' the man shouted.

Betsy continued scrolling to the right. A new image seemed to magically appear next to the Range Rover. A vehicle. She pressed play. The thumping turned to a harsh clattering as a chair was rammed against the door. Betsy blinked as the flash from a mobile phone signalled they had started filming her. The time on the screen said 21:50:31. Next to the Range Rover there was a black saloon car. It faced the camera. Betsy recognised the car as a Mercedes. It was parked so that the drivers were next to each other and could easily talk without having to leave their vehicles. The number plate of the Mercedes was clearly visible. The camera angle obscured the driver's face but Betsy could see the passenger seat was empty. She didn't have time to check other cameras to see if anyone was sat in the back of the car, but doubted there would be more occupants. The driver was holding something out the window, presenting it for Goncharov to inspect.

'Megan dear, black Mercedes saloon. Vehicle registration MF70DDP. I've got to go.'

The chair was smashed into the door again.

'Take a picture and call me,' Meg said.

Betsy ended the call. She took a picture of the screen on her phone then stood up. The window was crowded with people, most filming her with their phones. A woman's demented face screamed at her. Betsy recognised it was the woman from the front desk. The door shook from another hammering. Betsy scanned the small room. She leant over the fridge and tried the push handle on the fire exit. The handle levered down without difficulty, but the door didn't budge. The magnetic lock held firmly. She tried again, eliciting the same result. Another chair was smashed against the entrance door.

39.

The gunshot noise of the chair being smashed against the door continued. More people were yelling now. Betsy was breathing hard. Her eyes cast around the small office. They landed on the burger box. Inside it was a lighter. She grabbed it and clambered unevenly onto the swivel chair. It twisted left and right under the sudden demand of the woman's weight. She clutched the backrest for support, her fingers sinking into the tatty foam. The voices on the other side of the glass reacted to her movement, increasing in volume and aggression. Front-desk-woman leapt about like a deranged animal. She hammered a fist at the glass. The door shuddered again under a renewed assault. Betsy clicked the lighter until it emitted a limp flame. She held it to the ceiling, against a fire sprinkler pointing down at her. Her arm immediately started to ache with the effort of stretching. The sprinkler erupted into life, spinning in a frenzy. Water spat around the little office. A piercing alarm screamed throughout the building. Fire sprinklers in the main office simultaneously woke up. People ran for cover, clutching mobile phones to their chests as they ran. Startled yelling replaced the shouting at the door. The hammering stopped. The window emptied. Betsy's wet hair splashed across her face as she fell onto the desk, the chair spinning out behind her into a box of soggy paper. She snatched up her bag and bike helmet and launched her body at the bar on the fire exit. The door burst outwards. She clambered over the fridge and dropped onto a metal gangway outside the building. The slight breeze blowing at her from the purpling sky tasted of pure oxygen.

She found herself at the top of a set of metal steps. Leaning heavily on the handrail she half ran, half fell down the stairs, her wet hand slipping as she went. The main shopping complex was a hundred metres away across a patch of grass that sloped up from the office building. She started scuttling as fast as she could from the wailing fire alarms. The grassed area in front of her opened up like the no-man's land between two border posts. She snatched breaths and ran as if her life depended on it. Her sodden shoes slipped on the grass. Her hip screamed obscenities at her. She stumbled. Dropped the helmet. Grabbed it up. Expected the shouts of discovery to start at any moment and flinched at each cry. Every sound from the building thumped into her as if they were the bullets seared into her memory, blasting through a number plate and into her exposed body.

Betsy had nearly reached the corner of the main complex when she heard a shout clearly meant for her. A man yelled for her to stop. Turning a corner into the bright light she threw a glance behind her. People were spilling out into the car park, shaking water off clothes and wiping blurry mascara from eyes. A man was racing across the grass towards her.

Betsy hobbled past the main doors of the service station. Every step greeted with more protest from her hip. She reached the bike and donned the helmet. The man rounded the corner as Betsy pulled out of the parking space. She chanced a look over her shoulder. The man was at the entrance of the main complex. He hesitated then plunged through the automatic doors, out of sight. Betsy drove to the top of the car park and pulled up behind a row of cars. She dialled Meg's number and forced her phone into her helmet.

'Bets! Where are you?' Meg said.

'I'm out, leaving soon.'

Her breathing was ragged and her head swam in the tight confines of the helmet. She rubbed her hip.

'I'm working my way into the DVLA database with the registration number you gave me,' Meg said.

'Who is it?' Betsy said, eyes tight closed, breath harsh. 'Is it Heath, the Defence Secretary? I need to get to the reception to confront him.'

'I don't know,' Meg said, 'it's taking longer than I expected.'

'I need to know the name of the traitor. It's got to be Heath, why else would he have been skulking around the drop-off point?'

'Bets, you've got to give me more time,' Meg pleaded.

'There is no more time!'

*

Would someone, who had spent a large part of their existence balancing life and death decisions, have developed a sense of when death is approaching? Or rather, Betsy wondered, as her moped negotiated the tight streets of central London, after all the risks she'd taken in her life would her soul realise if it was approaching the moment of its end?

It felt like the end of something was close. She'd never liked guns, and didn't like the fact she'd had to use one now, when her career was well and truly over. She'd be powerless to resist any repercussions from so startlingly upping the ante, were any to be forthcoming. Much about the game had changed since the days she'd been active, officially so at least. There were some constants though. One of them being that pulling a gun on a Russian hood usually invites some sort of response.

She parked in a back street off The Strand, happy to walk the short distance to Westminster to attend the World Wide Treaty drinks reception in the Ministry of Defence. Meg hadn't yet told her what character she'd be inhabiting. Once the guest list had been accessed – not so difficult with an out of date operating system – Meg would insert Betsy's credentials. She'd uncovered the murders, the deceit, the lives traded. Now she had to confront Heath and reveal his treachery before he did any more damage.

She focussed on the job at hand. Partly on account of a professional echo calling from the past.

Mostly though to ignore the brooding darkness crowding her mind a step further back. She remembered an interview she'd once done with a member of the office who had been blown up in Iraq whilst embedded with a special forces team. The man had told her that he'd woken up on the day convinced he was going to die before sunset. He didn't know how, or where – he hadn't even been expecting to go out on patrol to meet an agent that day – but something inside him had told him he'd soon be dead. Betsy had tried to understand and didn't doubt the man's sincerity, but hadn't really bought into it.

Until now.

Until she rounded a corner and saw the Ministry of Defence rear up in front of her like the prow of a ship; Betsy bobbing in the water, about to be rammed under the hull. She was seized with the overwhelming feeling she was willingly moving towards the end of her life. The end of everything. Her course was as fixed as if the history of the life of Ekaterina Tereshkova, aka Betsy Trenmore-Halford, was running with the same assured confidence as the white lines in the middle of the road, accompanying her towards the final act.

40.

For a five-hundred year-old building the acoustics of the Henry the Eighth wine cellar, in the basement of the Ministry of Defence, were surprisingly good. Echoes from professional good moods landed softly. British officials, along with a global guest list of politicians, advisers and other functionaries, had successfully created a warm fug of contented political blather.

Andrew Heath was a natural at such events. Like many politicians he was most comfortable at the meeting point of a soft crowd and free booze. The political antennae were still on duty, but at least they could relax a bit and have a drink. English champagne, naturally. With mini-Yorkshire Puddings and Melton Mowbray pork pies, even the regional cuisine had been commandeered in the effort to promote just how brilliant everything British was.

Heath stood in a corner with his back to one of the pillars holding up the vaulted ceiling. Patrick Evans and David Passmore occupied the other two available corners. The last angle was taken up with a spiral staircase leading into the basement from a gantry running along two sides of the room. The gantry disappeared into the bowels of the Ministry of Defence at either end. At the point the two raised walkways met, at the top of the spiral stairs, there was an emergency exit.

Each Minister was managing his own ecosystem of international engagement. But they were minor celestial bodies, attended by the most basic satellites, compared to the bright light at the centre of the universe, which in this case was also in the centre of the room.

Sunlight beamed. With each solar flare a ripple of laughter would extend outwards as first the fluent, then the strugglers, then those with translators got the jokes. He was the beating heart of power, sending luminous energy pulses across the room.

Betsy shuffled around the room looking for the Defence Secretary. She'd been surprised Meg had so blatantly chanced her arm with a character, but not as surprised as the civil servant at reception who found that, yes, indeed there was a guest entry for the defence correspondent from Horse and Pony magazine. Betsy had explained her dishevelled and soggy appearance as a consequence of being caught in the rain. The young man had looked quizzical and slightly embarrassed but had, thankfully, been British enough not to challenge the old woman over the non-existent rain showers that afternoon. He'd hand-written a visitor's pass and wished Betsy a wonderful evening. She had muttered something about looking forward to covering Trooping the Colour before descending into the basement, cursing Meg's frivolity but glad also that her self-confidence had returned in their hour of need.

She briefly saw, through the crowd, Kathryn Fieldhouse. She wanted to speak to her, to warn her something bad was about to happen, but needed to get to Heath first and, anyway, wouldn't have been able to wade through the throng. Betsy raised a hand in acknowledgement. Kathryn's sullen face twitched a reply then turned away. Betsy might have cared for the slight once. A week ago. A lifetime ago. But now she was exhausted, mentally and emotionally.

Betsy fell into Andrew Heath's orbit.

'Minister, we need to talk,' she said.

'Oh dear, sounds serious,' Heath said to his guest, deploying a broad grin that revealed pastry between his teeth.

'I'll leave you to it. Nice to meet you Minister,' the man said.

'I know what you've been up to and it stops right now,' Betsy said.

'I'm sorry - ' a check of the scrawled name tag, ' – Ms Trenmore-Halford, I'm not sure what I've done to rattle the cage of the eminent Horse and Pony magazine.'

'Your little games.'

'Don't know what you're talking about,' said Heath, still with the smile, but also a frown now as he took in the entirety of Betsy's appearance.

'I saw you creeping about Wellspring Gardens last Friday,' Betsy said. 'And I'm not a journalist,' she added heavily.

The minister's smile faded.

'You saw me?' said Heath.

'Yes. Would have had it out with you there and then except some lunatic in a Millwall shirt objected to me parking outside his house.'

'Oh my God, that was you?'

'Yes, and I know what you've been up to. What the hell do you think you're doing?'

'Look, it's not what you think. I just needed some leverage over the Prime Minister. It's this bloody World Wide Britain Treaty.'

'Leverage? Jesus Christ, man. People are getting hurt.'

'I never meant for that to happen. I'm going to tell my wife everything tomorrow.'

'Your wife? It's the police you should be more worried about.'

'Well, yes, I accept there will be some questions to answer about the Ministerial code. What can I say? I'm a passionate man. Things got out of control.'

'Out of control? You're a senior politician Andrew, you knew the deal you were making.'

'Listen to me. I love this country and the PM's taking us down the wrong path.'

'I was nearly killed because of you.'

'What? I think that's a bit dramatic even for a Millwall fan. Look, if the PM wasn't going to see sense I had to make sure he wasn't around anymore. I'm doing it for the country even at the expense of my own reputation.'

'Sod your reputation. What about Marko Babić and Ravi Marimuthu?'

'I've no idea who you're talking about.'

'Typical. Don't try to wash your hands, Andrew, you're finished. I can prove what you've been doing.'

'Mrs - ' he gave up trying to remember her name, 'please, listen to me. I just need to kill off the PM. I'm going to see it through in the morning. I'll make a big statement.'

'Biggest statement of your life.'

'Exactly. It'll do for me, sure, but I'll take him with me.'

'A suicide bombing?'

'Well, again, you're laying the drama on with a trowel but I suppose so.'

'And what about the Russians?'

'Russian. Singular. There was only ever one.'

'Don't talk rubbish. I saw more than one. First, in Wellspring Gardens - '

'Well, she changes her wig every now and then.'

'Who?'

'Natalia. To spice things up a bit, you know.

'What?'

'Same girl each time though.'

'The one in Shepherd Market had a beard.'

A silence fell between the two. A waiter offering Scottish smoked salmon was waved away.

'What the hell are you talking about?'

'No, what the hell are you talking about?'

As Betsy stared up at Andrew Heath the politician seemed to grow an inch taller. A quizzical look spread across his face.

'I think this conversation is over, Mrs not-a-journalist. Now, if you'll excuse me.'

He tried to move away. Betsy stood her ground.

'Nice try Andrew. You can't brush this off. You're trying to kill the Prime Minister and, probably, everyone in this room. I've got proof. You're finished.'

Betsy's phone started ringing in her jacket pocket.

'Kill - ? You're demented. Kill the PM? What on earth are you talking about?'

Betsy fumbled the phone from her pocket. Meg was calling her.

'I've been having an affair with the same woman as the PM. I'm going to resign tomorrow and take him down with me. What are you talking about, killing people?'

Betsy turned away from the Defence Secretary to hear Meg.

'Slow down,' she said, 'I can't hear you. Start again.'

Since the Prime Minister's arrival the din of conversation in the cellar had grown very pleased with itself. The volume had increased accordingly. Betsy could just about catch a breathless Meg saying the words 'Heath', 'Evans' and 'South Mimms'. The rest was drowned out. She understood none of it. She saw a waiter with an empty tray disappear behind a large screen showing a picture of Henry the Eighth. Betsy hurried after him. She found herself in a narrow passageway with food stacked either side on trolleys.

'What was that? Say it all again, dear.'

'It. Is. Not. Andrew. Heath,' Meg said, over the noise of the party.

'Who is the car registered to?' Betsy said.

'Patrick Evans, the Foreign Secretary.'

'Evans? Christ. Heath's been having an affair. He's trying to scupper the treaty by bringing down the PM.'

'An affair? With the same woman?'

'Yes, it's not Heath. Evans would know all the surveillance targets as he would have okay'd them as Foreign Sec. He must have traded the lot. Shit and blast.'

'Who's there?'

'Everyone. They're all here. EU, Asia, Gulf. It's packed.'

'Get them out, Bets. Tonight's his last chance. It'll be a bomb. Evans will have got the Russians in somehow, fake employees in a services or building firm, posing as Poles, Romanians, anything.'

'A bomb?'

'Got to be,' Meg said, 'no other way at this stage. Get them out, Bets. As long as Evans is there it's safe. He'll make an excuse to leave before it goes off. You've got to stop him. Is Kathryn there?'

'Yes.'

'Betsy, you've got to get her out too.'

‘I will.’

‘Please hurry, Bets. Don’t let Evans get you. Speak later.’

Betsy hung up. She stared at the plates of canapés in the corridor, said ‘shit and blast’ again then hurried back into the crowded wine cellar.

Where she saw Patrick Evans climbing the spiral staircase with a phone pressed to his ear, smiling and waving back into the crowd as he headed for the emergency exit.

41.

Misha Niechenko could stand it no longer. Trapped in an interminably boring meeting, he was desperate to get out of the secure room. He checked his watch again – five past seven. The bomb was due to go off at quarter past and he had to ensure Kathryn's safety, now that the timings had been brought forward. He had an unregistered pre-paid phone in his office with which he'd planned to call in a bomb threat to the Ministry of Defence. His boss, Goncharov, would suspect him of double-dealing, but he'd soon be history anyway if everything went to plan, so it didn't matter what he thought. Provided Misha got to the phone.

Goncharov's nasal drone bounced off the hard bare walls of the secure room. He'd been lecturing Misha for nearly an hour on future targeting operations against dissident Russians living in Britain who were failing to place their assets at Moscow's disposal. There was no urgent need to have this discussion now, Misha thought, and definitely no reason to have it in the secure room, but his boss had insisted. He checked his watch again – six minutes past seven.

'I apologise if I'm boring you, Misha,' Goncharov said.

'Not at all, sir, it's just that I - '

'That you what?' Goncharov said. 'That you have an important meeting to get to? That you are not interested in your boss's ideas?' He affected a pained expression.

'No sir.' He couldn't help himself checking his watch again – seven minutes past.

'Oh, I understand,' Goncharov said. 'You're excited about the operation. Well, don't worry, boy, I've left instructions that we are to be informed the moment the team watching the building says the device has activated.'

Goncharov checked his own watch and showed yellow teeth to his deputy.

'Shouldn't be too long now,' he smiled, patting the younger man's thigh. 'I'll make sure you don't miss any of the action.'

*

'Patrick!' Betsy called, still immersed in the crowd. She pushed her way through the cramped cellar with just enough self-awareness not to be so rough as to invite the attention of the close protection officer standing near the Prime Minister. She could feel her anger rising fast. The Foreign Secretary looked back, but kept moving. Betsy fought her way towards the steps with increasing impoliteness.

'Patrick, wait!'

The Foreign Secretary wasn't hanging around. He'd reached the top of the spiral staircase and was turning towards the emergency exit. He hit the door like a train, to emerge at the foot of a narrow pedestrian ramp sloping up to ground level. The guard box next to the access road was directly above him. He saw a security guard, whose name he could just about recall, approaching down the slope.

'Excuse me sir,' the uniformed man said, 'this is a fire exit. It is only to be opened from the inside in an emergency.'

'Sorry, Trevor,' Evans said, 'this is a sort of emergency.' He held up a packet of cigarettes and grinned broadly.

'Ah, Foreign Secretary sir, good evening,' the guard said.

Trevor extended his security pass from the lanyard around his neck and tapped it against a small control box on the wall. A tiny red light changed to green. He spoke into a radio handset clipped to his shoulder.

'Control, Lima Four Three. You're probably getting an alarm at Bravo Two Two Seven. I've just cancelled it. Official business.'

Evans heard a tinny, 'roger that lima four three'.

'One minute only please, sir. I'll be back to check the door. And warn us in future would you?'

'Yes, yes, of course, sorry, Trevor,' Evans said, as he pushed a cigarette between his lips.

The security guard disappeared inside the building, leaving the door ajar. Evans stood still and stared up the slope. He took his first lungful of smoke. He hadn't had time to exhale it before the door was flung back on its hinges. Betsy rushed at the Foreign Secretary.

Evans turned and just had time to emit a smoky 'Who - ?' before he was gripped viciously by the collars and pushed against the wall. The cigarette fell from his mouth and hit Betsy's hand on the way to the ground. The momentary pain seemed to enrage her even more.

'Who are you? What the hell are you doing?' Evans said.

'You're not leaving,' Betsy said.

'I know I'm not leaving,' Evans said, 'I'm having a fag. Get your hands off me!'

'Where's the bomb?' Betsy said.

'What?'

'The bomb. Where's the bomb?'

'What the hell are you - '

With a fist she'd not formed in twenty years Betsy jabbed the Foreign Secretary just below the rib cage, aiming upwards.

He groaned and sagged onto Betsy.

'Don't treat me like an idiot,' spittle flew from her mouth. 'Your deal with the Russians and South Mimms, I know all about it.'

She allowed Evans to slump to the floor. He started sucking in air, winded from the punch. He stared at his attacker with wide eyes as her handbag swung back and forth into his face.

'Who on earth is South Mimms?' he managed between gasps.

'Last year. Fireworks night. Where were you?' Betsy spat.

'Last year? Fireworks? I was at home.'

'You were with the Russians.'

'What? I was at home, cancelling a long-anticipated dinner and fireworks party because '– a whoop as air rushed into his lungs – 'the PM demanded I spend hours on the phone talking about the future of the bloody Party. Now get off me!'

Over Betsy's shoulder the Foreign Secretary saw Andrew Heath emerge from the fire exit. The Defence Secretary stumbled to a halt and gripped the door frame, staring at Evans's desperate eyes underneath the old woman.

'Patrick?' said Heath.

'Get her off me!' said Evans.

Betsy took a hand off Evans's collar, gripped her handbag and threw it into Heath's face. The small links on the strap snapped and the bag, weighed down by her heavy plastic glasses case and backed up with a stiff arm, connected sharply. Heath's elegant nose erupted with blood and he fell back against the wall. Betsy returned her bloody hand to the Foreign Secretary's lapel and drew his head close.

'I'm not in the mood, Patrick. Where's the fucking bomb?'

'You've lost your mind, you stupid woman. What bomb?' Evans protested.

Betsy let go of the man's lapels and took his throat in her claw. Evans started choking.

'You're not having me, Patrick, you little shit,' Betsy said. 'It's over.'

Andrew Heath, slumped against the wall, held a handkerchief to his ruined nose.

'Who are you - ?' he managed.

Betsy stepped over the Defence Secretary and lunged for the fire door. Back inside the building now and nothing had changed. The crowd was thick below the gantry, and very noisy. Betsy flung her arms wide and started shouting. It had no effect. She moved along the gantry to be nearer the middle of the room. She leant over the rail running the length of the platform and shouted again. A few people looked up but nobody stopped smiling, chatting or drinking. She tried again.

'Get out. Everyone get out! she yelled.

Betsy realised the crowd would defer to the Prime Minister and even if he'd noticed he'd probably be waffling some nonsensical chaff about Brits not giving up that easily or time for one last drink, ha, ha, ha.

No movement. Betsy looked around. Further along the room the gantry disappeared through a set of doors. Just inside the doors was a fire alarm on the wall. Good. Even better, Betsy could see a security guard through the double doors, talking to – Kathryn?

Betsy ran at the fire alarm. She jabbed her thumb at the plastic cover, missing twice in her blind panic. The third time she felt it give way and an alarm started blaring. She leant over the railing again and yelled into the room.

‘Get out! There’s a bomb in here!’

Bemused faces looked round at each other. Some started moving towards the doors, but with little urgency. Betsy waved her arms and carried on shouting. The message seemed to be getting passed through the crowd. Activity increased. The level of noise was the same but it had undergone a subtle change in tone. The confident and worldly cadence had morphed into a meek and questioning search for reassurance. Heads swivelled, in the very human desire to find an authority figure to explain the joke. But no such figure presented itself. People started moving faster towards the emergency exits at the side of the room and up the spiral staircase. It was all happening too slowly, Betsy realised. Some guests were already at the emergency exit at the top of the steps, through which Betsy now saw Andrew Heath emerge with a bloodied cloth pressed to his face. Betsy remembered the security guard. She turned from the room and hurled herself through the double doors. The guard was indeed talking to Kathryn. He seemed in the process of answering a question she had just put to him.

‘No, I’ve had nothing on the radio,’ he said.

‘Kathryn, get the hell out!’ Betsy yelled.

The older woman then turned to the security guard.

‘There’s a bomb! I don’t know where and I don’t know what time it’ll go off, but it’s here. They’re moving, but too slowly. You’ve got to get them out!’

The security guard looked at Kathryn. The fire alarm screamed for attention. Although the MP said nothing, Betsy felt Kathryn bestow a permission on the security guard, an authority, an unspoken command. The guard spoke into his radio.

'Control, Lima Four Three, major incident declared. Am emptying the area around Bravo Two Two Seven.'

'Roger that, Lima Four Three. What's happening, Trevor?' the voice on the radio said.

'I don't know yet,' the man said, 'just get everyone out!'

Betsy felt herself pushed by the security guard back through the double doors. She saw Kathryn follow behind.

'Emergency exit at the end of the gantry, madam. Go!' the man said.

The room was almost empty, the last stragglers were being shepherded hastily through doors below the gantry by security guards. The last of the waiting staff were disappearing behind the screen with the Henry the Eighth image. Andrew Heath was still on the gantry. His face was bright red, with blood or anger, Betsy couldn't tell.

'Officer, this woman assaulted me and the Foreign Secretary, kindly arrest her,' he shouted above the wail of the alarm. Heath held Betsy's arm in a firm grip that halted the headlong rush for the emergency exit.

Betsy raged at the thought her life was about to end. She raged at the injustice of them winning, because of Andrew Heath's pathetic scene. She raged that she knew it all but didn't have time to explain. But with rage came purpose. With purpose came strength.

Betsy broke Heath's grip and pushed him away. She spun the Minister round and took hold of the back of his suit, shoving him towards the exit.

'Just get out, Andrew!' she shouted.

They reached the door. Betsy bundled Kathryn and Heath outside, followed by the security guard. She pushed them up the concrete slope. Guests were spilling over the lawn surrounding the building. Patrick Evans was nowhere to be seen.

'Control, Lima Four Three, that's the cellar emptied, confirm - '

Betsy saw the wall in front of her bulge slightly then felt herself lifted off her feet and thrown violently across the service road. Her world was at one moment bright white, then a murky yellow from a mixture of high explosive and brick dust. She lost all hearing and was left with a sharp ringing in her head, which felt like it had been slammed in a closing door. Her sinuses hurt. It felt like she'd dived deep underwater and not been able to clear her ears. She realised she was lying on the ground with her face in grass. She saw that her jacket had been ripped at her left elbow, which slowly transmitted a dull throb to her brain. The pain increased as Betsy blinked dust from her eyes. By the time she'd looked round to see other similarly prone figures slowly being revealed by the retreating smoke rolling up into the dark sky, the pain in her elbow had become overwhelming. She turned onto her right-hand side, gasping and cradling her left arm. The side of the building had collapsed. A huge chunk had been punched out of the wall. Betsy could see into the hole, unrecognisable now as a wine cellar, from which smoke and flame was still being emitted. The upper floors of the building sagged. They vomited desks and computers into the void. Betsy looked round at the figures nearby. She couldn't see Kathryn anywhere. The ringing in her ears was slowly replaced by other sounds: alarms, screams, and a metallic chirp, repeating every couple of seconds. She searched for the source of the noise and saw a uniformed man lying by her feet. The man was on his back, mostly grey from ash and dust, but with a big splash of white, which must be his shirt, Betsy reckoned, and a red gash down his chest. Had he been wearing a red tie? Betsy tried to remember.

'Lima Four Three. Come in Lima Four Three.'

Betsy heard the metallic chirp again.

'Lima Four Three. Come in Lima Four Three.'

Betsy saw, with what little clarity she had left, Operation Meadowland laid before her: trade secrets for the murders of officials making life difficult for the World Wide Britain treaty. A couple of teasers, just to build trust, then the biggy. Kill the Prime Minister and as many of the international negotiators as possible. Start again with new teams on both sides of the pitch. She wondered if MI6 had got the chef and the dog trainer out. Maybe they were floating past the fortress right now, face down in the Moskva River.

She heard the metallic chirp again.

'Lima Four Three. Come in Lima Four Three.'

Betsy saw some of the grey mess move at her feet. A hand reached up towards the man's head, immobile and surrounded by stones. The hand arrived at a rectangular lump next to the head and squeezed a switch.

'Control. This is Lima Four Three. Room clear,' the man said, and then he died.

42.

'As you know, the D Notice committee, or defence and security media advisory committee to use our proper name, seeks in no way to limit the freedom of the press.'

'Perish the thought,' Meg said.

'Far from it,' the official with the silver hair continued, 'given our links to the Ministry of Defence we know only too well the power a healthy democracy derives from a vibrant and perspicacious media environment.'

'Links to the Ministry of Defence?' more accusation than question from Meg, delivered with raised eyebrows.

'A sort of official-unofficial dotted line, if you like,' said the other man, from inside a grey suit straining against a middle-management paunch.

'Well I'm glad that's clear,' Meg said.

'So if you wish to go through with this idea of using your contacts in the media to write a story about the, ah, incident, it is neither our place nor our intention to tell you what you can and cannot print. We just asked you to this meeting to explain the wider context of the current reporting situation regarding the, um, event, in a spirit of friendship and transparency.'

'Not so transparent that you're covered by the Freedom of Information Act though, eh?' Meg said.

The first official ignored the barb. 'There may be information from other government departments with a bearing on the situation that you are currently unaware of and that we may be able to help with,' he said.

'All we ask is that you listen to our opinions,' the second official said.

'My mother used to say that opinions are like arseholes,' Meg said. 'Everybody has one.'

'Did she really,' said the first official, abandoning the effort of goodwill.

'Of course not!' Meg said with a flourish. 'It was her mother.' She pointed to Betsy, sitting on her left and, hitherto, a silent participant in the meeting.

'Ms Clover, we cannot force you to do anything - '

'Bloody right, mate.'

' – but we can advise you of potential consequences were you to print the story about the incident - '

'It was a bomb,' Betsy said. 'A great big Russian fucking bomb. That killed two people and - ' she broke off as her voice failed.

Meg turned to her and said softly, 'it's all right, dear.' She turned her attention back to the two officials on the other side of the desk in the windowless room on the fourth floor of the Ministry of Defence.

'What my friend was saying, was that we all know it was a bomb and if it hadn't been for the actions of the two ageing old crones in front of you, especially the actions on the night of my friend here, you would now be trying to manage the almighty shit-storm of having a hundred foreign dignitaries killed in your care plus, let's not gloss over, the Prime Minister.'

'All we're saying,' the first official tried, 'is that there are certain parts of government for whom it would be unhelpful right now to reveal to the public quite how close a hostile state got to committing such an atrocity.'

'You mean the spooks?' Meg said. 'They're worried we'll kick over the hornets nest and send all their - ' she turned to Betsy, ' – what do they call them?' she turned back and clicked her fingers, ' – clients, we'll send all their clients running for cover, terrified they can't be protected. Meanwhile, you, an unelected bureaucrat, get to decide what the British public are entitled to know.'

Having failed to build rapport, the first official stared hard at the two women and said, 'if you run the story you may find your personal data, revealing your backgrounds in the more shadowy areas of the state, is accidentally released the next time the Ministry of Defence is hacked. And there will be a next time. There always is.'

Meg smiled and leant across the table. She knotted her eyebrows and adopted an earnest voice.

'Raymond, my editor friend, gets twitchy whenever one of his journalists wants to put the word blackmail into a headline, but if I were doing a story on this meeting I'd be very tempted to use that naughty little word.'

'Nobody is seeking to blackmail anybody, Ms Clover. You may seek to print the facts, but between fact and truth is perception, and - '

'Oh don't be so stupid,' Betsy exploded. 'You're embarrassing yourself, you silly little man.'

'We can help you,' the second official blurted, in an effort to redeem the situation. 'We used to do it in the war with the V-bombs to prevent public panic. We can say it was a gas explosion.'

Meg looked at Betsy, then back across the table.

'If you boys are that interested, I know a walking tour that'll show you all round where the V-bombs landed, sorry, where the mysterious gas explosions occurred.' She waggled her fingers in exaggerated fashion either side of her head. The officials ignored the sarcasm.

'You'll get the exclusive. Well, your editor friend will,' the second man continued. 'Full access to politicians and officials, first interview with the PM, the full bells and whistles. How does that sound?'

'It sounds as if you lot still think you're Churchill,' Betsy said. 'The truth is so precious it has to be attended by a bodyguard of lies? That sort of thing? Forget it. Facts are facts. You start messing around with them, smudging the edges, blurring the lines, and before you know it, nobody knows what to believe any more. You've done the Russians' job for them.'

'I thought you ladies would take a more patriotic stance,' grey suit number one said icily.

Meg frowned and pressed a clenched fist to her mouth, elbow on the desk, as if contemplating deeply.

'By patriotism do you mean the habit of identifying oneself with a country, placing it beyond good and evil and recognising no other duty than that of advancing its interests?' Meg said.

'That's a reasonable summation', grey suit number two said.

'I didn't make those words up,' Meg replied. 'They're George Orwell's definition of nationalism. Heard of him? He wrote a book. I can lend it to you.'

The officials stayed silent.

'Your brand of patriotism is only one small goose-step away from that poison,' Meg said, 'and we will have nothing to do with it.'

The women stood up.

'You're making a big mistake,' the first official said.

'Maybe, but not as big as the one you just made trying to blackmail us.' Meg pointed at Betsy. 'She's not wearing that sling as a fashion statement! Her arm is smashed up because she acted when you lot had your heads so far up your arses you failed to notice a gang of Russian psychos had got inside one of the most secure buildings in the country. You want a healthy democracy you say, well that means you take the good and the bad, the rough and the smooth. You don't get to choose. My editor chum decides where the line is for his paper between what is in the public interest and what is interesting to the public. You should be thanking this woman instead of ignoring her this entire meeting. Let's go, Bets.'

Betsy got painfully to her feet and walked to the door. Meg followed. They were escorted through the building.

Outside, the women crossed the road to walk through the thin, grassed strip of Whitehall Gardens, running next to the Thames.

'I'd never say this in front of them, dear, but are you sure you want to let your friends write something?' Betsy said, looking back at the corner of the Ministry of Defence clad in blue plastic sheeting as repairs continued, contained within an exoskeleton of scaffolding.

'I'm done with the lies,' Meg said. 'They're still searching for the source in MI6 and I don't want to drop Jules in the shit so I may, *I may*, leave that bit out. But the Russians are in. The bomb is in. They can't get away with it.' She tossed her head towards the Ministry of Defence. 'And neither can they. Happy?'

'That's not an adjective I would immediately reach for to describe how I feel right now,' Betsy said, 'but I'm content we're more likely to have an impact on the opposition through your journalist friends than by letting those fools cover it all up.'

43.

Any normal parent – god or otherwise – would just be relieved their loved one had escaped obliteration in a bomb blast. Betsy had these feelings too, of course, but couldn't shake off another concern needling the back of her mind. Given the fortuitous fallout in London and Moscow from the discovery of the plot it seemed to her too coincidental that Kathryn should have been so close as to actually benefit from the bomb.

She hid the doubts well. Bright smile, smart jacket, bit of rare lippy for the unexpected lunch. She'd been surprised to get the invitation and very happy to take him up on the offer, even though her elbow still hurt from the blast. Still, always got to invest for the future.

Betsy smiled her thanks to the doorman holding open the entrance to the restaurant. Inside, behind a robust desk, another smile awaited.

'Good afternoon, madam, do you have a reservation?'

'Yes, although not in my name. I'm being treated today,' she trilled.

'Oh, how lovely. What name is the reservation in?'

'Niechenko. I'm a little late.'

The woman checked her screen. Smiled again.

'Don't worry madam, it's only ten past. This way please. They've already arrived.'

'They?'

Betsy followed the woman through the restaurant. It was busy, but not so crowded she would miss an attractive young man standing up to greet her with a smile capable of lighting the candles. She prepared herself but Misha was nowhere to be seen. The needle stabbed once more.

'Here we are madam, enjoy your lunch.'

She was about to correct the woman: sorry, wrong table, must be a mistake. Then realised: the only mistake had been hers. She felt cold, despite the warm summer rays piercing the windows.

'Hello Katya,' the woman said.

'Katya,' from the man.

Betsy said nothing.

'Please take the seat,' the woman said.

'What are you doing here?' Betsy managed to force from a dry throat.

'We're having lunch. With oldest friend.'

There were three place settings at the large round table. The restaurant staff had laid Betsy's close to her companions. She took her seat, stiffly.

'They have pickled herring here,' Svetlana Niechenko said. 'You still like Finland food?'

'What are you doing here?' Betsy repeated.

'Or burger perhaps.'

'We have come to see our son,' Anatoly said.

'But we couldn't be in London without seeing our oldest friend.'

'I'm leaving,' Betsy said. She stood.

'Yes, Katya,' said Svetlana, 'you leave. You always leave. Walk out on your friends again.'

Betsy looked around the room at couples, groups, smiling and enjoying life. She sat down.

'I had to go. I couldn't live with myself there. It was all a big lie.'

'Don't you dare,' said Anatoly. 'You think we didn't also know that? You think we liked it, had your choices? No. You did never think about anyone but yourself.'

'We knew all about you. Covered for your little adventures. Then you leave. Just like that. You were our friend. They tore us apart!' Svetlana hissed, leaning across her husband to throw the words in Betsy's face.

Anatoly took his wife's fist off the white tablecloth and drew it back, out of sight. The couple exchanged thin smiles.

'And for what?' Svetlana continued. 'You lose your family, your only friends. Are you happy, Katya?'

'My name is Betsy.'

'Where did your lies get you, *Katya*?'

Betsy felt light headed. The restaurant seemed louder than when she had entered, the lights somehow brighter. Why had Kathryn been near the bomb? Why had Jules missed the drop off in Shepherd Market?

Why had Misha set her up for this lunch? To punish her? To display the power he had over her?

She stood up, clutching the back of the chair. She felt old. The pride she had taken at a job well done, lives saved - even if the ultimate traitor was still out there somewhere – had evaporated. Maybe she was just a stupid, useless old woman after all.

'I – I'm leaving.'

'Yes, you leave,' Svetlana said. 'You go back to sad, lonely little life with smelly cat. I hope your lies keep you warm, *Betsy*.'

Katya stumbled through the restaurant, tears falling heavily on hot cheeks. She felt bruised, and not just from her elbow, from the inside too. From a soul that was screaming in pain. Faces turned to stare. She had to get out. To go somewhere, anywhere. But where could she go? Who was wondering about her day? Who was buying groceries right now, planning a nice dinner to share with her? Who would miss her if she never went home but, instead, expired right here, in a brief flash of light?

*

If there was any truth in the old adage about lies and pants, there would be a Great Fire of London every day of the week. Lies smoulder, even when the flame has diminished. Add fuel, oxygen and heat though, and they burst into life. Then the question becomes not how to start the fire, but how to control it.

Misha Niechenko and Kathryn Fieldhouse sat in bed watching the television news. A journalist with a serious face was speaking. Behind her, across a wide street, sat a grand building attended by manicured hedges. The sound was off, but a tag on the screen said: 'Live from central London'. Below that, running the width of the screen a banner headline read: 'BREAKING NEWS: Top Russian diplomats expelled'. The time in the corner of the headline showed it was ten past the hour. As the journalist spoke four black vehicles, two Range Rovers and two Mercedes, swept through the wrought iron gates. The camera swivelled round to watch them accelerate down the empty street of Kensington's embassy district.

'Angriest hack in Fleet Street,' Kathryn said.

Misha looked up from his mobile phone and said 'who?'

The curtains were drawn to stop the early afternoon sun dazzling the TV. Or warming the champagne. The screen cut to an aerial view of the Ministry of Defence. An arrow, next to a label saying 'Henry VIII Wine Cellar', pointed to the corner of the building wrapped in blue plastic sheeting.

'Jenny Boyle,' Kathryn said, pointing at the screen with her glass. 'Angriest journalist I've ever met. And that includes the hacks when they woke up after your bomb exploded.'

'Our bomb, baby.'

'Don't call me baby,' Kathryn said. 'And I still haven't forgiven you for not warning me the time had been brought forward. If it hadn't been for my godmother's theatrics I wouldn't be here now. And you'd be a very frustrated FSB Resident, *James*.'

She poked his leg under the sheets.

'Acting Resident. It's only temporary until they find a replacement. And a new ambassador,' Misha said, watching the journalist continue her soundless commentary. 'I tried. Anyway, it worked, and you're getting the praise for clearing the room. You should be thanking dear old Betsy.'

Kathryn's phone beeped. She looked at it and said 'hmm'.

'What's that?' Misha said.

'David wants me to go with him to the Foreign Office when he takes over.'

'Passmore plays the fool well. But he's sharp. Watch him. He knew how to fake the number plates and didn't let Dmitri film the video call with your Prime Minister in the service station. How is, what do you call him, Sunshine?'

'Sunlight.'

'Yes. How is Sunlight?' Misha asked as he stepped naked from the bed and walked the length of the flat to the kitchen.

'How much happier could a victorious Prime Minister be?' Kathryn called after him. 'Two major pretenders to his throne suspended and under investigation - that will eventually fizzle out, but who cares – and he's being lauded as the architect of the biggest push back against the nasty old Russians since the Cold War. Plucky and ingenious little Britain is looked to for international leadership once more. The effect has been, well, world wide, to coin a phrase.'

'Natalia was sad to have to say goodbye to Sunlight,' Misha called from the hallway as he returned to the bedroom.

'I'm sure she made it up to him. He's survived affairs before. He probably will again, just not great timing to be caught in bed with a Russian.'

'Oh I don't know about that,' Misha said, climbing between the sheets with a broad smile and a bowl of Kathryn's favourite guilty pleasure: chips. With mayonnaise.

ACKNOWLEDGEMENTS

My thanks go to Zoe, Cus, Paul, Diana, John & Mandy, who tolerated my experiments with straws and plastic bottles in their pool, Sam for a beautifully disturbing design, Jericho Writers, Debbie Young for her help in navigating the joys and pitfalls of self-publishing, Eve Seymour for editing and to you, for reading. Special thanks to Nic, for encouraging, nudging and badgering when Betsy wanted nothing more than to have a nice long sit down with a cup of tea.

Printed in Great Britain
by Amazon

27904980R10202